I ACCIDENTALLY SUMMONED A DEMON BOYFRIEND

USA TODAY BESTSELLING AUTHOR
JESSICA CAGE

Copyright © 2024 by Jessica Cage

Edited by: Alexa Thomas

Cover Design By: Night Witchery

All rights reserved.

No portion of this book may be reproduced in any form without written permission from the publisher or author, except as permitted by U.S. copyright law.

Contents

Dedication		VII
1.	Booty Juice	1
2.	Too much wine	17
3.	Soulmate	31
4.	Little Old Ladies	45
5.	Abducted	57
6.	Bonding?	73
7.	Detour	99
8.	Date with a witch	119
9.	Time to go home	131
10.	Sabotage	147
11.	Commitment?	161
12.	Crazy Ex-Girlfriends	177
13.	BDSM? Really?	183
14.	The Bitch is back	201

15.	First Death	209
16.	The choice is not yours	215
17.	Care for her	225
18.	And then comes Marriage.	235
19.	Training... Duh!	249
20.	A Total Natural	263
21.	I know Kungfu	277
22.	Two Tentacles and an Arm	287
23.	A cute little cottage	299
About the author		303
Thank you to our Kickstarter Supporters!		304

To the 30 something single girlies:

When dating sucks...

Summon a Demon!

I

Booty Juice

"He left his booty juice in my car!" I screamed at the phone as I frantically scrubbed the custom pewter leather seat. I'd waited four months for the color, and it was ruined after one bad date! My arms were already burning, but I was determined to erase every damn microscopic piece of evidence from my car. "I swear, I am *done* with dating!"

Of course, I'd said it a hundred times before. Hell, every single woman over thirty-five had, but what was I supposed to do? Give up? Maybe that was the answer: wave the white flag proudly above my head, buy a few cats, and head off into the mountains, never to be seen again.

"Girl, what?" my friend, who I video-called as soon as I got home, damn near choked as she tried to hold back her laughter. Her raspy voice was a stark contrast to my smooth flow. "Booty juice? What the hell is booty juice? Is that a new drug or some shit?"

"No! It's little drippings from the crack of his dirty ass!" I twisted my lips and pushed the perfectly coiled strands of my twist-out away from my face. I couldn't believe I wasted such a bomb hairstyle on what would go down in the hall of fame for horrible dates. "There is no way I am ever going to get this clean enough. I just need to buy a new car at this point. How can I sit my tacos on this seat now?"

"Tacos? Girl, stay focused, because you're losing me." The sharp snaps of Keri's coffin-shaped fingernails clicking together brought my attention back to the phone I'd propped up on my dashboard. "How the hell did he get ass juice on your car seat?"

"Bitch, his pants were so damn tight and way too small for his ever-expanding ass. You know, before we met, he kept saying how he'd gained weight. I thought maybe he had some cute love handles or something, but no! The man had to be at least forty pounds heavier than he was in *any* of his pictures, but his clothes, unlike his ass, have not gone up a single size." I tossed the scrub brush into the seat and threw my hands on my hips.

"Hold up. Wait a damn minute, please back up." Keri looked like she would pop a vein as she tried to hold her laughter. "How did the date go?"

"How did it go?" I stared at the phone propped up on the dashboard. "Let's see. He showed up late and bragged about how he was so well known at this spot. Oh yeah, he was well-known—so much so that the waitress looked disgusted when we entered the damn door. We sat down, and he made a fuss about not getting immediate service then went to the bathroom, where he apparently text me how beautiful I looked while pissing!"

"How would you possibly know that?" Keri squinted like she didn't believe me. I only wished I was making this shit up.

"He told me about it when he came back to the table!"

"No, he didn't!" She screamed and slapped her hand over her mouth. "I'm done. Why would he do that?"

"Yes!" I calmed myself before continuing. "Fast forward through awkward conversation and side glances from the waitress, and we finally get our food. This man starts inhaling his soup like I'm going to take it from him. Girl, it was so disgusting. He was sopping up the stuff with the bread, and it was everywhere. I felt like I was on a date with a toddler. And when he finally thinks to pick up the napkin, does he clean the soup dripping down his hand or all over his chin? No! He dabbed the corner of his mouth and stared at me like I was crazy for not eating. How could I eat after watching that?"

"Well damn. I didn't think it would be that bad." Shades of guilt covered her face, and she averted her eyes. She was the one who convinced me to go on the date.

I was two seconds from canceling when she insisted I give the man a chance. I would never let her live this down.

"After he finished the drink he ordered for me without thinking to ask me what I liked, he asked me to drive him back to his car. You know my overly nice ass said yes. So, I took him to where he parked, avoided an unwanted kiss, and the next thing I know, I'm looking over at his ass as he struggled to get out of my car!"

"Okay, so the date sounds like a nightmare, but maybe you're just inflating the booty thing to be more than it was because of how awkward everything else was. I mean, was it just like the top of the cheek?" Keri tried her best to erase some of the emotional damage, but it was no use. "I mean, it's not appealing, but it's not the end of the world either."

"No!" I whined and stomped my foot like a frustrated toddler. As my eyes fell on the seat, I shuddered. Flashes of ashy cheeks passed through my mind, and I thought I would lose the dinner I barely finished. "It was full ass crack. I'm surprised I didn't see ball hair! And then," another shiver passed over me, "I looked down at my seat and I saw it. A sweaty line of booty juice!"

"Girl," Keri laughed and slapped her hand on the table next to her. "You have got to stop calling it that. I can't take it!"

"Keri, what else would you call it?" I tapped my foot and narrowed my gaze at my dark-eyed friend as she struggled to gather herself. "I'm waiting."

"Um, something to remember him by?" Keri lost it. Her chubby cheeks turned bright red, and she laughed so hard, her jerking body hit the table, which caused her phone to topple to the floor. I stood there, annoyed, as I waited for her to crawl under the table and retrieve it, all while choking on her own laughter.

"Right, a lovely little memento." I stuck my tongue out as she finally came back into the frame. "You're not helping me right now!"

"I'm sorry." She snorted as she fixed her glueless wig, which had shifted during her struggle to grab the phone. "What are you going to do now?"

"I'm going to stand here in my sweatpants and favorite comfy t-shirt while I use every damn drop of cleaner I have in this house to get this mark of shame out of my seat. Dammit, and I just got my car detailed!" I rolled my eyes as I thought of the wasted expense. "Shit, I should send his juice dripping ass the bill!"

Keri tried to stifle her laugh, but it turned into a hideous snort. She smacked her hand over her face. "I'm so sorry."

"Keri, I'm glad you're enjoying this." I scowled and pointed my finger at the screen. "I come to you in my time of need, when my world is falling apart, and all you do is laugh!"

"You are so damn dramatic. Hold on, we need a conference call." Keri started tapping her phone screen. "The girls must know all about this."

"No, no." I shook my hand in the camera. "You go back and report to the henhouse. I can't. I have to finish this and then climb in my shower and scrub away the memories of this terrible... terrible night."

"Rayna." Keri sighed, softening her voice as she prepared to give the same words of encouragement all the booed-up girlies kept in their back pockets for their sad, single friends. "Girl, it's going to be okay. I promise, it gets better."

"It's okay, it really is." It took everything not to roll my eyes at her. "I just need about six months to erase the image from my mind and feel stable enough to try this again."

"Bae, you coming?" a deep voice called out in Keri's background.

"Is that Brandon?" I asked about the man who'd walked into my best friend's life eight months prior. Since the first time he flashed his bright smile at her, she'd been lost in the sauce of his love. The two barely spent any time apart, and it only got worse after he moved in with her.

"Yeah, we're headed out to see a late movie." Keri couldn't help herself. The goofy love smile stretched across her face.

"I guess the ladies will have to wait for your recap." I waved her off. "Go enjoy your mans."

"Seriously, all jokes aside, are you going to be okay?" Keri asked. "You've had a truly concerning string of bad dates lately."

"Yeah, I'm just going to conjure me up a boyfriend." I chuckled at the thought. "Eliminate the headache of all this."

"What?" Keri gawked. "Conjure a boyfriend?"

"Girl, it's nothing. I'm just joking... mostly. There's this fantasy book I read where the main character said this spell and boom, she had the perfect boyfriend." I thought of the magical storyline that had the perfect solution to modern dating. "All it took was a special candle, some oils, a feather, and a dance in moonlight. Then, just like that, the love of her life knocked on her door the next day. If only it were that simple."

"Well, let's not jump to using magic just yet." Keri shook her finger at me. "You know I don't play about stuff like that. My grandmother gave me more than enough warnings."

"I'm not that desperate...yet." I picked up the phone from the dashboard. "But you know, it would be nice if we could all get together. You know, a girls' night? We haven't done that since I became the last single girl in the group."

"Of course. I think we could all use it." Keri picked up her phone and started walking through her home, turning the lights off as she went. "We'll set something up for this weekend. I'll drop details in the group chat."

"Cool, have fun at the movie." I gave a quick wave as the call ended and turned my attention back to the tainted seat in my car.

Call me crazy, but I was determined to make the seat spotless, no matter how badly my arms burned. Maybe if I could get the damn thing clean enough, it would erase what happened, and all the previous bad dates along with it. Like the guy who massaged my hand and gave me a headache that lasted a week. Or the one who got mad at me for beating him in arcade games and took my rewards card so I couldn't get a prize.

But I knew no amount of scrubbing would erase the image of the man who wanted me to nurse him. *Yes*! He wanted to latch on to my titties like a newborn baby and *nurse*! I know I'm not a part of the itty-bitty titty committee, but that doesn't mean I want to be a wet nurse to a full-grown man!

The internal recordings of my mother's nagging played in my head. Every time we spoke, she went on and on about those damn fish in the sea. What she failed to realize was that the modern pollution of dating apps, social media, and #relationshipgoals had mutated the fish! As many times as I'd said it before, I really wanted to call it quits. Maybe that's what I needed: a nice long break from fishing. Part of me wished to keep the hope of catching a good one alive, but the cynical side of me was growing more and more with each disgusting encounter.

I ACCIDENTALLY SUMMONED A DEMON BOYFRIEND

"Fuck it. I'm buying a new car. This one is ruined." I slammed the door and headed inside to the oasis that awaited me in my bathroom. That was where I ran to recover when my days weren't as great as I'd hoped.

I'd worked hard building two careers, one in the arts landing my work in galleries around the world, and one as a digital marketer to Fortune 500 companies to give me a life of leisure. I took a nice chunk of my income to work with a designer who gave me the bathroom of my dreams, complete with a massive tub, heated stone flooring, a luxurious sauna shower, and yes, a bonnet warmer. You haven't lived until you've slipped a warm bonnet over a fresh twist down.

I expected to share the life I built with someone special, thought I'd have a partner to celebrate my wins with and even confide in when things didn't go my way. The older I got, the more I asked myself: was it so bad to enjoy it alone? I had a wonderful home, a flexible schedule, good friends, and loyal clients who kept my bank account full.

I may not have been able to get the car clean enough, but I would damn sure step into my shower and turn on that full body shower system to scrub the ick of the night from my skin, even to the detriment of my precious melanin. I hoped the shea butter gods would forgive me.

A week later, I sat alone with a ball of anxiety growing in my gut. "These bitches better not ditch me here!"

10:00 PM

The time popped up on my phone screen, and I rolled my eyes after checking the door again. It wasn't even my plan, meeting at this overpriced bar at eight on a Friday night. Something in my gut told me it was too good to be true. This was prime time for newly booed-up couples to go out on their cute little dates. Yes, I wanted the outcome to be different, but it'd be a lie to say I was surprised by those heffas bailing on me.

After sitting alone at the bar for nearly three hours reading a series of "I'm running late," and "I won't make it" text messages, I threw away any hope of seeing my girls. Each tap of my nail against the rim of the glass in front of me was another point of realization. I had to get used to this new life as the last single girl in the group.

We'd always promised each other that when we got into a relationship, we wouldn't forget our friends. We'd retain a sense of independence and connection with the girls. *Liars.* If any of them had been truthful, I wouldn't be nursing a drink alone in a bar while trying not to sneeze from all the competing scents of cologne.

The last thing I wanted was to have to go out and make new friends. At thirty-whatever, it was so hard to find genuine connections with people, and that wasn't limited to men. The idea of making new friendships as an adult sounded as appealing as detangling my hair with a fine-toothed comb. With everyone bringing their own bag of drama and prejudices, tiptoeing around them became a nightmare.

As a scuzzy guy in a cheap suit made his way back to my side of the bar, I peeped the quickest route to the exit. I'd avoided his advances twice already, and I didn't see how I would get away from the terrible breath and BO a third time without at least having to give out a fake number.

After a quick goodbye with Darryl, the bouncer who knew Keri, I made it to my car. When the door closed, I relaxed and silently celebrated having successfully avoided any more awkward interactions with the male species. I drove home ignoring the string of notifications on my phone. *I guess they finally realized no one showed up.*

"Maybe I'll get a cat," I muttered as the garage door lowered behind my car. There had been a stray cat lingering in my backyard before I got the fence put up. Maybe I could find him and give him a home. I glared at the soiled passenger seat. There wasn't a visible stain, but I knew what happened there. I'd never forget it.

Inside my home, a three-bedroom, two bath, corner lot beauty I got my hands on just before the market exploded, I got myself into a good mood. One bottle of cherry Moscato and a 90s R&B jam session later, and I was dancing around my home to Deborah Cox and feeling fuzzy. When the room started spinning, I flopped down onto the plush white sofa that cupped my ass like the horny boyfriend I wished I had.

"This is some bullshit." I sighed and looked over to see the book I'd told Keri about still sitting on the coffee table.

To Conjure Love. The book that had me wishing love was so dang easy. True, the couple in the story still had trials, but damn it. One good spell, and the man of your dreams just drops into your lap. What girl wouldn't want it to be that easy? No more swiping left on twelve hundred duds just hoping a decent guy would show up. No more going to stupid meet ups praying the love of your life was feeling equally pathetic and signed up for a singles mixer.

I picked up the book, flipping through the pages, and sighed. "Wouldn't it be nice... I could try it. I mean, what would it hurt?"

Giving up on the silly idea, I tossed the book aside on the couch. The damn thing bounced off the plush peach couch cushion and somehow slid underneath the mosaic coffee table I'd picked up in Bangladesh. When I bent down to pick it up, I couldn't help but laugh. The book had fallen open to the exact page where the spell was laid out in full detail, and what did my drunken mind think?

How could I not do it? The universe clearly wants me to, damn it!

The words on the page moved in psychedelic waves as I tried to focus on the list of ingredients. I needed a lavender scented candle, moonlight, and three oils: jasmine, sandalwood, and patchouli.

Thank you, oil sample kits. I had each one and even added a little lavender to the mix, since lavender was my favorite. I read over the spell.

In the cast of moonlight, touch the mixture of oils to your wrists, neck, chest, and forehead, then light the candle and recite the spell.

"Simple enough," I said and started mixing the oils in a small bowl.

After mixing the oils, I opened the curtains over the large bay window where I typically sat to read. The moon was full and looked like someone had reined it in closer to Earth. I don't think I'd ever seen it take up that much space! That alone should have told my drunk ass not to be messing with magic, but I kept the dream alive. The moonlight washed into the room, and I hummed.

The bench beneath the window operated as additional storage and was the resting grounds for the tools of my candle making obsession. Lifting the pillow topped lid, I found the perfect candle sitting right on top. It was a large red gothic attempt that was coincidentally perfect for love-summoning magic. I'd used Ylang Ylang oil in the wax, so it would be fragranced as well. Again, this should have been a sign for me to stop. When I was sober, I didn't believe in coincidences!

With the candle ready, it was time to do the spell. My head was still spinning from all the wine, but I dabbed the oil mixture on my inner wrists and neck before pouring a healthy amount down my cleavage and then touching it to my forehead.

Next, I lit the candle and positioned myself where my full body was lit by the moonlight. The hairs on my arms stood as I recited the spell.

"Light of the moon, heat of the flame, bring me the one whose soul knows my name," I called out to the moon, as if it would somehow make this fictional magic real. Then, I closed my eyes and whispered it three more times. When I opened my eyes, I stood there looking around the room, like I'd actually expected it to work. "Hello? Magical boyfriend, are you there?"

When there was no response to my call—not that I really thought there would be—I blew out the candle and closed the curtains, cutting off the soft moonlight.

"Not even magic can help me," I huffed as I chugged the last of the wine and headed for the shower. Someday, maybe, I would get a man, but a spell from a random fantasy novel wasn't going to be the thing to make it happen.

I wasn't ashamed to admit I spent half an hour in the shower. I'd just gotten a new detachable shower head that made the experience... so much more enjoyable. It wasn't until the water got so cold my nipples pebbled that I glided out of the bathroom, breast bouncing free, a towel wrapped around my chubby waist. The music was still playing, and it was about three seconds before I was swaying my hips to the rhythm.

I was dancing my heartache away when I saw something—something that made my heart pound in my chest, and I hoped like hell it was because of the wine. I stopped in my tracks and slowly turned to the figure. Surely, it would disappear like the phantom image you can never quite catch. My slow turn wasn't slow enough though, because as my view shifted, the figure was still there.

"You called?" the deep voice spoke from the corner where the apparent intruder stood.

"Oh, hell no!" I bolted for the door, titties flopping with each step. There was no way I was staying there. I didn't care who he was. What I wasn't going to do was sit around and find out what sick shit he wanted to do to me.

Just before I made it to the door—damn me for wanting such a big ass bedroom—the figure appeared in my way. I hadn't seen or heard him move, but he was there. I skid to a halt, nearly falling on my ass, and in a moment when I should have been terrified, the wine in my system told me it was time to laugh. And I did. I doubled over, clutching my sides.

Why the hell was I laughing when there was an intruder in my home? Because the man in front of me had horns! Actual horns that sprouted from his forehead. His skin was dark with a purple tint, and he had to be at least a foot taller than me. When I stopped laughing, shoulders still bouncing with soft chuckles, I looked him up and down. I noted the dark nodes along the length of his bare arms and the even darker energy that radiated from him.

My brain refused to accept this as reality. This wasn't an intruder intending to rob me. It was only a dream, a figment of my imagination. I learned a long time ago not to be afraid of the creations of my own mind.

"Damn, I must have fallen asleep." I glanced back over my shoulder at the bathroom door. "I knew that shower felt too damn good."

"I'm sorry?" He cocked his head to the side. "Why have you called me here?"

"Oh, well, fuck it. If it's a dream, I'm going with it." My mind was already spinning with ideas of how to turn this dream from horror to something a lot more fun. "At least I can get kinky while I sleep!"

"A dream?" his voice rumbled with annoyance as I moved closer to him.

"You have horns!" A hiccup interrupted my giggle as I lifted my hand up to touch them. "I like your horns." My eyes dropped to the black slacks that covered his lower half. "Do you have another horn?"

I ACCIDENTALLY SUMMONED A DEMON BOYFRIEND

"Are you okay?" He frowned at me and I smiled. He looked damn near human in his features: wide nose, sharp jawline, and only a slightly inhuman look to his flesh. For what I assumed was a demon of some sort, my brain had created him to look more like a man I wouldn't turn down for a second date.

"I'm great, but you can make me better." Feeling inspired by all the romance and demon smut novels I'd been reading, I pulled the knot loose on the towel and let it fall from my waist. "Make me better, demon bae. You are a demon, right? I read demons come with interesting... tools."

"I am a demon." He frowned, and those subtle ridges became far more pronounced. "Where did you read about demonic tools?"

"Don't worry about the tools." I brushed off his question, took a half step back for leverage, and then leapt into his arms. "Fuck me, demon."

"I will not." He refused my request, but he didn't put me down.

"You say no, but you're gripping my ass right now. Hey, this is my dream. I summoned you, which means you have to do what I want. And what I want," I lifted in his hold to put my boobs in his face, "is to be fucked!"

I leaned in to kiss him, and he hesitated. Rarely had I been rejected by a man my mind designed, but maybe that was the twist to this dream. This was a demon. He would be hard to get. So I persisted, moving my lips against his and licking them like they were my favorite flavor of ice cream. It was after my thigh rubbed against his dick, awakening his demonic tool, that he succumbed to me.

"Dammit," he muttered beneath my kiss, and I couldn't help the smile that spread across my face as he tossed my ass on the bed like I weighed nothing at all.

"That's right, demon boy!" I cheered, but he stood at the foot of my bed staring at me.

"You're intoxicated." He shook his head at me almost like he was disappointed in me. *The nerve of a demon judging me for having a drink or two.*

"So what if I had a little wine?" the hiccup slipped through my lips. "I know what I want. This is my dream; you're supposed to do what I want."

"This is no dream." He stepped closer to the bed.

"Whatever you say." My brow lifted as I examined him. *This has to be a dream.* "I know what I want right now. That's you, naked."

"Are you sure what you're asking for?" he said it as if his lower half hadn't already betrayed him. I could tell by the sudden tightness of his pants that I wasn't the only one who wanted it.

"What the hell are you waiting for? Strip!"

And he did. No more protest. I'd broken the resistance of the dream and took in the view of the demon man as he removed the weathered clothing from his body. The man looked amazing. Fit body, not too muscular, brawny arms and chest with a slight pudge to his stomach. It was when he dropped his pants that my mouth fell open. I'd like to say I didn't salivate at the sight of his dick, but I did. It was large, pulsing, with the same nodules that marked his arms, only smaller and with beneficial placements. "Oh, my God."

"Do not praise God when looking at my dick," he ordered.

"Oh, my... devil?" I frowned and forced my eyes away from his member to look up at him. "Whoever is responsible, they did a good job."

"I suppose that's better." He pulled my legs apart and dropped to his knees in front of me. "Let's get you ready for my *tool*."

"Well damn, get me ready!" My giggle quickly turned into a deep moan as his face dipped between my thighs.

Though I only saw one tongue, it felt like he had at least four working between my legs. Every time I looked down to try to catch a glimpse of what magic he was working to make it feel like he was both licking my clit and swirling his tongue inside my pussy at the same time, my eyes slammed shut with another orgasm. The man had only put in two minutes of work, and my hands were clutching the sheets like we'd been going rounds.

I squealed as he pushed my legs higher, lifting my ass just high enough for that third tongue to explore another hole, a hole I had never explored before, and dammit if it didn't feel amazing. I gripped my legs, amazed at my own flexibility as I helped him gain access.

Next thing I knew, he flipped me over onto my stomach – ass tooted in the air – and slapped my cheeks, groaning as he watched the recoil. I looked back at him, and I swore the horns on his head grew as he stared at my ass. One hand braced the bed near my face as he leaned into me. The weight and heat of his body added to my growing excitement, and when the head of his dick pressed against my lips, my pussy started dripping, ready to accept him.

"Breathe," his deep voice rumbled in my ear, and I almost said something smart mouth. Almost.

My eyes widened as he slowly entered me. The sensation was unlike anything I'd felt before. Inch by inch, nodule by nodule, he forced my walls to expand and mold to him. For a demon, he was gentle... at first. But the moment my pussy started throbbing, gripping around him and growing wetter, begging for more, he abandoned that gentle shit. Each thrust sent him deeper into me, and he picked up the pace so much that the headboard slammed against the wall, echoing each stroke.

Just as I adjusted to him and started pushing my ass back against him, he flipped me back over.

"I want to see your face," he said, and a moment later he was back inside me. "Show me how much you like my tool."

I saw a dark glint in his eyes, the lift at the corner of his lips, and then, I felt it. The nodules on his dick moved! I didn't understand what was happening at first. This unfamiliar feeling was like a cyclone inside my pussy, better than any vibrator I'd ever had.

Encouraged by the motion, I flipped the demon onto his back, grabbed his horns, and rode him like he was the mechanical bull at the rodeo bar that always had too many women in line for me to bother trying to hop my ass up there, but this bull was all mine. I had no idea when this dream was going to end, but I was going to take every damn orgasm I could get. Hell, maybe I'd remember the details of his dick, make a new prototype, and become a millionaire when it hit the market! I bounced my ass on top of him wildly until he gripped my hips, forcing me to ease up.

"Take your time, woman," he ordered and before I could protest, his dick revved up inside me and pushed me into another orgasm.

"Oh. My. G-" I started, but his hand covered my mouth.

"Say it again, and I won't leave you with enough strength to even think his name," he warned.

This time, it was me who had the devilish grin as he pulled his hand from my face. I looked him straight in those dark eyes and knew my next words would be playing with fire. Match lit!

"God," I said and then squealed as he flipped me over and fucked me so good, that at one point, I swear, I forgot the lord's name.

2

Too much wine

The lazy smile stretched across my face as I awakened to a warm sensation over the length of my back. My first thought was this was the body heat of a big sexy man lying next to me. My second thought was, *"Get real, girl. The only man you have is the one in your dreams."* What should have been a gentle return to consciousness was a series of sharp sensations that made me want to shove my head under the damn bed. Why the hell did I drink so much wine, knowing damn well anything over two glasses gave me the worst damn headache? I tried sitting up, but my head felt like water circling the drain.

With the bright sunlight pouring into the room, there was no way I was going to get over the mind splitting pain. The first thing I had to do was close the damn curtains. The second thing was to find the pain killers, guzzle some water, and go back to bed.

"Alright, girl," I muttered to hype myself up to trek across the room. Damn me for wanting a large master suite that put my window a nauseating ten feet from my bed. It was only me in the damn house. I didn't need that much space. "You can do this. Just a few measly tasks, and then back to bed."

I took a deep breath and then rocked my way out of the bed and onto my feet. The moment my feet touched the floor, I gasped as the throbbing soreness between my legs kicked in.

"What the hell?" I pressed my hand against my pussy to ease the pain. "My period just ended. I know damn well it ain't coming back again."

But then, I realized this wasn't period pain. No, this was something else. It'd been so long since I'd had sex that I hardly remembered what the aftermath felt like—the wobbly legs, the remnant throbbing, the need to pee!

I'd had dreams that felt real before, but this was another level entirely.

"No dream is that good," I muttered, and despite the mysterious discomfort lingering between my legs, I focused on the goal. Close the damn curtains. I wrapped the sheet around my naked body and forced myself to move.

Moving like a calf fresh out the coochie, I'd just about made it to the window when my knee slammed against the edge of the decorative table I'd sworn a hundred times to get rid of. Damn me for accepting the eyesore just because my friend got it for me. I loved Nevia, but her taste was terrible.

The thing was a pepto pink, with blue and green stones down each curved leg. The top was a mosaic stone with unfinished edges that had left several marks on my knee. It clashed with everything in my house, so I hid it in the bedroom where no one could see it. At least with the dark blue accent wall, it didn't look as terrible. That's what I told myself, anyway. I didn't want to hurt her feelings by tossing it in the storage closet. People pleasing only hurts the one doing the pleasing.

"Son of a bitch!" I cursed and jumped back on unsteady legs, which landed me flat on my ass. "Ouch!"

"Are you always this clumsy?" the deep voice spoke, and I froze. It sounded familiar, but I didn't know why. No matter how familiar it was, no one was supposed to be in my damn house.

Not only was there an intruder in my home, but they'd made themselves comfortable and apparently had the audacity to comment on how clumsy I was. Fear and anger were all I needed to force the effects of the hangover to the side. I sprang to my feet and snatched the closest thing I could find to defend myself: a calf-high boot with a chunky heel.

Sure, the boot may have done some damage, but I could hardly think of ways to wield it after seeing who was in my home. I turned around, and there, in all his glory, with his dark, purplish-black skin, was the damn demon from my dream. Instinct told me a lot of things—run, get a better weapon, puke—but what I did was scream. The loudest, gut-churning scream I'd ever produced in my life. If I'd ever cared to make friends with any of my neighbors, one of them might have come running to check on me.

And then, flashes of the dream returned. Images of me jumping into his arms, pressing my tits in his face, and holding onto his horns while riding him were sharp reminders of what I'd done. I slapped my hand over my mouth to cut the sound and then over my pussy as I recalled him prepping me for his *tool*.

"That was a dream." I shook my head and whispered to myself. "This must still be a dream. You're not real. I'm still dreaming. How much wine did I drink?"

"You're not dreaming." His words cut down any hope I had of explaining away what I hoped was a fucked-upside effect of drinking too much wine. "You called me here, and I came."

"Called you here? I didn't call you here!" I thought through the night before. "I went out, came home, drank, danced, and then-"

"Then what?" he asked.

"The book. Oh shit. I read the spell from that book, but that was fake. Not real!" I dropped my hands to my side, and the boot smacked against my calf. "There is no way any of that really happened. I'm dreaming. I have to be!"

"I don't know how many times you're going to make me say this, but you are not dreaming." He crossed his arms, and those plump lips twisted with his frown.

"Oh yeah, the hell I am." I pointed at him with the boot. "Because if I'm not, you're really a demon. A demon I summoned with a made-up spell and then had wild and unusual sex with."

"That part is true." He nodded, and the collar of his black button-up shirt shifted around his neck, revealing more of his purply black skin.

"This isn't real. This isn't happening. You aren't real!" I screamed, waving the boot in the air.

"I can assure you, I am," he grunted. "And yelling that I'm not, won't change that fact."

Determined to prove him wrong, I chucked the boot at him, using his horns as targets, and it made a satisfying yet terrifying thud as it hit him on the head. I swear, I expected it to fly right through him, that his body would just fade away like in the movies. That didn't happen. There was no cool effect or relief to come with the realization that I just had an overactive imagination.

"Why would you do that?" He rubbed the side of his head, and his face turned into a mask of annoyance punctuated by his furrowed brow.

"No, nope, nah. This isn't happening." I pinched myself as the last resort of breaking what had to be a dream, but I didn't feel the numb sensation of fake contact I expected. The pain shot through my flesh, and I cringed. "Fuck! That hurt!"

"I'm not sure what you expected that to feel like," he grunted, still rubbing the sore spot on his head. "Or why you insist on harming yourself and me?"

"I expected it to feel like nothing because this is a dream!" I whispered, my eyes darting around the room. "Because you know, in dreams, things don't hurt. They feel oddly unreal."

"Did last night feel oddly unreal?" He smirked, his brows raised with his question.

"I-" I choked. "Last night, shit."

"This is not a dream. You can keep saying it is, but that won't make it true. Neither will it make the bite mark you left on my neck any less real." He pointed to the impression of my teeth on his dark flesh.

"Shit, I did that?" I leaned forward slightly, just enough to see the marks on his skin. "Damn."

"Once you grabbed my horns, you went a little wild," he huffed. "Can't say I've ever been told to, 'Giddy up, boy' before."

"You're a demon." I disregarded his comment as more images of the night flashed through my mind. "A demon with horns and a rotating dick. And I fucked you?"

"Sounds about right." He nodded. "Though I don't know where you got the spell from. We didn't do much talking."

"Wait." I looked at his forehead, where moments ago there were two horns, but was now smooth flesh making him look much more human. "Where are your horns?"

"Safely tucked away." He rubbed his forehead. "I can hide them when I want, and I didn't want to set you off again. You seemed to be turned on by them, and I thought it would be nice if we actually had a conversation about what's happening here."

"I wasn't turned on by your horns!" I defended myself.

"Are you sure? I could have sworn your eyes lit up when you first saw them, and then you couldn't keep your hands off them."

"It was a dream!" I stomped my foot in protest.

"No, it wasn't." He smirked. "And you know, our dreams are where our deepest desires get to shine. Do you think it says anything significant about you that when you thought you were dreaming, your response to a demon and his horns was insatiable arousal?"

"Who the fuck puts a spell like that in a book if it actually works?" I couldn't debate with him anymore. I felt like my chest would explode. Soon, I was struggling to remain calm, and every glance at the demon made it harder to keep my lungs functioning. "That's insane!"

"Someone who probably didn't think it would work." He leaned against the wall behind his back and crossed his arms over his chest. "Authors are studious creatures. The best ones really do their research. Doesn't surprise me that one might stumble across an incantation, think it's a dud, and pop it in a book."

"This is sick. This is. Oh my God." My breaths became shallow struggles for air. "I think I'm going to be sick."

"Calm down." He held a hand out to me but remained on his side of the room. "Just breathe. I don't need you passing out on me."

"Nope, definitely sick." I ran past him, clutching the sheet wrapped around my body.

He grunted as I pushed him out of the way and headed for the bathroom. I nearly missed the toilet as the contents of my stomach shot out, splashing into the water. After what felt like an hour of puking, my stomach was finally empty. I sat on the floor of the bathroom and wiped my mouth with the sheet. I'd have to burn them anyway. No way I could keep sheets I'd had demon sex on.

When he appeared in the doorway with purplish black skin and a wide grin, I looked up at him and never felt so much regret in my life.

"Oh shit. Okay. That was real. I actually fucked a demon." The hollow sound that crawled up my throat was half sob, half dry heave. "I'm never drinking wine again!"

"You fucked a demon," he chuckled, nodding slowly. "I doubt that's going to keep you off wine, though. If anything, I'd suggest you look into some support groups. Are there any other addicts in your family?"

"Great, I fucked a demon who thinks he's funny. What do you want from me?" I asked. There had to be a reason he came and still hadn't gone back to hell. "Not my soul, right? Please say you're not here to drag my soul back to your underlord."

"Underlord?" He scoffed. "Look, I'm not the one who summoned you."

"Fine—go." I waved my hand, shooing him away.

"Excuse me?" He cocked his head to the side. "You're sending me off?"

"Summoned, fucked," I cringed. "Job done. You can go now."

"Right. Well, I'm glad you enjoyed yourself." He winked at me, and then his horns appeared, as if he thought they would trigger something in me. When he didn't get the response he'd hoped for, the pressure built in the room. It felt like invisible hands wrapping around me, pressing in on every side.

And then the demon disappeared.

Turns out, my stomach wasn't completely empty. I vomited for another twenty minutes after that.

"I'm so sorry we didn't make it," Keri started her sad apology as soon as I stepped across the threshold to her newly-painted apartment. The smell was nearly as overwhelming as her blabbering. "There was just so much going on. You know how it can get. I-"

"Yeah, yeah. Whatever." I waved her off as I scanned her apartment for any anomaly.

There was nothing out of place, no demon visitors standing in the corner waiting to taunt me. It was still Keri's boho style with the large rustic area rug, tall plants, massive oil paintings that covered the wall, and patchouli incense burning in the corner on a glass shelf. It was her favorite scent. She'd recently done an accent wall in Castleton Green, which I knew because she'd called me talking about how every green she'd found before had too much *army* to it.

"Girl, what are you doing?" Keri closed the door and followed me. "Are you okay?"

"Keri..." I turned to her, whispering like a kid about to be scolded by the principal at school. "You will not believe the shit that happened to me last night."

"Damn it. What happened? Please don't tell me some perv slipped something into your drink. Is that why you stopped responding last night?" Keri put her hands on her hip. I could already see the legal side of her mind gearing up. "We'll find them. They have security everywhere. I didn't get this law degree for nothing. I may not be able to throw hands anymore, but I will throw their ass in jail for fucking with my friend!"

"No, nothing like that. And I stopped responding because I was pissed about being stood up!" I paused, mentally comparing an attempted assault to an actual round of midnight acrobatics with a demonic entity. Which one deserved more outrage? "Actually, I think this is worse. I mean... yeah. It's way worse."

"You're freaking me out. What happened?" Keri grabbed my arm and pulled me to the couch to sit next to her.

I stared at the new piece of furniture that looked out of place with her stuff. She'd thrown a few fuzzy pillows over the modular nightmare, but it still didn't feel like it belonged there.

"Is this his couch?" I tried to keep my tone from edging toward critical as I ran my hand across the grey material. "Doesn't really seem like your normal style."

"Rayna," Keri snapped her fingers, "focus. Tell me what happened."

"Right. Okay, so I'm sitting there pissed off about my friends standing me up and leaving me alone in lonely single land." I shot Keri a side eye. "So, I go home, crack open a bottle of wine, and start vibing on my own. And you know things are good. I'm not exactly happy about being by myself, but as a single girl, you figure out a way to make it work. Anyway, do you remember that book I told you about? The one about the girl who says a spell and magically creates the perfect boyfriend? Well, I may or may not have opened that book, let the moonlight into my crib, lit a few candles, and performed the spell."

"So what? That's nothing to be embarrassed about, Ray." Keri's eyes widened as she locked onto a distant memory. "Remember when we used to get together and do that thing at sleepovers? The spell that's supposed to let us lift someone with our fingertips? What was it? *Light as a feather, stiff as a board.* That never worked."

"Okay, but..." I felt my face warm with embarrassment. "This may sound insane, but I think it may have worked."

"Maybe it's the lack of caffeine in my system, because that three-hundred-dollar piece of junk espresso machine I just got crapped out on me, so I may need you to correct me. Did I just hear you say you did a spell, and that spell created a man for you?" Keri looked at me with those mothering eyes. Whenever she felt concerned for me, which happened far more than I care to admit, she would get those eyes. The expression meant she'd be ready to call my therapist. Luckily, she didn't have the number. "Please tell me I'm trippin' and that is not what you just said."

"You're not, and that is what I said." I felt the knot form in my throat. Was I really telling my friend this? For a moment, I thought I'd lost my mind, but what I felt was real. "Only, I wouldn't exactly call that thing boyfriend material."

"Girl, what the hell are you talking about?" Keri slapped me on the shoulder. "Stop playing around, Rayna."

"Keri, the spell worked!" I stood from the couch and paced circles around the bulky coffee table that Keri said she never wanted. She hated furniture that broke up her open spaces. "That dumbass author I usually fawn over put an actual fucking spell in her book. I did it, and it worked!"

"Right." Her word trailed off as she watched me. That concern grew more prevalent in her expression as the corners of her lips dropped and her eyes narrowed.

"Don't look at me like I have one foot in the white room." I pointed at her. "I know that look."

"I'm not saying that, but maybe it's time to see your therapist?" Keri stood and met me at eye level. "I mean, it sounds to me like you may have had a little too much to drink, and that inspired some vivid dreams."

"Dreams that spilled over into this morning? I woke up, and he was still here!" I pointed to the floor as if we were standing in my home instead of hers.

"And where is he now?" she asked, that gentle counselor voice in full effect.

"Gone," I whispered.

"Gone? Where?" She looked at the door, as if he would appear there.

"That's the thing. The man, the thing I conjured, was…" Suddenly, I couldn't say it. It was ridiculous. No wonder my friend was so concerned about me. Maybe I'd finally lost it. Sir Booty Juice had broken me.

"Was what, Rayna?" Keri pulled me back to sit down on the couch. She positioned herself between me and the door, like she was afraid I would take off running.

"Never mind." I brushed it off. "Let's just talk about something else."

"You know damn well that's not gonna fly with me." Keri touched my shoulder. Her voice took on that familiar quality of a caretaker concerned for her patient. "Ray, you can tell me anything, no matter how insane it may sound."

"Remember what you just said." I pointed at her, and she nodded. "I think, I mean he was a demon, and he went back to, I guess, hell."

"Rayna," she said. And there it was: pity. Pity for the sad single friend dreaming up demons to fill her time. Keri's shoulders dropped, her lips pouted, and her eyes said, *my sad single friend has lost her mind.*

"Don't look at me like that!" I fussed and moved further from her on the couch.

"Look, I'm sorry we ditched you, but girl. You can't possibly believe what you just told me." Keri shook her head.

"I swear, Keri. It sounds insane. I know it does. Just think about how it felt for me." I took a deep breath to calm my stomach. There should have been nothing left to expel, but the way she looked at me made me feel sick again. "Anyway, I told him I wanted nothing to do with him. He disappeared. I puked and passed out."

"Puked and passed out?" Keri sighed. "Sounds to me like a terrible hangover and your insanely active imagination. Look, I'm sorry for bailing on you last night and I will make it up to you. I really think you should call your therapist. You're still seeing the same one, right?"

I didn't know what I expected to happen. Keri wasn't the type to jump on a crazy story without proof. It made her a good lawyer. The problem was, I'd dropped this in her lap, and I had no way to validate what I told her. Looking my friend in the eye, I gave up. I'd have to deal with this on my own. Keri was my best friend. If she didn't believe me, no one would.

"Yeah, maybe you're right." My shoulders slumped with defeat. "It felt so damn real, though."

"I'm sure it did." Keri shook her head. "How much wine did you drink?"

"Maybe a bottle?" I tried to recount the night again but couldn't see past the images of me grabbing onto horns with one hand and twirling my towel over my head with the other. "Maybe more?"

"Let's not do that again." Keri patted my knee then stood. "Now, I'm dragging you with me. If I don't get another coffee maker, I'm going to scream. He wanted that damn thing with all the bells and whistles. I asked for a simple machine with a timer. That's not too hard. No, he had to get the coffee machine from hell, and after it spit hot milk all over the kitchen, it stopped working!"

I should have known better than to think Keri would stop after picking out a new coffeemaker. The woman went from department to department, each new aisle sparking a memory of some other random thing she needed for her home. When the first store crapped out, she forced me back into her car so she could cart me to the next. I should have driven my car, but I just wanted to get away from my thoughts, and I figured Keri's eventual chatter would keep my mind occupied. Even her constant conversation wasn't enough to keep images of those dark eyes and purplish black flesh from invading my mind, though.

Four hours later, we were back at her house. After promising Keri I would get some rest and check in with my therapist, I was allowed to leave. Back in my own car and starving because Keri was on a strict diet and surviving on smoothies and celery sticks, I headed for my favorite taco spot. I smacked the steering wheel when I pulled up to see the line of people standing outside. It was my favorite spot for a reason, and Saturday afternoon was always a busy time.

I parked, but instead of jumping in line, decided it was best to take a walk. The restaurant wasn't far from a cute little park with paths that led to a nice-sized pond. It was a spot I often went to whenever I wanted to eat my tacos and clear my mind in peace. It was the perfect place to wait for the crowd to die down.

It felt strange walking the path without three steak tacos in hand, but I was sure the effect would be the same. The sounds of nature, of animals rustling, and birds swimming in the pond, would clear my mind. No more thoughts of demons. As I reached the end of the path that opened to the hidden gem, I sighed.

"Get it together, girl. Clearly, it was a dream," I muttered as I tried convincing myself that tall, dark, and horny was a figment of my imagination. He had to be.

My preferred bench was open. It was the only one that wasn't under trees, so it wasn't covered in bird poop like the others. Sitting down, I dropped my head back, stared at the cloudy sky, and filled my lungs with slow breaths as the cool breeze moved across my skin. I had to slow my breathing if I was going to gain any control of the rising anxiety. The strangling sensation had been building ever since I left Keri. It was a dream. It had to be. There was no other logical explanation for what I experienced.

"Maybe the wine was expired," I mused aloud, and a snorty laugh that quickly made me self-conscious trumpeted from my mouth.

I scanned the area to see if anyone heard the embarrassing sound. It wasn't until that moment that I realized I was alone. It wasn't uncommon to find the secluded area empty, but the complete lack of activity suddenly felt nauseating. There were no geese or ducks to watch from the corner of my eye, because I didn't trust the damn things. No squirrels battling over fallen nuts, no sounds of children playing at the park just on the other side of the hidden area. It was totally silent. I looked at the water, and even that was still, undisturbed by the breeze that brushed my skin moments before.

"What the hell?" I muttered, and as the words crossed my lips, a chill moved across my spine. "Alright, time to get the hell out of here!"

One thing I'd learned in my thirty-something years was to listen to my damn instincts. That gut punch that followed the chill told me to get out of dodge. I stood from the bench, casting one last worried glance at the water, and then turned to leave. I made it exactly one and a half steps before my eyes found the source of the sudden concern. Standing at the edge of the path was an unmistakable beast, a demon.

The thing locked eyes with me, lowered its head, and laughed!

3

Soulmate

My inner voice screamed for my body to move. As panic swelled, my legs froze, and my eyes widened. Because what the hell else was I supposed to do? The thing that stood in front of me was nothing like the man I'd almost convinced myself was just an elaborate figment of my imagination. There was nothing human-like about it.

This thing looked like the backside of a bull and smelled like the bird shit I avoided sitting on. It had at least six horns that grew so long, they wrapped around its head in spirals. They reminded me of the wire at the top of a barbed fence and circled his head like a makeshift crown. Instead of flesh, it looked like its skin was the same as the bark that wrapped the trees nearby. Oddly deceptive flowering decorated its arms and chest, as if welcoming its victims. I imagined the thing hiding in the park, waiting for someone to get too close.

The thing was massive. My eyes slowly scanned from the enormous clawed feet, up the branch-like legs, past the bloated torso and heaving chest. And then I focused on its face: the lifeless, soul-crushing face. Its jaw slacked and revealed yellowed pointed teeth as it labored to breathe like an asthmatic being forced on a nature hike. Its eyes glowed red. If I imagined what a demon looked like, this was it. Hellish, murderous, ready to take a life. My life.

This wasn't the human-like man hunk that fucked me senseless the night before. This thing was ugly, and the longer I looked at it, the more I felt my self-control slip. Terror became my captor. Logic told me to run, but the fear of what this thing could do to me made that impossible.

It stood on two legs, putting its head at least three feet above my own. The thing was a giant, and it looked hungry. As soon as the thought passed through my mind, a snake-like tongue shot out of its mouth and covered every inch of its face in sticky moisture before retreating. How much could devouring me do to satisfy this thing? Yes, I had some meat on my bones, but I couldn't imagine I'd be anything more than an appetizer before it ran off to consume something more filling.

If there wasn't a horror movie rule about looking a monster in the eyes already, there should be, because the moment I did, my stomach boiled with regret. Beneath the thick, furrowed unibrow were two menacing, glowing eyes. As if taking my eye-contact as a challenge, the ugly beast growled. Its lips were so thin they were hardly distinguishable from the rest of its face. When those crust covered corners lifted into a crooked smile, I could almost hear a demonic voice taunting me in my head. *'I got you right where I want you'.* I dared to look away, to find a route of escape, and when I did, the damn thing charged at me.

It took two seconds for the sound of its large, hooflike feet pounding against the ground to send a jolt through my body. The fear that froze me in place just moments before became the fuel I needed to move again. Prickles rushed across my limbs as I turned on my heel and ran as fast as I could. There was another path I could use to escape the area. I knew damn well I couldn't fight it off, but I sure as hell wasn't going to just stand there and let the thing take me out. My only alternative was to try to run away, and what a sad attempt it was. The heat of its touch spread across my skin before I realized what had happened. I'd made it a solid six steps when long, branch-like fingers wrapped around my shoulder and neck and pulled me back.

I closed my eyes, expecting to feel the sharp bite of its uneven teeth ripping through my skin. I just knew it was going to eat me, but it didn't. My feet left the ground, and wind rushed past my ears as it let me go. I opened my eyes to see the ugly demon getting further away, my arms and legs flailing at my sides. *Did this fucker just throw me?* I questioned a moment before my ass hit rocks and dirt. My teeth gritted when I felt the sting of flesh pulling from my forearms as I slid across the rocky ground and tried to shield my head from the impact.

Groaning from the pain, I rolled over just in time to watch the ugly thing turn and stomp towards me. It grunted with each step, as if it was a mile-long run. As it neared, I could have sworn the damn thing was actually laughing at me. That's right, mock the pathetic human prey. If I wasn't sure I was moments from losing my damn life, I might have come up with something witty to say about its struggle to breathe and disgusting body odor.

I can't believe this is how I'm going to die. The thought raced through my mind, leaving me dizzy as I watched the monster close in.

There really was nothing else I could do but speculate on the coming moments. In the time it would have taken me to get back to my feet, it would already be on top of me. Funny how thoughts worked faster than action in real time. Though I was confident in my capabilities, I hadn't quite reached the level of delusion it would take to believe I could outrun a damn demon or fight it off.

Then, my thoughts shifted as I recounted everything that happened, and before long, I was mentally beating myself up about picking up that damn book. I had no business experimenting with the ritual or making fun of something I knew damn well was not to be played with. I could all but hear my grandmother scolding me from the grave. It was with the imagined berating of my family's matriarch that my luck shifted.

I watched as the demon, who was just a few feet from me, stopped in its tracks. It didn't take much to realize there was another force at play. Its legs and arms twitched, and the muscles strained across its body, rippling with building pressure as it still tried to reach me. This was the time to run, but my body was hurting from the fall. It didn't matter. I gritted my teeth, moved to a sitting position, and started scooting away as its face twisted into something painfully unsettling. I almost lost my shit when its eyes bulged from its face.

The consumption of countless books, movies, and TV shows told me it was time to get the hell out of there. Whatever was happening, however mysterious, provided the opening I needed to get up. I stood, taking careful steps back from the demon despite the ache in my limbs. All I needed was a moment, just enough time to tell if it could get me. Nothing happened. If it could have, it would have grabbed me. I didn't question my luck—I turned and ran.

As my feet pounded against the grass-covered path, I heard its death gargle, like the sound of someone drowning. Yes, common sense told me to keep my head forward and run, but I couldn't help it. Never would I talk about the crazy white girl in the horror movies who just *had* to stop and stare. Curiosity craned my neck back toward the scene.

What I saw made me slide to a halt. It was him, the demon I wanted to believe my mind crafted for momentary pleasure—the one I'd fucked senseless. He held the massive body of the treelike demon over his head like a wrestler in a death match. With gritted teeth, he lifted it higher and turned toward the water.

"Go back to hell," he seethed with barely-contained fury as he tossed the body away from him.

It splashed into the water, and to my surprise, it sizzled as if the water was acidic. I slapped my hand over my mouth as the massive body quickly dissolved and disappeared beneath the surface. If the smell was terrible before, dissolving it only made it worse. I gagged as a breeze carried the sickly odor over to me.

Demon boy turned around to look at me, and when our eyes met, every moment of the previous night flashed through my mind again. He took a step toward me with an odd look of concern on his face, and I bolted. I got the hell out of there! No, I didn't thank him for saving my life or for disposing of the demon. If he could do that, who's to say he wouldn't turn on me?

All I could think of was getting to my house. Once there, I would be safe. I'd made it back to my car and ignored the questioning gazes from the people still in line for their food. I peeled out of the parking lot, nearly hitting the curb, and had to remind myself that this wasn't a movie. No plot armor would keep me safe from dying in a car accident. I had to chill, but I was constantly checking the rear-view mirror the entire drive, as if I would spot demon boy flying behind me.

"Get it together, Rayna," I said to myself as my hands gripped the steering wheel so tightly, my knuckles turned white.

Against the stacking odds, I made it home, and as the garage door closed, leaving me in darkness, it hit me. *Bitch, you live alone!* My dumb ass ran away from a populated area—with *witnesses*—to the solace of a home so well insulated, my neighbors wouldn't even hear me if I screamed. Apparently, demons could pop in and out of places at will, so what was stopping them from popping into my hallway just as I stepped inside and dragging me back to hell?

"Brilliant," I muttered as I stared at the empty passenger seat and once again wished my greatest concern was the sweaty ass drippings left behind by a horrible first date. "All that, and I still didn't get my damn tacos!"

I pulled my phone from my pocket, relieved that I hadn't lost it in the commotion. There was no way in hell I would go back for it. A few taps on the screen brought up Keri's face, blowing kisses at the camera. My thumb hovered over the call button. Did it make any sense to call her? The woman already made it clear she didn't believe me, and that hadn't changed. If nothing else, telling her would have her activating the calling tree and initiating some kind of intervention with the rest of our friends, an embarrassment I didn't need to endure.

If Keri didn't believe me before, she sure as hell wasn't going to believe me now. I could almost hear her voice. *'Sure, Rayna. All that happened, and no one else heard or saw a thing?'* I stared at the phone a moment longer as I ran down through the mental list of people I could possibly call. Everyone I thought of would immediately tell me the same thing: seek help.

Maybe they would think I was pathetic, that I'd been on my own too long and was losing touch with reality. The worst part was, I was wondering myself if maybe I hadn't made it all up just to give some type of excitement to my life. Had I really summoned a demon? Had I really then fucked said demon for the better part of six hours? And had I really just watched that same demon kill another one and send him to a sizzling underwater grave?

No one else reacted to what happened. No one saw or heard a thing, and it wasn't like that thing was *quiet*. Maybe my mind was slipping. What would that mean for the rest of my life? Could I still run a business this way? Leave it to me to consider work before my safety.

Those questions and several others circled in my head until my growling stomach was louder than my worried thoughts. I needed to go inside and eat. All the issues and worries of my fading sanity would have to wait.

After gathering myself, I opened the door to activate the motion sensor lights. My nerves were completely shot. The rush of adrenaline got me home, but the moment I parked the car, I felt my body crashing. *What the hell had I just witnessed? Why did no one else come to help me? Had that thing worked some kind of spell? Was that why it was so empty by the pond?* My mind raced with questions I couldn't possibly answer.

All I knew was I had to get in the house. From there, I could figure out what to do next. Carefully, I tiptoed from the car and through the double garage, which suddenly felt way too big, and up to the door into my home. With each step, I paused and waited, as if some demonic alarm would go off and alert them to my location. In my frazzled mind, it seemed logical that sitting in the car apparently made me invisible to them. I made it a foot away from the door and stared at the doorknob. *What if it burned to touch it?*

"Get the hell over it. It's not like they booby-trapped the damn thing!" I fussed at myself before grabbing the knob. Yes, I flinched. Yes, I felt silly as hell.

"Alert. Alert. Garage door. Alert. Alert." The security system scared the hell out of me; I'd forgotten to deactivate it before opening the door. I ran over to the panel and fumbled entering the security pin, only just avoiding a call to the police. No, I didn't need cops showing up at my house while I was clearly in a paranoid state of mind.

With the door shut and the alarm set, my stomach growled again, and at the same time, the skin on my arm stung. I looked down to realize I was bleeding. I'd scraped my arm worse than I thought when I fell. *Dammit, that's going to leave a scar.* The first order was to clean and bandage my wound. I also changed out of my dirt-covered clothing and mourned what was once my favorite pair of skinny jeans.

In fresh clothes and with my wounds cared for, I made a beeline to the kitchen. Threat of demon attacks or not, a girl had to eat. I turned on my lo-fi sounds as I limped around the kitchen—anything to help calm my nerves while I put together a meal of random things that had no business on a plate together.

While I worked, the adrenaline that rushed through my veins settled, and then came the rush of pain. Why the hell I thought I could be thrown around by a demon and not be severely injured was beyond me. I popped open the bottle of ibuprofen I kept in the drawer by the sink and tossed three pills into my mouth.

When I finished my chaotic collection, I sat down in front of a plate of leftover chicken, a bowl of sweet pickles, a side of spinach dip, and a bowl of spicy popcorn. I frowned at the collection; something was missing. Then, it hit me. I ran to the fridge and grabbed the leftover crab macaroni from two nights ago. My ass did a little happy dance while I quickly warmed it up, then returned to the meal and prepared to dig in.

"What are you eating?" The deep voice scared me so much, the fork went flying out of my hand. When I looked up, I was no longer alone. Demon boy sat in the chair across from me, crab macaroni on his face.

"Dammit, don't do that!" I should have been terrified and possibly running for my life, but maybe my hunger made me delusional, because I busted out laughing before quickly slapping my hand over my mouth when I saw the crab meat dangling from the tip of his nose. "My bad."

"That smells foul." He picked a napkin from the table to wipe the food from his face. "How can you eat like this?"

"My meal smells no worse than your sizzling demon friend." I shrugged.

"Well, I wasn't preparing to eat him." He finished wiping his face.

"Not something you guys do?" I asked. "Cannibalism?"

"Did it look like we were friends?" He went back to my earlier statement, carefully avoiding the accusation. "I killed him. If we were friends, would I have done that?"

"For all I know, that's how demons play." I picked up the piece of chicken and took a bite, quickly following it with a sweet pickle covered in spinach dip.

"You're no longer questioning my existence?" He frowned at me, and I thought he might actually pout.

"I figure if I'm losing my mind, I might as well steer into the skid." I got up and headed to the refrigerator to grab a bottle of soda. "Besides, I can talk to you about you being a demon. If I mention it to anyone else, they'll look at me like I need to be locked away for my safety."

"Speaking of your safety." He watched me carefully as I returned to my seat. "What the hell were you doing out there by yourself?"

"Excuse me?" I slammed the drink down and rolled my eyes. "I'm a grown-ass woman and I do what I want. That's what I was doing out there. Who do you think you are, coming up in my house and questioning me about what I'm doing?"

"It's not safe," he spoke in a strained voice, visibly trying to keep his cool. I could already tell I tested his patience, and I wasn't planning on stopping.

"Well, it's not like demon attacks have been common in my life. Why would I have thought that a place I visit damn near once a week would suddenly be dangerous just because you popped up in my bedroom?" I narrowed my eyes. "Are you going to lecture me about how I need to stay safe? Is that what's happening here? Because if it is, let me trade this soda for a glass of wine."

"I can't pop up here every time you're in danger," he scolded me. "Be more careful."

"I'm sorry." I looked over my shoulder, searching for someone who wasn't there, because he clearly wasn't talking to me. "Who asked you to? Do you see them here?"

"You did!" he said through tight lips. "Do you not remember the ritual you did under the moon?"

"I said words, you came here. We did what we did, and I sent you on your way. I didn't call you back up here." I chewed on the thought for a moment. Had I unknowingly called out to him while running for my life? "Yeah, no. I didn't do the spell again. You just appeared."

"I think you're smart enough to know it's not as simple as telling me to go away." He leaned forward on his elbows. "You read those fantasy books; don't they cover how all this works? It's not all fiction, obviously, so apply the same logic here."

"Why the hell can't it be that simple?" I huffed. "I don't want you here. Yes, I've read a lot of those books, but this is the first time anything like this has ever happened to me, so don't act like I'm supposed to be the expert on getting rid of unwanted demons. Besides, that spell was supposed to bring me a soulmate, a loving, doting man who would kill big bugs and build custom bookshelves for me, not some angry ass demon who thinks he can tell me what to do."

"That ritual ties us together." He huffed, clearly annoyed he had to explain himself. "You asked for a soulmate, and you got it. A tie between two souls. I know you weren't exactly expecting it to work, or expecting it to bring you a demon, but here I am." He leaned back in his seat and shook his head. "Unfortunately for you, I'm not exactly a well-liked guy where I come from."

"What does that mean?" Suddenly, it felt like I couldn't breathe. A tie between two souls and a demon who wasn't well liked—what the hell had I gotten myself into?

"It means that smelly demon won't be the last to come after you. They know about you, and they think you're a weak point for me."

"So, what? Your enemies are now my enemies?" I could feel the air leaving the room. "There's some demonic target on my back because we fucked?"

"Not because we fucked, but yes." He nodded. "Demons have energy signatures, and mine is now intertwined with yours."

"Oh, well, fuck me." I flopped back in my seat and placed my hand on my chest to steady my breathing. "This can't be happening."

"I did that already. Do you want me to do it again?" He grinned, and his horns grew with the spread of his lips.

"Very funny, demon boy." I pointed to his forehead. "You can put those away."

"Do *not* call me that." He frowned, and his horns vanished again.

"What? Demon boy? Is that not what you are?" I smirked. "I like it. It fits you just fine."

"My name is Metice."

"I'm sorry, did I ask?" I teased him.

"Why are you acting like I've done something to you? I didn't recite a spell that snatched you from your home and dragged you across realms," he fired back.

"Whatever." I sipped from the cool drink and then swirled the cup in my hands. The ice clinked against the glass, marking the seconds that passed as we stared at each other.

"That's what happened, in case you weren't aware. One moment, I'm enjoying myself in the hellscape watching an interesting performance between two dovetail demons, and the next, I'm here, on… Earth." He said the word like it left a foul taste in his mouth. "And I have to keep coming here for you until I figure out how to sever this infuriating link between us."

"I didn't know the spell would work." I rolled my eyes, refusing to take any responsibility for his woes. "Like I told you, it was a silly thing I found in a book.

I thought it was fiction. And I didn't specifically call out to you because, until a few seconds ago, I didn't even know your name. I'm just as put out by all this as you are. Trust me, I had no wishes to be stalked by demons today. If you want to air out your grievances, find the author who put the spell in the book."

"Why did you do it?" He leaned forward, looking at me as if he could see right through to the truth he felt I would hide from him.

"What?" I frowned and leaned further back in my seat.

"Why did you work the ritual?" he clarified his question. "You didn't think it would work, so why do it?"

"I was drunk, horny, and thought it would be funny." I shrugged then played with the food in front of me. "Does there need to be some deeper meaning behind it?"

"Funny?" He grunted. "You thought it would be funny to play with magic?"

"Yeah." I couldn't believe it, but his stare made me nervous, like I would choke on my words. "Maybe not funny, ha-ha, but more like funny, I don't have to feel so pathetic after being ghosted by my friends who chose their boyfriends over me. They left me sitting alone in a bar to be hit on by every scuzzy man who stumbled into that place. The shit was depressing. So yeah, I came home, cracked open a bottle of wine, and had a silly little moment to lighten a heavy night. It wasn't supposed to work!"

"Sounds like you need some better friends." He watched me with dark eyes, trying to penetrate the invisible wall I frantically built around myself. "That still doesn't explain why you fucked me."

"I thought I was dreaming." I dropped my head on the table, pushing my plate aside. "Remember the horny part? It's been a *long* time since I got me a little something something. Hell, the real-world dudes ain't giving what they're supposed to be giving. So yeah, in a dream, standing across from a muscular, mostly human-looking man, with an apparently rotating dick, I hopped on it. I'm still trying to figure out how you got your dick to do that."

"It does a lot of things," he smirked as his eyes glinted, almost teasing me.

"Oh?" I raised a brow and dropped my eyes but was disappointed to find my target blocked by the edge of the table.

"Eyes up here, please." He pointed to his face. "Do you realize you're not dreaming now?"

"Yes." I looked across the table at him. "I don't want it to be true because it means you and your demonic buddies won't go away, but I know this isn't a dream. If it was, I'd be able to rewrite this moment and not have to deal with any of this."

"Okay, so you realize you're awake." He leaned closer. "So, tell me, Rayna, why are you aroused?"

"What?" My eyes widened, and I squeezed my thighs together to stop whatever he thought was happening. "I am not!"

"There's no need to be embarrassed or lie about it. I can smell it, your arousal." He chuckled and leaned back in his seat. "I thought you were only attracted to me because you thought it was a dream, but I can feel your heat from over here."

"I'm not a damn dog. I'm not in heat!" Because I didn't know what else to do, I started cleaning the table. I hadn't even finished eating, but his intense glare had me putting things away, anything to avoid his accusing stare.

"Say what you want, but you're aroused." He stood from the table, crossed the room, and invaded my space. His horns grew with each step, and I swear, it felt like watching his dick get harder. "Your pulse quickens, your pussy is wet, and I smell it. Your body wants me, Rayna."

"You're delusional." I moved away from him, scooting around the large granite island. "I don't know what drugs they have in hell, but you need to ease up off them."

And then I questioned if I was the one on drugs, because he disappeared. One moment, he was walking toward me, the next, he was gone. *Good. Let him be gone.* I took a deep breath, thinking he might actually leave me alone, but of course, he wouldn't make it that easy.

I took a step back and felt the warm body of a man—a demon—behind me. His chest pressed against my back as his arm wrapped around my waist, pulling me closer to him. I gasped as he placed his lips next to my ear to whisper his next words.

"I'm not delusional. I'm darkness, and if you're not careful, I'll devour you." Warm breath brushed against my neck before his lips met my flesh. His kiss lingered on my pulse point, making my heart race and my legs tremble. "Keep yourself safe—unless you want me to drag you to hell with me."

Before I could come up with something snappy to say about hell freezing over before I'd allow that to happen, he was gone again. I waited longer than I cared to admit for him to pop back into view. He didn't. I rounded the island and sat on the stool. Right in my line of sight was the wine rack, the decorative piece holding the bottles of sweet nectar that got me into this mess.

"Shit, I need a drink."

4
Little Old Ladies

Of course, I got very little sleep that night. I swear, every little sound had me jumping out of my damn skin and reaching for the five-hundred-dollar collector's baseball bat that was no longer in its pristine casing but now propped up against my nightstand. It wasn't much, but I hoped it would at least give me enough time to run away—if I didn't fall on my ass from delirium first.

When I finally slept, my dreams were invaded by a shapeshifting demon with adjustable horns, a rotating dick, and a terrifying backdrop of the underworld. My mind concocted images of a blazing landscape filled with demons, the darkest voids, and hellfire. Despite the scenery that belonged more in a horror story than an erotic one, the narrative shifted from fear to fucking. Each time, I woke up just before the demon ripped my clothes off and banged me into oblivion.

And yeah, I was pissed about it. It was hard enough being horny, but horny and terrified was an unnerving combination. By the time morning came, I felt like shit. The sun peered through the sheer curtains, making me wish more and more that I wasn't such a cheap ass and had shelled out the extra hundred bucks for the actual blackout curtains. The cheaper version just didn't get the job done.

"Sunday morning. The demons should stay away. God, I hope so," I muttered as I threw my feet over the edge of the bed. "Too bad I gave up the church scene years ago. Maybe someone there could actually help me out with this."

Now, I wouldn't call myself a religious type, and I also wasn't one to believe in anything like demons, but in the last twenty-four hours, I'd already seen two in real life, one far more disgusting than the other. I could almost hear the raspy voice of my aunt, a bible-thumping nutcase, shouting from the rooftops about Jesus returning and dousing us all in holy water.

Every time I thought of it, I laughed. How could I not? My cousin Phil scared the hell out of the old woman while wearing a scarred face mask with makeshift horns he'd crafted out of twigs and tape. After that, she went on a week-long tirade of "cleansing" the youth of the family. If we came within three feet of her, she would splash us with foul-smelling liquid and then trap us in a bear hug and pray for our souls. When I told my mother about the smell, she teased me that it must have been toilet water. She said it was a joke, but to this day, I believed it was.

After careful consideration of recent events, I decided it was best to stay in. There was nothing on my to do list that called for going outside anyway. The last thing I wanted was another encounter like the one I'd had at the park. Unfortunately, the self-inflicted restriction backfired. It was like being a hormonal teenager. The moment when your parents told you not to do something, suddenly, it was like the world would end if you didn't get to experience it right then and there. I tried distracting myself with various activities, like online games, streaming shows, paint-by-numbers, and anime, but of course, my mind kept wandering back to the land of demons.

After making myself a bowl of broccoli cheddar soup, I decided a good book was the thing I needed. I put the bowl to the side and began my search, and of course, my effort to find something on my ever-growing TBR that captured my attention didn't work. Sorting through the stack of books only made me spiral about my current situation. Reading was what got me into this mess; who the hell would have ever thought reading a spell from a novel would work? I tossed my third attempt at escaping into the carefully crafted fictional world to the side and then had a thought.

"It worked once," I said to myself. I shrugged and then went on the search for more spells. "I *swear*, one of these books had a spell for tripling your income or something like that. I still need to buy a new car thanks to that too-tight pants wearing asshole."

I muttered to myself as I continued my search for the book, and after coming up empty, I gave up. Maybe it was a good thing. It wasn't as if the spell had gone according to plan. "Fuck it," I huffed as I grabbed my bag and headed for the door before curiosity actually killed the cat.

I had no idea where I was going as I pulled out of my garage. I just needed to get the hell out of the house. I tried calling my girls up, to get some companionship in my moment of fleeting sanity, but once again, none of them answered their damn phones. *I really need to make new friends.*

As I drove, I went down the list of people I could call and felt weird at how short that list actually was. I refused to call my mother, who would only bore me for hours before eventually getting on my case about how old I was getting. I had the nerve to be in my thirties, unmarried, and with no kids. How dare I!

My dad would have been a good choice if he lived anywhere near me. After he retired, he moved seven states away and spent most of his time golfing, so there was no way I could just hop on his couch for the afternoon. He would have definitely kept me entertained with tales of the good old days. I could just hear him bragging about mackin' on young girls and how fly his jheri curl was.

Instead of stalking my friends or blowing up their phones until I found companionship, I chose another route: the friendship of strangers you don't actually have to talk to. The movies. Sure, watching things at home hadn't worked a damn for clearing my mind, but that was different. A big dark theater full of strangers might be the thing to help. I pulled up to the theatre, opened the app on my phone, and purchased a ticket to the next showing, an action movie about three young girls battling aliens in outer space.

"Perfect." I rolled my eyes. "At least it's nearly sold out already."

Inside, I paid for the grossly overpriced snacks, got the largest slushy they offered, and headed for my seat. And the damn theatre was empty, not a single person there. Any other time, this would have been my dream, but when demons were looking for me, it made my stomach twist into knots. I almost turned and left until two little old ladies entered behind me. Maybe the people who bought the other one hundred seats were just running late. Yeah, that was likely, five minutes before the movie was supposed to start. Nothing to worry about there!

But that was okay, because no demon would attack with grannies around…right? Wasn't that like a horror movie rule? Grannies and babies were off limits? I wouldn't know, because typically, I was too afraid to sit through a full horror flick. I'd always make up an excuse to leave, no matter how ridiculous it sounded. *Oh, look, a fax just came in!* They didn't believe me, but they let me off the hook every time.

I settled into my seat, took several deep breaths, and started chomping on handfuls of popcorn as the movie began. The previews were interesting, mostly comedy and action. I made a mental note to check out one about single women abducted by aliens. Wasn't too far off from my current lived experience.

Yeah, being in the nearly empty theater had my nerves on edge, but the movie was good. Once I got into it, I damn near forgot about everything. From the moment the first weird creature appeared on the screen followed by an afro sporting badass who kicked its head off its shoulder, I was stuck! It was about twenty minutes into the movie when the unexpected explosion made me jump so damn hard, I almost fell out my seat. I looked around to make sure no one saw me.

Of course, no one noticed. The damn place was still empty. I checked on the grannies to see if they'd survived the shock, but they weren't there.

"What the hell?" I lifted from my seat to get a better look at the empty chairs, expecting to spot the tops of grey curly hair in the lower seats, but they weren't there, and that nagging feeling in my stomach started again.

I squinted to scan the theater. There was a faint hope that the little old ladies had chosen better seats, considering no one else entered after them. I would find them eating their own snacks, so engrossed in the film that they hadn't noticed how weird my ass was acting.

And then, the paranoia kicked in. My stomach twisted. If they were shuffling around through the darkness, I would have noticed. The movie was good, but it wasn't that damn good. I hadn't seen them leave. That spark of intuition nudged me and said it was time to get the hell out of there. I picked up my sling bag, threw it across my shoulder, and headed for the exit.

As much as I was enjoying the movie, something didn't feel right, and that was reason enough to miss the ending. I made it to the exit and pushed against the swinging door, but it didn't budge. I leaned all my weight against it, but the damn thing refused to move. The thin hairs on the back of my neck stood, and I felt the change in the energy in the room. With the building tension came the sounds of explosions blasting over the speakers. The movie grew more intense, and as the sound rose, so did my blood pressure.

I pounded my fist against the doors, but no one answered. Could they even hear me? Would they think my cries for help were just a part of the movie? There was barely anyone in the damn place anyway. Most people were spending their Sunday at church or sucking down mimosas at brunch, not in the chilly theaters watching women fighting aliens. Still, what else could I do? I banged on the door until my fists hurt from the impact then switched to kicking the damn thing.

"Help!" I screamed. "The door is stuck! Is anyone out there?" My throat burned from yelling, and still, no one came.

I looked over my shoulder and damn near kicked myself when I saw the glowing exit sign. In case of emergency, use the exit, not pound on the door like a maniac. I abandoned the useless door, hoping for better luck with the emergency exit.

I was a foot away from what I hoped would be my salvation when I heard it. The sound created such a fear in me that I skid to a halt just short of the door. I turned on my heel to the sound of bone chilling laughter. My eyes almost fell out of my head. Those two little old ladies with their blue-grey hair and large eyes stood at the top of the steps, mouths wide and displaying sharp teeth as they cackled.

"What the hell?" I spoke, but I couldn't take my eyes off them.

They stood there, holding hands and watching me. Their wrinkled brown skin, deep-set eyes, and grey curls bobbled as they continued laughing. One lifted a thin finger at me as she laughed, like I was putting on some kind of one-woman show, my act timed and crafted with the perfect comedic punch lines.

"What the hell is so funny?" I couldn't help myself. Irritation broke through fear, and I yelled at the woman.

"Oh, you'll find out," they said in unison and then did something that made my stomach twist into a knot.

The little old ladies wrapped their arms around each other then, in a process my mind wasn't creative enough to imagine, they fused together! They melted into one form, like two scoops of ice cream on a hot summer day. Their bodies swirled and blended until they were indistinguishable from each other, their legs and arms sticking from places where they didn't belong, and soon, I was looking at one oddly shaped body with two heads. Each head continued laughing as their faces mutated. Their chins elongated as their ears pressed into the side of their heads before disappearing altogether. I watched, completely disgusted, as gray hair transformed into whiskers above wrinkled foreheads and yellowed eyes resembling a mutated cat.

"Oh, hell no." I took a slow step back, and then the damn thing started humming. That was the eerie ass sign in every horror story I'd ever read. Things were not about to play out in my favor. The cackling turned to something more sinister. It was time to get the hell out of there.

I turned and bolted for the door, and I made it. For a short moment, my dumb ass actually thought I was going to get out of there. But just like the first door, it didn't budge. I threw my full weight against it, and even though I heard the latch click, it still didn't open. My last hope was that it would at least sound the alarm, that someone would know I was in danger, but again, nothing happened. The soft light from the exit sign flickered above my head, and then it went out. Every damn light in the theater went out leaving me in darkness with that creepy ass humming.

"Fuck. What the hell was his name?" I squeezed my eyes shut, focusing on the conversation I had with the demon in my kitchen. If I needed him, he had to come, right?

The emergency lights switched on just in time for me to catch sight of mutated demon bitches coming straight for me. I had no way out. My eyes darted around to find a path. What could I do? Run in circles and hope they got so tired that they gave up trying to kill me?

That's exactly what I did. I darted to the other side of the theatre, away from the exit. Luckily, the blended mess wasn't agile, and instead of making a smooth turn to follow me, it crashed into the door where I had just been standing.

"Dammit," I cursed at myself as I darted back up the steps. "What the hell is his name?"

I didn't have much longer to figure it out. The humming turned to cackling again as the monstrosity corrected itself and made a path for me. I knew I wouldn't be able to keep outrunning it. I ran again, twisting though the seats and glancing over my shoulder at the thing to make sure it wasn't getting too close. And in true horror girly fashion, I looked back while trying to turn around a seat and fell flat on my ass.

That was it. I lost my edge, and the thing was closing in. It got close enough for me to smell its horrible breath, and apparently, that's what I needed to remember his name.

As I scooted across the floor trying to regain my footing, I called out his name.

"Metice!"

Absolutely nothing happened.

He didn't magically appear to save my day. Nope. No big dangerous demon to fight the crazy cat bitch. What happened was that mutated granny cat monster kept coming for me. If I hadn't finally made it back to my feet, it would have got me. I dodged the clawed hand just in time. Back on my feet, I jumped up two rows, ran across the room, and when I saw it had followed my path, I ran back down the steps.

I could see a sliver of light coming through the emergency exit. The impact from when the mutation slammed into it earlier had bent the hinges and forced the door to open just enough to let the light in. That was my way out. All I had to do was outrun it a little longer, and then I'd be free.

I was surprised at how my body responded. Here I was, asthmatic, overweight, and knees aching with the age I pretended wasn't on my license, while hopping down the stairs like they were nothing. Despite the unimaginable acrobatics I'd done, the demon was already closing in on my tail. The wicked voices blended with another round of sickly laughter.

Was he ignoring me? I couldn't help the thought that flashed through my head. *Where the hell was that damn demon?* I was in trouble. He said he could feel me, so why hadn't he felt any of this? At the bottom of the steps, I had a little too much momentum and skid across the floor, slamming into the wall beneath the screen.

The damn thing was now hopping over the chairs. I had no time. I darted for the door, pushing my body and ignoring the nasty sounds behind me. I made it. I made it to the door, and... it didn't open! Despite the slither of light, the hinges were so badly bent, they fought against my efforts to open the door.

"Fuck!" I cried out as I turned and watched as the monster came for me.

I looked at the steps. Okay, time to go back up? The demonic old ladies must have read my thoughts, because just then, the fused being split with a disgusting sound like muscle being ripped from bone. Once they were two bodies again, they headed in different directions. That was it. They were going to corner me. I'd have nowhere to go.

"What the hell happened to you'll come when I call?" I cursed beneath my breath and then tried one more time to call the demon who started this mess. "Metice! Get your dark ass over here and help me!"

That time, something changed. The atmosphere shifted with a new sense of tension, followed by a quick flush of heat that pulsated around me. My skin tingled, and for a moment, that tingle turned into red hot fire. And then, just as suddenly, it stopped. The two ugly old ladies must not have noticed it, because they continued to close in on me. The one to my right leapt through the air, and I threw my hands up to shield myself from her attack.

"Aacck!" the choking sound came before the thud of a body slamming into the wall.

I looked up to see the old lady on the ground, and just in front of me, the demon with the rotating dick. *Finally*.

Metice turned to the other one just as it changed its course, abandoning efforts to get to me. It screeched, no longer laughing when it saw its other half limp on the floor. The thing actually attacked him.

He jumped back and grabbed the bony arm reaching out to him, dodging the spiked fingertips as he threw her into the theater screen. She clawed at the screen, leaving rips through it as she slid to the floor.

Metice turned to me, but before he could say anything, the first lady jumped up again, her neck hanging brokenly from her shoulders. She still laughed and pointed at him, and then, faster than I thought possible, she also charged him. Her little body had to be fueled completely by her thirst for retribution, because she moved like she was an extension of the shadows.

"Watch out!" I screamed and pointed to the threat behind him.

He turned around just in time, and this time, he didn't toss her to the side. His fists slammed through her chest, ripping out the heart, which he dropped to the floor and stomped. You'd think having your heart ripped out would be an instant death, but it took a moment for the mind to realize what happened. I watched in horror as her sinister eyes moved from Metice's face to his bloody hand, then finally to the gaping hole in her chest. Then, with a weak sob, she crumpled to the floor.

Metice wasted no time. With her down, he returned to the other and completed the same task. He pulled the bodies together, then removed their heads from their shoulders. Headless, their bodies melted and gave off a nauseating smell that had me gagging within seconds. I didn't know who would have to clean that up, but I didn't envy them.

"I dare you to get up from that." He spit on the sizzling body.

"I'm never going to get that smell out of my nose," I choked as the contents of my stomach threatened to evacuate.

A mixture of orange, brown, and green oozed from their orifices as their bodies disappeared, leaving burn marks everywhere they touched.

"What did I tell you?" Metice snapped and marched over to me, his finger pointed in my face.

"Don't point at me like I'm some child for you to scold." I slapped his hand away then pointed right back at him. "I did nothing. I went to a movie by myself. It's your buddies who won't leave me alone!"

"We're going." Metice grabbed my arm, but of course, I pulled away.

"Keep your hands off me." I brushed my hair from my face and adjusted my bag, which was sliding down my shoulder. "Where the hell do you think you're taking me?"

"Somewhere where you will be safe, and I don't have to keep dropping everything to come save you from yourself," he answered.

"My house isn't far from here." I huffed and headed for the exit. "I'll go there. You won't have to worry about me."

"You're not going back to your house. It isn't safe." He did that creepy reappearance thing and was suddenly in front of me. "I'm taking you home with me."

"Your home? In hell?" I stepped back from him. "You have got to be out of your mind if you think I'm about to let you take me to hell."

"There is no way I'm leaving you here," he grunted. "I cannot keep dealing with these distractions."

"Yeah whatever." I sidestepped him, my sling bag knocking against him as I once again headed for the door. Maybe I was losing my damn mind. None of this could be real. I refused to believe it. Keri was right: I needed to call my therapist. Hell, maybe I needed to be on meds.

Then, he did that creepy shit again. *Poof*! There he was, blocking my exit. "Seriously?" Metice's massive hands grabbed my arms and pinned them to my sides. Of course, I couldn't move. He was a demon and strong as hell.

"Get your hands off me. I'm not going to..." My vision went dark, and my mind hummed with dizzying energy as the theatre and the sounds of an alien invasion disappeared. There was a loud pop and fizzle before I could get the last word out of my mouth.

"Hell." I blinked, suddenly standing in front of a massive window and looking out onto the hellscape I saw in my dreams.

I pinched myself. It was the typical test of reality. If I felt it, it was real, not a dream I could wake up from. After the sting of my self-inflicted injury subsided and the weight of my new reality settled on my shoulders, I screamed bloody murder.

5
Abducted

"Are you done?" Metice rubbed his ear and shot me a look like I'd have to pay his doctor bill for the broken ear drum. "You need to stop pinching yourself, unless that's some kind of kink you haven't shared with me yet."

"Am I done? Are you serious?" I screamed. "I'm in hell. I'm in hell. I'm actually in motherfucking hell!"

How could he ask me such a stupid question? My heart pounded in my chest, and what felt like a severe tension headache wrapped around my brain as I tried to process what was happening. If I were thinking straight, I would have been sucking on my inhaler in between borderline hyperventilating.

"I think you ruptured something." Metice shook his head and tapped his ear like he was tuning an instrument. "I may be deaf in one ear. Say something quick." He plugged his left ear and leaned in with his right.

"I don't give a fuck about your damn hearing! You actually brought me to hell!" I started swinging, slapping the demon upside the head, neck, and shoulders. "Are you out of your fucking mind? Take me home. Take me home!"

Metice dodged my next two swings, but I kept aiming for him. It only added fuel to my rage when he spoke without effort, despite my attacks.

"I told you exactly what I would do if you kept getting into trouble. I'm many things, but I'm not a liar. Yes, you are in the hellscape." He caught my wild swing before I made contact with his face. "If you hit me again, I will chain you to the wall. Again, I am a lot of things, but I speak the truth."

"Why? Why would you ever think bringing me to the place where demons actually live was the best way to keep me safe from the demons who are after me?" That was when the second wave of panic hit me. I backed away from him and scanned the room like I was running from the cops. "They can probably tell I'm here now, sense my presence. Can they smell me? Oh shit, what if they heard my scream?"

"Right, because all of hell heard that." He laughed in my face, like I wasn't having a total mental breakdown. "Yes, it was loud, but not that damn loud. Don't be so dramatic. I just need time to figure this out without having to pop to Earth every five minutes to save you. Now, if I let you go, do you promise not to swing on me again?"

"I'm not promising a damn thing." I narrowed my eyes. "I'm also not one to tell lies."

"Right." He dropped my hand and turned his back to me. I swear, it was like an invitation to try him.

Before I could decide if I wanted to test the limits, he turned back around and handed me a pen and paper.

"What is this for?" I stared at the items in his hand, not taking them.

"It's for you to make a list of whatever you need from your place. I'll go retrieve whatever you ask for." He pushed the items at me again. "I'm trying to be accommodating."

"I don't want you going through my stuff." I slapped away the offered pen and paper.

"Fine, you can make do with what I have here." He shrugged. "I doubt I have all the frilly stuff you humans use for cleaning, but the lava rocks make for a good exfoliant."

I looked around and realized he was right. There was no way he had what I needed, and I had no idea how long he planned to keep me there. The home was carved into what looked like a cavern but had odd touches of modern amenities. There was an actual door and windows that looked out onto a strange landscape.

We were high in the air and overlooking a small lake. Metice apparently liked isolation. To the left, I could see tall rock formations, six of them. They looked like pillars created from stone, but I could tell they were a part of the earth, carved by time, not by man. In the distance, there were thick clouds dancing across a reddish sky. To the right were hills covered in trees with red mossy tops. I could see nothing on the ground beneath the canopy.

Inside, the furniture kept the same aesthetic as outside. Dark red and brown leather covered everything. Every tabletop looked to be made from the same stone as the pillars, even the floor. I imagined he cut a hole in the side of the seventh pillar and made it his home. He even had what looked like a kitchen, and I hoped like hell that one of the other doors led to a functioning bathroom. I had no idea what it would be like to wash my ass with lava rocks, but I didn't want to find out.

"Fine." I held out my hand. "Give me the damn paper. I can't believe this is happening. Maybe I really am losing my mind."

After finishing the quick list of things I could remember needing to survive, I handed it over to him.

"Do you really need all this?" he grunted after reading the paper, which had items spilling over to the back side of the page.

"Do you want to hear me complaining the entire time I'm here?" I crossed my arms over my chest and huffed at him. "If not, I suggest you bring back everything on the list."

"Infuriating," he muttered before the energy in the room tensed with power, and then, Metice disappeared from sight.

"You're the infuriating one!" I yelled at the empty room. "Damn asshole! Acting like I asked to be here."

I stood there like a moron, waiting for him to return. I don't know why, but I thought he would pop right back in, arms full of the things I requested. Apparently, he didn't have those kinds of powers. After a few moments, I gave up and decided the best way to pass the time was to invade his privacy.

How could I not? I was standing in a bachelor pad in the middle of hell! Yes, I was still freaking out, heart racing and struggling to breathe, but I had to distract myself from that. It was the best way to handle it. First, I took in the bigger picture. The dark walls were curved, smooth, and looked like they were covered in tar. I pressed my hand to it, expecting the slick surface to be sticky, but it wasn't. It was cool to the touch and even sent a shiver up my arm into my shoulder. Maybe that was by design. Cool walls to keep the heat from hell out.

Surprisingly, his furniture was soft and covered in what felt like the finest imported leathers. I didn't think a demon would care about stuff like that. Candles were used to light the space, which I assumed meant there was no electricity in hell. How unfortunate. There were a few doors that led to other rooms, plus one that looked like it was made of a heavy metal I assumed was an exit. I was *not* about to be going through that one.

The first door I opened turned out to be his bedroom. The space was massive, simple in decoration. A large bed sat in the center. Candlelight lit the space just as it had in the other room, and along the walls were books stacked nearly to the ceilings. I couldn't help myself; I had to find out what books this demon liked to read. I was impressed. As I went through the collection, I found a ton of titles, some familiar but most not. There were ones so ancient, they looked like they would fall apart if I breathed too hard near them, and others had alien texts on the covers. I wondered how vast the universe was and how many worlds Metice had been to. Clearly, he wasn't just a pest for single women on Earth.

"There is no way I'm actually in hell." I plopped down on the large bed. His library was interesting, but not that damned interesting. I was in hell, captured and taken there by a demon who was now going through my things to bring me a list of supplies. How was this my life? "Whoever is writing my story has a funny sense of humor." I dropped the book I'd been holding onto the bed.

Just then, the bag hanging around my chest vibrated, and I damn near jumped out of my skin. "Shit!" I screamed before realizing the sensation came from the bag I'd managed to keep with me during the fight with the mutated grannies, not a demon coming to drag me deeper into the pits of hell. I fumbled with the zipper to open the bag and pulled it out. I gagged as I saw the message on the screen.

Booty Juice:

I had fun. When can I see you again?

"How about never!" I fussed. "Be glad I didn't bill your ass! Wait, how the hell do I have service down here?" I stared at the phone and then tapped the screen, hoping whatever sliver of service I had was enough to get a call out.

At first, nothing happened, but then it connected, and my heart raced. The phone rang several times, and I almost gave up hope, but after the fourth ring, the screen lit up, and my friend's face appeared. Keri looked like she was just waking up. Her bonnet hung off the side of her head, as if she was fighting her own demons in her sleep.

"Girl, do you know what time it is?" Keri coughed to clear her throat.

"Keri, I need your help," I whispered, because as far as I knew, the walls had ears and a mouth to report everything I said to Metice.

"What's wrong?" Keri leaned in. "Where the hell are you?"

"I-" I thought about what I needed to say. Keri already thought I was out of my damn mind. How would she accept the news that I was in hell? "You have to keep an open mind and understand that I am not losing it."

"That's a comforting lead in." Keri struggled to turn on the light by her bed, which illuminated her pissed off expression even more.

"Hold on." I thought it was best to show her better than tell her. I left his bedroom and walked out to the open room with the massive window that overlooked the underworld. Thinking this was the best way to prove my point, I turned the camera to the window and waited for Keri to respond.

"And I'm looking at what, exactly?" she asked.

I turned the screen back on myself and sighed. "I'm in hell."

"Cool. Can I go back to sleep?" Keri rolled her eyes.

"What?" My heart dropped. *She doesn't believe me. Great.* "I just told you I'm in hell!"

"What did you find, some AI generated filter or something? Is this for that game you were talking about creating at one point? Looks pretty impressive." Keri yawned, a sign she was done with the conversation. "I'm happy for you, but couldn't you have waited until the sun was up to tell me?"

"Sun? What?" It hadn't been that long since demon boy kidnapped me. It was barely the afternoon when it happened. How could it be that late? "Look, Keri, I know that this sounds insane, but I'm telling you. I'm in hell!"

"I love you. I do, Rayna, but this is too far." Keri sighed. I knew what she was thinking. It was a part of the reason I was in therapy. "What do you need to bring you out of this, because I'm seriously worried about you."

"I'm not lying," I pleaded with her to believe me.

"Look, I gotta go. My alarm is going to sound off in a couple hours, and I really need sleep before dealing with those horrible people I call coworkers. Please call your therapist. I'm worried about you."

"Keri-" I wanted to beg her to believe what I was saying, but the call ended. I thought of calling someone else, but the air tensed with a now familiar feeling. He was coming back. I hurried, turned the phone off, hid it in my bag, and sat awkwardly on the large chair by the window.

A moment later, Metice appeared in front of me, holding four bags and staring at me like he wanted to wrap his hands around my throat and end it all. The bags fell to the floor with a thud, and I had to stop myself from laughing in his face.

"Did you really need all of this...stuff?" He pointed to the bags. "How long do you plan on being here?"

"I don't know, you tell me." I leaned forward and narrowed my eyes at him. "Unless you're ready to take me back home, I need every single item on that list."

"Including the half-finished crochet project?" He lifted the bag that had my yarn falling out of it.

"I finally have some time on my hands." I shrugged. "Who knows, maybe I'll get inspired to finish it. And you don't have electricity here, so I need something to do while I wait for whatever you think you need to do while I'm here."

"Of course," he grunted.

"This isn't right. You can't just kidnap someone." I rolled my eyes. I expected him to give in and tell me I could go home or at least argue a little more. "I have responsibilities, a job, people who rely on me for things. Am I supposed to sit here and allow my life to fall apart while you do whatever it is you need to do?"

"I don't care what you do. You have plenty of stuff here." He moved the bags from the floor to the sofa beside me. "I even brought your laptop, though there is no internet connection in hell. I got one of those portable batteries for you. Its solar charging, so you can keep it powered up by sitting it next to the window."

"There's a sun in hell? I mean, I know there's light out there, I just assumed in the underworld, you didn't have a regular solar system." I looked out the window, and for the first time, I processed that there was a source of light in the sky and a warmth carried by that light.

"Please stop trying to compare my world to the various lores you humans have created. This isn't the hell you think it is. It's more like another planet far away from Earth. We have our own sun. We even have our own power supplies, though they aren't compatible with your devices. It should work perfectly fine."

"Perfect, I can draft emails that will never be sent." I rolled my eyes.

"The appropriate response is thank you." He waited.

"There are rules against these kinds of things. Snatching someone up and refusing to let them go home isn't okay." I wasn't about to thank him for a damn thing. So what, he brought me a battery pack—he still had me there against my will.

"Do you honestly think I care at all about your human laws?" Metice stepped back from me and looked me up and down like he was assessing my soul. "I thought you were smarter than that."

"What am I supposed to do here? You want to investigate, fine, but what do you expect me to do? Just sit in this cave hidden away?"

"That's exactly what I expect." He pointed to the bags full of items. "Work on your crafts, write in your journal. Hell, work on that screenplay you never finished. Do whatever you need to keep you from annoying me while we figure this out."

"How the hell do you know about my screenplay? Did you go through my things?" I grabbed my laptop and pulled it to my chest, as if that would erase the knowledge from his head.

"Isn't that what you sent me there to do? I can't help it if I can read." He finally sat on the chair across from me. "Honestly, it started off pretty good. That's what took me so long. Started reading and lost track of time."

"That is a violation of my privacy!" I shouted. "How could you do that?"

"Don't worry, I won't tell anyone about your fascination with alien porn." Metice snorted, and his horns grew.

"It is not alien porn!" I defended my work about a woman whose blind date turned out to be an alien.

"Sure." He leaned back, and his shoulders shook with laughter. "Now I know why you were so quick to fuck me when we first met: working out scenes for your story. I wonder what your dreams are really like."

"Shut up." My face actually warmed with embarrassment. "This isn't right." I felt like I would cry—the embarrassment, the fear, the lasting denial. It became too much. "I shouldn't be here. You shouldn't have taken me from my home."

"Yes. You've said that already." His laughter stopped, and he straightened, voice turning serious. "Are you always so repetitive? If so, it's going to make this a lot more difficult to get through."

"Do you honestly expect me to sit here and say nothing?" I asked. "What would you do in my position? What do you want me to do?"

"I don't care what you do, just as long as you don't leave this room. You have everything you asked for. Hell, read a book." He pointed to his bedroom. "I have plenty, though some of them you won't be able to understand. Whatever you do, make the best of it. I can't keep popping to Earth to help you when I have things to do here. Until I find a solution, this is the best option." He stood from the chair and looked over his shoulder at the door. "Speaking of which, I have to leave now. Stay put."

"Where the hell would I go?" I asked as he turned and walked away ,leaving me sitting with the pile of my belongings. "It's not as if I can poof my way out of this place like you can."

For the first hour, I worked on my crochet project. After several attempts at solving the riddle of the hood I wanted to attach to the top of the crop shirt, I unraveled most of it and tossed it back into the bag. And of course, boredom led me right back to snooping. Hell, he'd gone through my stuff, even read my damn writing. He had lost all rights to privacy in my book.

This time, I opened a different door and was so damned thrilled to find what resembled a bathroom. There was no working toilet, but there was a large stone tub. How he filled that tub I didn't know, because there wasn't a faucet in sight.

"Does he wash his ass at all?" I frowned then tried to erase that thought, because if he didn't, I'd probably get some sort of secondary skin disorder after the nasty, sweaty sex we had together. It would be just like me to trade the booty juice jerk for a dirty demon who didn't understand what soap was.

Too disgusted by my own imagined skin disease, I gave up on trying to figure out how anything in the room worked. Stepping back into the main room, I intended to go through my things and organize them as much as I could, but there was a knock at the door. The same door Metice used to leave his home. The door he told me not to go out of.

"Oh, now you want to have some damn manners?" I joked as I opened the door, expecting it to be the brooding demon showing his odd sense of humor. It wasn't him. I choked on my words the moment the door opened, and I saw who was waiting on the other side. "Oh, shit."

I stood there, face to boobs with a demoness who stood at least a foot taller than me. I couldn't help myself. My eyes scanned the long legs, muscular torso, plump breasts, and bright green skin up to the angular face with large eyes and full lips set in a tight grimace as she realized I wasn't who she was expecting either.

Delayed common sense kicked in, and I pushed the door closed, but the green giant stopped me. Her hand, fixed with sharp black claws, grabbed the edge of the door and pushed it back at me. I stumbled back, avoiding falling, and watched as the unannounced visitor entered Metice's home.

"Look what we have here. Is Metice bringing his hunts back home?" A deep, sultry voice crossed her lips as she spoke. "And he's not even sharing. How unlike him."

"Hunts?" I choked. *Was that what I was? Had he hunted me? Was he going to kill me?* I snapped myself back to focus. Now was not the time to go on a paranoid search for answers to questions that didn't matter.

She inhaled the air like she could use it to tell her a story and then frowned. Apparently, she didn't like what she learned.

"Who are you?" Large orange eyes narrowed as the demon examined me the way I had her just moments before. "Why are you here?"

"Excuse me?" I might have been scared shitless, but it felt like I was being accused of something.

"Where is Metice?" She changed her question.

"As if I would know that." I shrugged. "He dropped me here then left."

"Well, aren't you annoying?" She crossed the room. "I could kill you in an instant. You know that, right?"

"Yeah, but I'm already in hell, so how much worse could things get?" I took a half step back.

"You smell," she sniffed me again, "interesting."

"That new natural deodorant," I couldn't help my mouth even in the face of danger. "I swear, they say it's long lasting, but that's a lie."

"What the hell are you doing here?" Metice asked from behind the woman, and my asshole unclenched. If he was there, it meant she wouldn't hurt me, and I didn't have to worry about shitting my pants.

"I dropped by to see a friend." She turned her back to me to face him. "Heard you've been having some trouble. I'm starting to understand why."

"Someone reporting my business to you?"

"You're a popular guy. A lot of people are paying attention, and rumors fly fast down here. Regardless, that's not important." She pointed over her shoulder at me. "What is this doing here Metice? A live human... you know that is against the rules."

"And you know I don't give a fuck about rules." Metice glanced around the woman, and his eyes locked onto me. "Just like I know you don't give a fuck about me being in trouble. Leave."

"Ah." She walked over to him placing her hand on his jaw. Metice backed away like her touch burned his flesh, and her lips twisted into a scowl as she snapped, "Don't you miss me, even a little?"

"I miss the silence when you weren't here." He stepped aside and pointed to the door. "Get out."

"Fine." She sucked her teeth and tossed an annoyed look over her shoulder at me. "But I'll be back."

"Don't bother." Metice sounded like he was holding back so much rage. This woman had a physical effect on him. He balled his fist at his side, and the veins stood along his arm. "I have nothing to say to you."

"You be careful with this one. Trouble follows wherever he goes." the nameless demoness spoke to me but kept her eyes on him. "You might just end your fragile human life earlier than expected."

I wish I'd said something back to her, but I didn't. My mind was spinning with thoughts of my future, this demon, and the potential of losing my life. I stood there like a deer in headlights as she left. When the door shut and the latch clicked, my brain snapped out of its paralysis.

"Ex-girlfriend?" I asked when Metice neglected to address the elephant in the room.

"What?" Though he was looking right at me, his mind was clearly somewhere else. He snapped into focus.

"The way she looked at you. The touch on your face." I mimed the affectionate action. "I'd say that's an ex. She didn't look happy to see me here either."

"You're not entirely wrong," he confirmed my theory.

"Didn't think I was." I looked at his empty hands and frowned. "You didn't bring me anything to eat?"

"Excuse me?" he muttered, and we were back to him being annoyed not by the unannounced visitor but by the human he kidnapped.

"I've been sitting in your dungeon for hours and you're not even going to feed me?" I wasn't really that hungry, but I had to change the topic. I didn't care about what issues he had with his ex. I didn't want to know any details that didn't concern me getting my ass back to Earth.

"I-" He stammered. Whoever that was, she'd really did a number on him.

"Right, you're selfish." I threw my hands up and returned to the sofa. "Kidnap me then starve me while you run around hell. Thanks."

"If you want something to eat, just ask," he snapped back. "It's really not that complicated."

"Why should I have to ask for you to consider my needs?" I had him. I could see it in his eyes. The spell was broken, and the sassy demon boy was back.

"I'm sorry, are you my wife now?" He scoffed and sat across from me. "What's happening here?"

"Just practicing." I shrugged.

"For what?" he asked.

"We're soulmates, right? That's what you said. Meaning we'll be stuck together forever." I carved my lips into a scheming grin. "How do you think it's going to be? You and me, together for an eternity. I wonder if I'll get some of your immortality. Do you think I could live here forever with you at my beck and call?"

"Not if I can help it." He looked like he was going to be sick at the thought.

"Well, until you figure out how to fix this, I'm going to need you to be anticipating my needs." I laid back on the sofa, stretching my arms above my head. "And right now, this human needs to eat."

"No wonder you were trying to use magic to make a man for yourself." He pointed at me. "No real one in his right mind would deal with you."

"If I pretend to be upset by that, will you find me some food?" I stuck my tongue out at him.

"I'll get you food when you ask for it. Nicely." He sat forward. "I'll wait."

"Excuse me?" I rolled my eyes at him. "Ask nicely?"

"I didn't cause all this. You did." He narrowed his eyes, and I swear the hair on the back of my neck stood at attention. "If you want to eat, you'll politely ask me to supply you with a meal like a good girl."

"You're out of your mind." I rolled my eyes. Had I read that line in a book, I would have been swooning, but in reality, it made me want to pop him in his thick forehead.

"Maybe, but I'm not the one who will starve to death," he doubled down. "In fact, I can go months without eating a thing, one of the perks of my particular brand of demon. I've never watched a human die from starvation. If I keep you here, I can use this as an observation for my notes. I wonder how long that would take. Time moves slower here than it does in your world."

"Fine." I gave up, because I could no longer tell if he was joking. Would he seriously watch me starve to death as if I was some sort of science experiment?

"Fine?" While my smile faded, his grew with a seductive tilt. "Are you going to be a good girl, Rayna?"

I could feel my face warming when he said my name. Okay, so maybe that dominance thing wasn't just hot in the books. Maybe, in real life, it had a little weight to it.

"Can you pop your demon ass to Earth and bring me back a burger?" My question was rude as hell, but it had to be. I couldn't be too sweet with my request. Regardless of the power he clearly held over me, I would never make it that easy.

"Is that the nicest you can ask that question?" He leaned back and narrowed his gaze at me. "I think you can do better than that."

"I'm pretty sure humans start to stink when they're starving to death. Foul breath, flatulence, and diarrhea." I rubbed my hand along the supple surface of my seat. "I can't imagine that would do well for your soft leathers. I mean, this is a comfortable spot to decay."

"That is disgusting." He frowned.

"I know, right? But hey, at least you'll be able to satisfy your curiosity, right?" *If Metice wants to play with me, he better learn quickly that I'm skilled in mind games.* You don't grow up with fifteen boy cousins and not come out of it with a few lessons in how to twist a man's mind.

"Fine." Metice stood from his seat. "I'll get you some damn food."

He rolled his shoulders, and the atmosphere tensed. I doubted I would ever get used to that feeling. And then, the demon disappeared.

"And fries!" I called out, knowing he wouldn't likely hear me. "Damnit, I hope he doesn't forget the fries."

6
Bonding?

I waited patiently for him to come back. Luckily, this trip didn't take nearly as long as the first, and within a few minutes, the tall, dark demon stood in front of me holding a bag of food. He led me to the dining table, a huge slab of polished lava rock, and laid out the meal.

"You got me seventeen burgers?" I gawked at the layout. "Exactly how much do you think I can eat?"

"How am I supposed to know? Judging from the meal you had the other night, it didn't seem like you were all that discerning when it came to your food."

"Discerning?" I laughed and gestured towards the feast. "This is enough food for a family."

"Well, I didn't forget your fries." He held up the brown bag of greasy fries. "I tried one. Actually pretty good."

"First time?" It was funny to me to think about him eating Earth food. Of course, that led me to the consideration of what he actually ate, and that thought took me back to the demoness. She mentioned he hunted humans. Did that mean that, for Metice, I could have been on his meal plan? I shuddered at the thought.

"Actually, yes." He sat down at one of the high-backed chairs and pointed for me to join him. "Like I said, I don't eat much, and anytime I travel to new worlds, trying the local cuisine really isn't something I'm worried about. Though I have taken a few cooking classes. I guess it's an oddball hobby."

"What do you usually do when you travel?" I asked as I unwrapped the first burger.

"You curious about me now?" He watched me closely and popped another fry into his mouth.

"Your friend mentioned something when she was here before you got back. She said you didn't typically bring your hunts home." I laughed nervously. "She thought I was one of your hunts. Is that what you do when you go to new worlds? Do you hunt for prey? Do you bring it back here to study?"

"That makes me sound far more interesting than I really am. If you must know, when I go to a new place, I'm there to study. I learn what I can about the culture. I collect books, and I bring them back here to read." He pointed to his bedroom. "I'm sure you've seen my collection. That's just the surface. There is another level of my home that I'll show you later, full of books and artifacts."

"Well, that doesn't really sound like the life of a man who would have so many enemies." I took a bite of the burger and sighed as my stomach rejoiced. Apparently, I was a lot hungrier than I thought I was. "How could there possibly be so many other demons who hate you?"

"That's the unfortunate life of a reformed man in hell, one who wanted to escape another more devious lifestyle." Metice turned his gaze to the window, as if he saw something I didn't. I followed his line of sight and only saw the darkened sky. "Unfortunately, there are people from my past who don't want to let me leave it all behind."

"And I take it she's one of them?" I looked at the closed door where I first saw the tall green demoness.

"Yeah, she is, actually. She's the one trying to pull me back into that world." He looked annoyed. "I keep telling her to let it go, but she doesn't want to. She lost a lot when I turned my life around."

"Will you tell me more about her?" He'd piqued my interest, and my mind instantly went on a race to figure out their relationship dynamic. Was she a jilted lover, a scorned boss, or was her life on the line because of him?

"You want to know more about her?" He tilted his head as he continued to watch me eat. "Why?"

"At first, I wasn't going to ask. I figured the relationships you had before I came into your life were none of my business, but the truth is, I'm a part of your life now, however temporary. Those relationships, some apparently not on the greatest terms, come knocking on your door, and considering you won't tell me how long I have to stay here before I'm allowed to go home, I should probably know what to expect." I pointed to the door again. "I mean, your enemies have your home address, and apparently, you don't have the best security system here."

"You're right. You should know." Metice pushed the bag of fries away from him. "The thing is, I'm not really sure how much I should tell you."

"You think I can't handle it?" My body tensed with a sudden wave of annoyance. The man had already ripped me from my world; now, he wanted to keep his secrets. How was that fair?

"That's not it. I've seen you in action. I'm pretty sure you can handle a lot of things." He slid the compliment in there, and yes, I caught it. I raised my brow, questioning the sentiment, and he brushed me off.

"You were saying?" I winked at him before he continued.

"There are things about my world that must stay secret. Rayna, you're smart, smart enough to connect the dots, and I worry if you do, there won't be a way for you to really go back to your life the way it was before all this happened. I give you a lot of shit about casting the spell that brought us together, but I know you didn't mean it. Since you didn't mean it, the best thing for us to do is to figure out a way to reverse it and send you back to your life, unaffected by mine."

"That's not what I expected you to say." I finished the last bite of burger and followed it with a sip of soda. He'd brought seventeen burgers and one drink. "So, what can you tell me? Is there anything I can know that won't put my life at risk?"

"I'm sure there is." He nodded. "But it's pretty boring information, and I'm tired. I think we should get some rest."

"We?" I took another long sip of the drink. "As in both of us?"

"Are you not tired?" he asked me, and it was like the question pulled a yawn from my gut.

"I-" My eyes darted to his bedroom door as I tried to force the yawn back down my throat.

"There is another bedroom," he laughed. "We don't have to share a bed. In fact, I'm sure you will like it better than the one I have in there. I fixed it up for you."

"You did? When?" It surprised me that he would do anything like that. Honestly, the entire exchange was unlike any of our past conversations. I missed the banter. It was better than the awkward bout of nerves taking over my body.

"That's not important." Metice stood, grabbed my things I had organized near the sofa, and headed for the door to the far right of the room, the one I hadn't explored because the visitor distracted me. It opened to a staircase that led down.

The bottom of my stomach jumped into my throat as I realized I was following a demon who was leading me further into his lair. This couldn't be good, right? I should be rejecting this. I was the girl in the book who I rolled my eyes at and turned the page, hoping her foolishness didn't get her in more trouble. It always did!

I kept my nervous thoughts to myself and followed him down the narrow stairs and into the room below. It opened to another living space, one that looked far more modern than the one above. If I thought he was the type to have guests come over, this would have been a space for it.

This secondary living space had floor to ceiling windows that lined the wall to the right of the steps, making it feel like you would fall into the abyss below. It was then that I got a clearer view of how his home was set in the side of a mountain. It wasn't another pillar. The natural formation expanded from either side of the home and created what felt like a fortress.

In the center of the room was a massive, grey, u-shaped sectional big enough for my entire friend group to sit comfortably. There was a stone fireplace just behind it with additional seating. To the left were three white doors that blended in with the soft color of the stone walls. He took me to the first.

"This is your bathroom." He pushed the door open and stepped to the side.

"Wow." I was shocked to find what resembled a full human bathroom, complete with a functioning toilet and a standing shower. It looked nothing like the archaic lavatory I'd seen next to his room.

"Is it up to your standards?" he asked as he walked through the bathroom to the door opposite the one we entered.

"I mean, there's no eucalyptus, but this will work," I joked and almost snorted when he rolled his eyes at me.

"I'm glad it's sufficient." He shot a glare over his shoulder then opened the next door. "And this is where you will sleep."

Instinct said to say something smart, but I couldn't. I was too shocked by what I saw. A large bed sat in the center of the room. Clearly, Metice had an issue with walls touching the bed, but I was okay with that. To the left was a wall of floor to ceiling bookshelves overflowing with books.

To the right was a desk with a laptop stand, and stacks of notebooks, the cutest teardrop light hanging just above it.

There was a floor to ceiling mirror, and the back wall had soft lilac curtains hanging from the ceiling. There was no window, but it added to the ambiance. Soft candlelight lit the space, and the smell of lavender filled the air. He'd taken time to create this for me. I had no words.

"When did you do this?" I walked over to the bookshelves, and when I saw titles I knew and loved, my heart fluttered. "You couldn't have done all of this just now or today?"

"I set it up the first night we met," he admitted as he sat my things on the large chair next to the desk. "I had a feeling this would happen. Not that I wanted it to, but I'm the type to prepare for all possible outcomes."

"That was what, a day ago? How could you do this in so little time?"

He cocked his head and grimaced. "Don't you remember I told you time is different here? One day here is equal to about seven in your world."

"Oh shit." I never considered there would be a time lapse issue, but it made sense. "Okay, but how did you know what books I like?"

"You slept that night. I didn't." His look felt heavy, like with just his eyes, he could strip my clothes away. For a moment, Metice was lost in his own imagination before he focused back on the topic at hand. "I'll admit, I did a little snooping while waiting for you to wake. I hope I got the right ones. Some of the titles were hard to remember, and I had no way of knowing which ones you'd read or not. I also found similar titles and organized them the way you had yours. By author."

"Oh." What the hell else was I supposed to say to that? This was a demon. He was supposed to be mean and aggressive and scary enough to make me want to run away, but in that moment, I felt myself softening to him. That internal voice that said 'give him hell' quieted, and that optimistic one popped up. *Maybe the spell did it right. Maybe he's the man of my dreams.* I quickly shook that off. He couldn't be my perfect man! He was a damn demon!

"I thought it would make it easier for you to be comfortable here." Metice's deep voice rumbled in my ear and pulled me from my conflicting thoughts. "Like I said, I know you didn't do this on purpose, but if you're going to have to stay here, there's no reason for you to feel so out of place. I get it. This isn't your home, but it's going to have to do for now. I promise, I will get you back home as soon as possible."

"About getting me back home. "I turned to face him, putting my back to the bed. "Do you have a plan you want to share with me? I mean, I know you said there's a lot about your history, your friends, and this world that I shouldn't know. I get that part, I do, but I should at least be able to know the plan for my future. How exactly do you think we're going to solve this? How do I get home?"

Metice chewed on the questions. He looked at me like he was trying to solve a puzzle, and my stomach flipped. *Was this the moment he told me I could never go home? Was I supposed to see this room and forget about my life?*

"I'll tell you all of that in the morning. For now, please rest. Take a shower and try to get as much sleep as possible. Then, we'll talk. Is that fair?" he asked.

"I guess that's fair." I didn't want to give in, but it made no sense to fight him on it.

"You should have everything you need." He nodded toward the bathroom. "If not, let me know, and I'll make sure you get it."

"Thank you," I said reluctantly. Why the hell was I standing there thanking the demon who kidnapped me? Why wasn't this more traumatic? Again, I stood there questioning my own sanity as he left me alone.

After staring at the books a little longer, my body screamed at me. I really was tired. How long had I been awake? Metice had mentioned that time moved at a different pace than on Earth, but what was the conversion? One to seven. How long did that mean I'd been awake? It suddenly felt like I'd been up for days. My body ached, and my skin tingled with the prickles of exhaustion. I also felt filthy. All the running around the theatre had me sweaty, and my pits told the recap of the battle with every whiff.

"Shower, then sleep," I muttered.

In the bathroom, I was happy to find not a detail had been skipped. My favorite bodywash and even the African net sponges for my skin were there. Unfortunately, I couldn't figure out how to get the temperature in the shower just right. It had two settings, ice cold or boil your ass until your skin melts off. I jumped in, scrubbed up as fast as I could, then hopped out.

I dressed in my nightgown, stuffed my wild hair into a bonnet, opting not to comb it because my arms were already tired just thinking about the work it would take. I didn't think I'd be able to sleep, but I did. The bed felt like floating on clouds, and the moment my head hit the pillow, I was out like a light.

It was the sound of light tapping on the door that woke me from a dreamless slumber. I really thought I would have haunted dreams filled with demon sex, but I didn't. After I woke, it took me a minute to remember where I was. When I saw the wall of books instead of my crappy black out curtains, my reality slowly set in again.

"Rayna?" his deep voice called out before he knocked again. "Are you awake?"

Without thinking and tempted by the delicious aroma of breakfast, I rolled out of the bed, kicking the plush comforter aside and stumbled over to the door. When I swung it open and saw his face, the truth of my appearance slapped the front of my brain.

"Uh…" I stood there, face warming with embarrassment and hoping my left tit wasn't hanging out of the side of my damn shirt.

"I got food." He stepped aside and pointed to a new table set up in front of the massive windows.

"Um, give me a minute?" I closed the door in his face and ran to the bathroom.

I could have screamed when I saw my reflection. I looked like death rolled over. My bonnet of course did *not* stay on my head. I swear, those things run for the hills the second you fall asleep. So, there I was, right tit a thread away from exposure and the entire left side of my head flattened.

"Why didn't I look in the mirror first?" I muttered and went to work fluffing out my hair. When that was done, my disappointment only grew as I found the mental capacity to examine the rest of my reflection.

Could I be anymore disgusting? My right eye had that terrible sleep crust, there was dried drool on my damn lip, and both my eyes looked like I spent the night crying. That demon wouldn't be able to keep his hands off me after seeing me like that.

It took me ten minutes to get myself to a mildly presentable state. After setting a warm towel on my face, my puffy appearance returned to normal. Maybe I was allergic to hell. That had to be a good thing, right?

I threw on a lounge suit, matching pants and hooded top, and returned to meet my captor.

"Sorry," I said as I exited the bedroom and found Metice standing and staring out the window.

"Everything okay?" He turned to me, body outlined by the rising sun adding a soft halo that brought the purple tones of his skin closer to the surface.

"Yes, I just wanted to wash up." I nodded and pulled the door closed behind me.

"Got that crust out of your eye, I see." He laughed and pointed at my face.

"Seriously?" And any of those inappropriate butterflies that his kindness the night before left me with died like winter had suddenly rolled in.

"What?" he laughed. "Look, I got food. Food makes human women happy, right? Be happy."

"Right." It was a good thing. I didn't need to be having flutters when I thought of him. The annoyance that made my lip curl was better. Safer.

I sat down at the table, and yes, the meal was amazing. I wasn't sure where he got it from, but there were eggs, bacon, hashbrowns, waffles *and* pancakes, and an assortment of fresh fruit. Again, too much food for me to eat alone, but he didn't seem to care about the waste.

He watched me eat for a while before interrupting my chomps and moans of delight.

"So, the plan," he started. "You wanted to know what it was."

"Yes?" I looked at him over a forkful of eggs.

"Breaking the link between us is going to take a lot more time than I think either of us wants, but I think I've found a temporary solution that will at least allow you the chance to go home sooner than later. I just need a few days to make it happen."

"What's the solution?" I asked. As long as I got a get out of hell free pass, I was going to take it.

"There is someone. You might think of her as a witch. She's a magic worker, very powerful for the right bargain. She can cast a spell that will shield you from other demons," he explained.

"Shield me?" I dropped my fork. "What does that mean? They won't be able to hurt me?"

"They won't be able to see or sense you at all." he clarified. "Right now, they are able to track you because my essence is now intertwined with yours. It's an energy signature, like a calling card. If we can cut that off, you'll be safe while I solve the bigger puzzle."

"Okay?" I leaned back in my chair and looked out over the hellscape that looked even more menacing in the light of day. In the distance, I could see large beings moving around, but I couldn't make out any details. "This is a lot."

"It's the only way I will feel comfortable sending you back." He gave the explanation I didn't ask for. "I can't keep you here forever, but letting you go back unprotected isn't an option either."

"And you can't keep popping to Earth to save me, I know." I straightened in the chair. "Then what?"

"Then, you go home." he answered. "And I stay here. I know there is an answer to this, a way to dissolve our bond, but the people who have that information...well, it's going to take some time to convince them to share it."

"Do I get to know what that is?" It sounded like he already had an idea of what we needed to do, but he wasn't sharing. "I mean, you know something already, right? Maybe I can help."

"I don't know enough now to share. If I do, you'll waste your time trying to solve a riddle I only know a piece of." There was something like apprehension that flashed across his face. His right eye twitched, and his lip curved down slightly at the corners. He knew a lot more than he was telling me. "As soon as I figure it out, I'll let you know."

"You're the boss." I gave up.

"Eat. You need to get your strength up. I'll be back in a few hours."

"You're leaving?"

"Like I said, I have to find the right bargain." Metice left me alone with the mountain of food and a head full of spinning thoughts.

I spent the day staring out the massive window and hoping the creatures I saw flying in the distance wouldn't see me. When I wasn't examining the strange landscape of peaks and valleys, I tried to busy my mind with tasks. I worked on the shirt and unraveled it again. I opened my laptop and tried to write, but nothing came. I tried to contact home, but the weak ass connection I once had was no longer there.

The best thing I could do was lock myself in my room, away from the window, and curl up with a book. I'd gotten through two romantic comedy novellas and fell asleep in bed.

"Rayna?" Metice stood over me when I woke up. "Sorry, I knocked, but you didn't answer. I have dinner for you."

Outside the room, the table was covered with the same ridiculous layout. Way too many burgers and fries and one sad little drink.

"You know I do eat more than burgers, right?" I rolled my eyes at him, then peered at the food. "Is this the same food from yesterday?"

"No, I got it fresh. Is there a problem?" He was rightfully annoyed. "At least I didn't forget you require food. Having to eat every day is such a waste of time."

"Excuse me for not having the metabolism of a snail like you. It's just…" I paused. "You don't have to get so much. One burger is enough. This is wasteful."

"One of these days, when I do something nice for you, you're going to simply say thank you. No complaints or snippy observations." Metice sat down at the table. "And just so you know, Earth snails eat at least once a day, so you have exactly the metabolism of a snail."

"Oh, shut up and kiss my-" Metice held his hand up to me and pointed to the table.

"Don't get defensive just because you were wrong." He winked. "Just sit down and eat."

The meal started awkwardly. I ate a burger, he popped a few fries in his mouth, and we both stared out the window. It was one of those moments when I knew I had to apologize, but I damn sure didn't want to. Metice was right. I was the one who read the damn book and played with the spell. He didn't summon me. Still, I didn't want to take the blame. Fuck that grown woman, healing journey shit. Date after nauseating date left me feeling a little silly; it wasn't supposed to turn into a demon and a trip to literal hell.

"I'm sorry," I finally broke as I poked at the second burger in front of me. I wouldn't eat it; it was just something to focus on so I wouldn't have to look him in the eye while tucking away my pride.

"What?" Metice had just popped another fry into his mouth and nearly choked on it when I spoke.

"I don't mean to be rude, but-" I paused, trying to figure out what exactly I wanted to say. No, I didn't want to be rude to him, but I didn't want to be his friend either.

"But you have your defenses up because you're a human who was ripped from your home and brought to hell?" He finished the thought for me and was pretty close to accurate with his assumption. "It makes sense."

"That, and the fact that you're a man. I haven't had the best run with men lately, so I'm a little more rigid when it comes to interactions."

"That doesn't make sense." He shook his head and crushed the empty fry bag.

"Why not?" I sipped from the drink.

"You're rigid about men, but you want one so bad you would cast a spell?" He watched me closely, examining every shift in my expression as I considered his question.

"It's complicated." I pushed the drink away from me and looked him in the eye for the first time. And those butterflies came back. Dammit.

"Clearly." He rolled his hand through the air gesturing for me to continue. "I'm a smart man. I can handle complicated."

"Look, I wish I could shut that part of my brain off that wants companionship. It would sure as hell save me a lot of heartache. The dating pool is full of piss and poor decisions, and the few of us still brave enough to swim in it are coming out with infections."

"That's colorful." He frowned. "But it explains a lot."

"It does?"

"You aren't the first woman to do this, cast a spell with the intent of summoning a demon lover. You may be the first one to do it without knowing it, though." Metice cleaned up the mess on the table when he realized I wouldn't be eating anymore food.

"How did that even work? That's been bugging me. I mean, sure, I had some ingredients, but I'm not a witch. I don't have any powers of my own." It was a question that rolled around in my head since that first day. Fake spell or not, it worked, and that part didn't make sense. I'd never used magic before, and though my mother and grandmother didn't play around with it, neither of them was a witch either.

"I have my theories about that, but I haven't confirmed anything." Metice looked at me, and I saw his hand twitch like he wanted to reach out to me, but he restrained himself.

"What theories do you have?" I stood from my seat and helped him put the last of the trash away.

"When I went to Earth to study the world, I found so many disconnected bloodlines, people who were displaced and lost touch with their roots. A lot of those people were descendants of magical beings. More often than not, when things like this happen, it's because one of those descendants tapped into the power they didn't realize they carried in their blood."

"You think I'm descendant of a witch?" I thought about it. "Well, slavery was a thing. My family lost all knowledge of where we're from. I guess I never thought about the possibility of something like that, though I didn't exactly believe any of this was real to begin with."

Our conversation continued with a lot more ease after that. He shared little about him, and I shared a lot about me. It was like once I started, I couldn't stop talking. It felt safe because, well, who would he tell? I told him about my childhood, my schooling, even my friends. I gave him the rundown of how I met each of them, saving Keri for last.

"I've known her since we were in the fifth grade. We met in the cafeteria on the first day of school and have been inseparable since." My heart warmed when I thought of Keri. She really had been there for me through so much. Yeah, she was wrapped up in her man, but I knew she'd come back around once things settled. It was okay to be lost in the newness of it all.

"Doesn't sound like a good friend," Metice commented as we moved from the table to the oversized couch. His words felt like a smack in the face after I'd just been internally praising my best friend.

"What do you mean?" I plopped down across from him.

"You tell her you were visited by a demon, and her response is to tell you to seek help?" His body quickly relaxed into the couch, and he looked more comfortable than I could ever remember seeing him. "You've already forgiven them, especially Keri. I can tell that much, but I'd expect them to have more concern for your safety."

"Not everyone believes in demons. I know I didn't until..." I trailed off.

"Until you hopped on me?" He laughed and exposed his horns.

"You can put those away." I rolled my eyes and waited for the horns to vanish again. "The others don't know, and Keri has her reasons for that response."

"Sounds like you're making excuses for her," he challenged me while his eyes moved to look out the window.

"I'm not. See, it's been about a decade, but there was a time when I had a mental break. I was seeing things, imagining all sorts of freaky shit that caused me to have a break with reality and disrupted my life. She was there for me, but it took a lot for me to come out of it." It hurt to remember what was the most difficult time in my life. "Keri is just afraid all that messiness is going to happen again. I'm afraid that it will ruin our friendship if it does."

"Hmm." He looked at me in that critical way. He was on a mission to investigate a mystery. I was that mystery. "What was it like? Your break with reality."

"They call it derealization," I started and paused. "I saw other worlds, creatures and strange alien-like people. There were times when I was so detached, it felt like I was on another world entirely. I felt like I lived four full lives in the span of a few months, and when I came back to my true reality, I broke. I couldn't believe anything was real. I couldn't fathom that the lives I had in those other worlds were all a fabrication of my imagination."

"That sounds heartbreaking." Metice moved closer to me. His body radiated heat that calmed my stirring spirit. I said nothing, because on some level, I wanted him closer. Thinking about that time in my life was painful, so any comfort in that moment was welcome.

"It was. I had to mourn the loss of so many relationships that never really happened." My mind went back to those days of looking in the mirror and seeing my young face again. I'd lived a long life; I had a family in one of those worlds. Then, I woke up one day, and I was back in my suburban home, and everyone around me acted as if nothing had happened. "And I've been in therapy ever since. Luckily, I found someone who didn't make me feel like it was wrong to miss those people and mourn the relationships."

"I see."

"What is it?" When I looked at him, I saw it again: he knew more than he let on.

"Nothing. Just a thought, but it's probably unfounded." He shifted his weight away from me. "You should get some more rest. I won't keep you awake any longer."

Metice abruptly stood and left me there alone on the couch. It made no sense, but that stinging pain of embarrassment sparked in my chest. I placed my hand over the ache and looked at the door where he'd exited. Of course, it felt shitty. I'd just revealed that I had one toe in the crazy house, and he ran away. How else was I supposed to feel?

The next two days went the same way. Breakfast together, alone for the day, and dinner with an abrupt ending after a revealing conversation. I kept telling myself I wouldn't tell him so much about me, but I'm a chatter head after a good meal. Each feast was far too much food for me to eat alone, and most of it went back into a bag at the end of the night. I wanted to ask him what he did with the leftovers but was afraid he'd say he just dumped it outside somewhere. A disgustingly wasteful act.

The third day was different. When I exited my bedroom to join him for dinner, I found the table set for two. There were two plates, both filled with fresh cuts of steak, potatoes, vegetables I couldn't identify, and a glass of wine.

"What's this?" I looked at the modest meal. "No burgers?"

"You didn't seem to enjoy the food last night. Thought you might want something different." He pulled out my chair for me to sit. "If you don't like it, I can get something else."

"No. This is fine." I sat in the offered chair. "Where is this from?"

"It's not from your world," he answered shortly. "I'm not sure you want to know much more than that."

"Um." I looked from the plate to him as he sat across from me. "Is this safe for me to eat?"

"Yes. I wouldn't have brought it for you if I didn't think it was safe." He lifted his glass. "Trust me, its fine,"

"Right." I was skeptical. How would my body digest this food? All I could imagine was having my bowels blow out in hell. Not ideal.

"Would you like me to take the first bite?" he offered.

"I'm not sure what that would prove." I took a deep breath and cut into the steak. With Metice watching, I popped the piece into my mouth, and as the flavors danced across my tongue, I moaned. "Oh my God."

"There you go again, praising your god," he teased. "I told you I don't like it when you do that."

"You said not to do it when looking at your dick. This steak isn't your dick." I popped another piece in my mouth and wiggled in my seat. "What is this? It just melts on my tongue."

"Yeah, it's pretty good." He leaned back in his chair watching me.

I sipped from the drink, ate some of the potatoes, and then turned back to the meat. After a few more bites and sips of the drink that was stronger than I gave it credit for, I just couldn't take the idea of eating it alone. It was blowing my mind how the flavors shifted each time. First, it was savory, and then, there was a hint of sweetness, and the third bite brought a touch of spice. It was the perfect combination.

"You have to try this." I stood up from my seat with a piece of steak hanging from my fork.

"What are you doing?" Metice looked at me like I was losing my mind. "I have my own. Sit down."

"Sit down? Okay." I didn't return to my seat like I was sure he meant. Instead, I sat side-saddle in his lap.

I should have questioned my actions then. Yes, the steak was good, but it wasn't good enough to make me jump into this man's lap. The only thing I could think of was that the meat was so delicious, and I had to have him try it. Clearly, I was already intoxicated by the alien drink. My head spun like I already drank half a bottle of wine, even though I'd only had a few sips. But two plus two was equaling seventy-five, and my senses were out the damn window.

"Rayna." He leaned back from me.

"Just take a bite and tell me it isn't the best thing you've ever had." I pushed the fork in his face, forcing him to eat the meat, and he did. My eyes were glued to his lips. He slowly chewed the bite of food, and his eyes closed, marking his enjoyment. There was a small drop of juice that landed on his lip, which I used my thumb to remove.

"Isn't it so good?" I licked the juice from my thumb as he swallowed the bite.

"Yes." He cleared his throat and looked down. "You're in my lap."

"Would you like me to move?" I asked. "Are you uncomfortable?"

"Yes." His eyes moved back to my face. "I am."

"Okay, I'll move." I placed my hands on his shoulder, stood, and moved my right leg over his lap, lowering myself until I was straddling him. "Better?"

"Have you lost your mind?" He looked me in the eye but didn't remove me from his lap.

I reached back and grabbed the cup of wine, took another deep swig, and then gave it to him.

"Drink." Before he could refuse me, I pressed the cup to his lips, and he took a sip of the dark liquid, again leaving drops on his lip. With my mind spinning with the effects of the alien alcohol, I cleaned the drops with my tongue. "Tastes so good. I mean, it's almost better than the steak."

"Rayna." My hips slowly rocked, and he grabbed my waist to stop me, but the heat from his hands felt like encouragement.

"Yes, Metice?" I asked as the heavy wave of arousal crashed against me.

"Do you know what you're doing?" There was a new gruff to his voice that had my pussy wet.

"Just tasting," I said, but I didn't finish the answer. I leaned in and kissed him. "I don't want anything to go to waste."

"Are you going to claim this was a dream?"

"Huh?" I asked against his lips. "You taste so good."

"If you keep doing that," he grunted.

"What? What will you do, demon boy?" I teased. I knew what calling him that would do.

He growled and lifted me from his lap to sit me on the table. "You're playing with fire."

"I'm already in hell." I grinned and grabbed his dick through his pants. "Might as well have a little fun, right?"

"Last chance." He grabbed my wrist pulling my hand away from him.

I pulled my hand from his loose grip and slipped it into his pants. I stroked his dick and looked him in the eyes as he grew in my palm. "Last chance for what?"

"Alright." He lowered his mouth to my ear. "But this time, you're going to tell me you want it."

"What?"

"You heard me, Rayna." His hand slipped into my top and beneath my bra to grab my breast. He teased my nipple between his fingers as he continued. "Tell me you want it. Tell me what you want from me."

"Mmm," I moaned. "I want-"

"Yes? What do you want, Rayna?" His horns appeared, slowly growing as he waited for my response.

"I want you to fuck me, demon boy." The devilish grin stretched across my face.

"You asked for it." He smiled, and the plate behind me hit the floor.

"The steak." I pouted.

"You want steak or dick?" He dropped his pants, revealing the heaving length. "I can go get you another piece of meat if that's what you prefer."

"Dick. I choose dick." I nodded and licked my lips.

He pushed me back on the table and removed my pants.

"Let's get you ready." He dropped in front of me and had a different meal.

"Dammit!" I slapped the table with my hand and moaned as he used that split tongue on me. It rolled over my clit and slipped both in my pussy and my asshole. Within minutes, I came so hard, I kicked the chair over. "Yes! Please! Don't stop."

But he did stop. After my second orgasm, Metice stood in front of me, horns erect as he removed his shirt, a black button up. Completely naked, he grabbed my hips and slid me down the table and onto his dick. He slipped inside and held me there.

"What are you doing?" I squirmed.

Metice picked up the glass of wine and took a sip.

"I'm savoring it." He pulled me forward until I was sitting up, dick still inside me, and placed the cup to my lips. "You should too."

I drank from the cup, holding eye contact as the warm liquid moved down my throat. Next, he grabbed my plate, the one that hadn't hit the floor, and picked up the steak. He held it to my lips. "Eat."

I bit into the steak as ordered, and while I ate, he pulled my tit into his mouth and teased my nipple with his teeth. He moved between my breasts, and the sensation combined with the taste of the food became so overwhelming, I came again.

As I moaned with my orgasm, I pulled his head away from my chest and fed him the rest of the steak. Metice ate as his dick revved inside me, rotating in my pussy and rolling over my g-spot. I rocked my hips and gripped the edge of the table.

"Metice," I moaned his name and pushed against him.

"Yes, Rayna?" He swallowed the last bite of meat. "Tell me what you want."

"I can't take it anymore." I grabbed his hips pulling him further into me. "Give it to me."

"Give what to you? I'm already inside of you," he teased.

"You know what I mean."

"Do I?" He pushed me back on the table and lifted my legs to his shoulders. His dick slowly slipped from me until just the tip remained inside, and then he thrust forward, slamming back into me. "Is that what you want?"

"Yes!" I cried. "God yes!"

"What did I tell you?" He pounded into me again. "Do." *Pound.* "Not." *Pound.* "Praise." *Pound.* "Your." *Pound.* "God."

He flipped me on my stomach and held my arms to my side as reins to control his thrusts.

"You know my name. Use it," he ordered.

"Metice." His name passed my lips in a deep moan.

He leaned down and bit into my shoulder. "Louder."

"Oh. Fuck. Metice!" I cried out. "Yes. Fuck me, Metice."

He pulled the plate over, putting his fingers in the potatoes and then in my mouth. "Suck."

He ordered, and I did. I ate the food from his fingers, using my tongue to clean every morsel. Then, he stopped, pulled me from the table, and put me on my knees.

"Suck," he instructed.

And I did.

"Yes. Just like that." He grabbed my head, pushing his dick further down my throat until I gagged. He pulled back, but I gripped his ass and forced him forward. I loved to choke on it.

I kept sucking, and my eyes watered from the constant gagging, but his dick suddenly tasted like raspberries, and I couldn't stop. *Was this another customizable feature?*

"Shit, I'm not ready to come." He picked me up, flipped me upside down, and ate my pussy while he walked over to the couch.

Next thing I knew, I was on my back, and his tongue was exploring every hole I had.

"Wait, please." I begged after coming twice more.

He stopped and climbed up my body, kissing my stomach, tits, and neck before he made it to my mouth. And dammit if that tongue wasn't just as good in a kiss.

"You begging for mercy?"

"I just—" I caught my breath. "Dammit."

"No breaks," he said and then flipped me on my stomach. "You asked to be fucked, Rayna."

And he was back inside me. Slow strokes teased me, this time without the revving. He took his time, kissing my back as his hand gripped my hair. Soon, I was dripping wet, pushing my hips back, encouraging him to give me more. He lifted my stomach from the couch until we were both vertical as he fucked me.

I threw my hands above my head, but he grabbed my wrist pulling them back to him.

"Keep your hands on me," he groaned." Hold on."

"Yes," I moaned, reaching behind me to grab his waist as he thrust inside me.

"Good girl." He slapped my tits and teased my nipples again, sending sharp but pleasurable sensations through my body. *Dammit, I loved that.*

I fell forward and looked back at him. "Smack my ass."

"Oh, you like the pain huh?" He grinned.

"Yes." I threw my ass back at him. "Smack it."

"Beg for it." He rubbed my cheek, preparing the surface for the coming sting.

"Please, Metice. Please smack my ass." I bit my lip and waited.

He gave me what I asked for, and I cried out in pleasure. "Yes!"

After four more slaps that left my cheek red, he flipped me on my back. "Take this dick like a good girl."

This time, he brought the rotations back, and I was about to lose my damn mind.

"You're so big," I moaned as I pulled one of the cushions from the couch. "Dammit."

"I can get bigger." He leaned in. "Would you like me to get bigger for you, Rayna?"

"What?" I gasped.

And then, he grew. *Inside me.* Metice stretched until I couldn't take anymore.

"How the hell?" I felt his dick in my stomach. "How did you do that?"

"I'm going to stretch you out." He took one of my breasts into his mouth and slowly pushed my walls further and further until I could give him no more room. Then, he started pounding my pussy again, and I lost it.

"Stretch me!" I cried and smacked his ass. "Fuck me! Don't stop!"

And he didn't stop. He fucked me through the night—on the couch, in the shower, in the bed, and back to the shower—and then he left me, legs weak, body limp, mind spinning.

I woke up on the fourth day with one of the worst hangovers I'd ever had. My head felt like a freight train had run me over, and my body was sore from the acrobatics of the night before. Metice fed me again before he left, but my mind felt like I'd been sucking on helium.

I avoided eye contact and stared out the window. It wasn't until he left that I decided we had to talk about what happened. After a day full of nervous thoughts and failed attempts to get my phone to contact the human world, I waited by the door for him to return home.

Only, I didn't get to bring up the topic of our unexpected night of fucking. Because when Metice walked through the door, he was covered in blood.

I ran to his side as he stumbled into the room. "What happened to you?"

"I found the right bargain." He coughed, and more blood spilled from his mouth onto the floor. "We go to see the witch tomorrow."

.

7

Detour

"Let me help you," I fussed as he brushed my hand away. I sat next to him on the leather couch with a towel and a bowl of water.

"I'm fine. I'll heal," he groaned after lifting his arm too quickly. It was then I recognized just how badly hurt he was.

"Obviously you'll heal, but that doesn't mean I can't help." I pressed the towel against a bloody wound. "These are going to scar."

Metice didn't say anything. Beneath the eerie moon, he watched me clean the blood from his skin. I couldn't look at him because I was terrified. How could I not be when the demon who was supposed to be protecting me from the rest of hell looked like he was near death? My mothering nature pushed my terrified inner child into a corner. After I finished his left arm, I moved to the other and followed that with his chest, shoulder, and finally, the cut above his eye. I had to change the water in the bowl six times before I was done.

The entire time, he sat there silently watching me. We didn't talk, not about his wounds or the night before.

I could see him already healing before I finished cleaning the wounds, but I couldn't stop myself. I felt the need to help him. Metice had to be okay, and there was something in me that pushed me to make sure of it.

It wasn't until after he fell asleep when I finally found my way back to my room, and for the first night since I landed in hell, I couldn't sleep at all. All I could think about was, what the hell was possibly strong enough to do that to him? And what if that thing found me? From there, I wondered about the bargain he'd made. What exactly did he have to give up to protect me? How did that exchange leave him in such a terrible condition?

They left him bloodied and beaten. And he'd suffered all that just to make sure I could go home safely. It wasn't right, and the thought brought on the heady sensation of guilt. Of course, I should feel guilty. Because of a drunken mistake, no matter how indirect, I'd hurt him. Metice was in pain, and it was my fault.

I didn't want to care as much as I did. I didn't do it on purpose, but it didn't change the fact that my actions had ramifications. And the demon, who was mostly an asshole to me at first, had softened. In the days we spent together, over the meals we shared, I realized he wasn't so terrible.

And as I lay there in bed, surrounded by books, I had to accept something. In the time I spent with Metice, I grew to care about him. I shared so much of myself, it would have been impossible not to feel a developing bond. And though he'd told me very little about him, he listened. He was attentive, and he remembered things about me.

Not to mention the sex. Yes, I was drunker than I ever imagined I could get off a few sips of wine, but I wanted him. It wasn't just that once. Over the days of talking, of growing closer, my curiosity about him increased. I often found myself watching his lips as he talked, his ass as he walked by, and wondering what it would feel like to have him hold me.

I looked around the room full of things he's picked out just for me, and I couldn't help but feel that he cared about me. Yeah, we gave each other shit, and we would continue to do so, but something was happening there, something I'd seen in movies and read in books. There was a connection between us, one I had to sever, because there was no way in hell I was going to fall for a demon. I didn't want him to be hurt, but I sure as hell wasn't signing up to spend the rest of eternity with him. I'd picked up that book and put it back the hell down.

There was something else bothering me. Since I admitted my truth to him and told him about my history and psychosis, I had been questioning myself. Why hadn't I called my therapist the second I saw him standing in my bedroom? Why had I just accepted that this insanity was the truth? For a long time, I wanted to believe that those lives I experienced were real, that I didn't just make it up in my head because that felt like an easy explanation for what I experienced. When he appeared, he gave me a reason to believe I wasn't crazy.

Then, I thought about those people, the ones who I came to know and love, the ones I'd been forced to mourn. Maybe they were real. Maybe they were out there, living in another world that I'd somehow accessed. Metice said it—there were magical beings on earth. Could I have inherited that ability from one of them?

Then, there was the fleeting hope that I could somehow find my way back to them. It was insane to think about, but it felt better to have talked about it, even with the one who I partially believed was just another break in my psyche. And now, he was hurt. So what did that mean? Did it mean I was breaking further? Did it mean I would have to mourn the loss of yet another figment of my imagination? Even if I believed the phone would magically work again to contact my therapist, the damn thing was dead because I'd forgotten to charge it. I was on my own, and he was hurting. I had no idea what I was going to do.

The next morning, after getting maybe twenty minutes of sleep, I gave up the effort. Metice still wasn't awake. I showered, dressed, and waited for him at the table. When he appeared, he had no food. He looked tired, but the wounds that previously covered his body were gone. His eyes were dark and his horns, which he'd had hidden since I got there, were erect on his head.

"Are you okay?" I stood and met him at the bottom of the steps. "How are you feeling?"

"I'm fine. How are *you* feeling? Did you sleep at all?" He shifted the attention back to me.

"No. I couldn't." I scanned his arms and lifted his shirt to check his chest.

"Excuse me?" he said, and I looked up to see his dark eyes on me. "What are you doing?"

"Just wanted to check your wounds. They were pretty bad." He was right: he'd completely healed, not a mark on him.

"I'm fine. You, however, look terrible." He grabbed my face and peered into my eyes. "You should have rested. Going without sleep is only going to make this more difficult for you."

"Like I could sleep while worrying about you. Maybe you shouldn't come home all bloodied and beaten like that," I fussed and slapped his hand away. "Besides, this entire experience has been difficult. So there really won't be much of a change, now will there?"

"Do you think being stubborn is a sport you can win?" he asked, and when I opted to stare out of the window instead of answering him, he continued. "Well, we better get going. We have a long way to go, and I need to make a stop along the way."

"You mean we can't just pop over there like you do?" I thought he would be transporting us to wherever he had in mind.

"No. That's a skill I use mostly when I'm away from this world. To do it here can be considered rude, especially to the person we need to see. When I'm home, I travel like everyone else."

"Do you at least have wings?" I pointed out the window where I'd seen several flying beings before. "You can fly us over all the other demons?"

"Do you think if I had wings, you wouldn't know about them by now? Have you ever seen me sprout wings and take flight?" He crossed his arms and waited for a response.

"Your body does a lot of things I don't understand." I glanced down at his dick. "And I assumed you didn't show me all your tricks. Remember, you said I can't know everything about you."

"Right." He followed my eyes. "To answer your question, no, I don't have wings. Don't worry, it won't be too difficult to get where we're going. We have transport. You don't have to worry about tiring your fragile human body with walking.

"Transport?" I asked, and Metice turned and headed back up the stairs.

Getting out of his home was a trip. The heavy door led to a long flight of stairs that spiraled about twelve times before we reached the ground. By the time we made it to the lower level where another door waited, I was out of breath.

"You do that every day?" I pointed back at the spiraling staircase.

Metice shook his head and opened the door. "You should work on your stamina… outside of the bedroom."

The door opened to a view of the lake I'd seen upstairs, and I felt fresh air for the first time in days. It washed over my skin and tickled my nose. Then, I realized the air in hell smelled like warm apple tarts. Where I expected lava, hellfire, and burning souls, there were tall trees, colorful skies, and strange animal sounds. I looked for the source of the squawking but found nothing.

The transportation he mentioned was a carriage, a gothic thing made mostly of what I assumed was iron or some other heavy metal. It had four windows on either side, thick maroon curtains draped across them. In front was an empty driver's seat, and on each side was a door with handles that looked like claws stolen from a large bird.

Oh, and there weren't any adorable stallions pulling it. Instead, there were what I dubbed hell horses. What else would you call a horse at least three times the size of a shire horse and coated in a flaming liquid that dripped from their flesh and left scorched marks on the ground beneath them?

"What the hell?" I gawked at the horses and flinched when one turned to look at me with scorching red eyes.

"You know, while you're here, you should really come up with a new phrase." Metice laughed and opened the door. "Get in."

"I never would have imagined you would ride around in something like this." I winked. "It's a little girly."

"You're calling this girly? This is top of the line!" He flicked the metal frame of the carriage with his finger, and the sharp ping echoed around us.

"It has frilly curtains on the inside!" I pointed at the windows.

"Those frilly curtains can stop a bullet." Metice looked genuinely offended for a moment before he put on that nonchalant mask again. "Call it what you want, I guess. It's not my usual ride, but I didn't want to bring too much suspicion to myself while carrying such precious cargo."

"Precious cargo?" I placed my hand over my heart and fluttered my lashes. "Is that how you think of me?"

"Get over yourself." He knocked my hand away from my chest.

I took a step closer to him and then froze as the largest of the three hell horses made a noise like a damn tiger. The sound reached beneath my skin and terrified me. At least they were frightening creatures. Maybe they would be enough to keep any other demons from trying to interfere with our trip.

Once the shock wore off, I got in the carriage. Metice closed the door and jumped in on the other side.

"Um, who's driving this thing?" I pointed to the front of the ride where the coachman's seat remained empty.

"They know where they're going." He leaned back and shut his eyes. "Just relax and enjoy the ride."

A moment later, I was holding on for dear life, because those damn horses took off like they'd been fed jet fuel. Here I was, bracing for impact, and he was snoring. There was no chance of me relaxing. Even when I did ease into my seat, one of the horses would make that terrifying sound and scare me back to my senses.

Eventually, I worked up the nerve to peek out of the covered window at the unfamiliar territory we traveled through. Hell was beautiful. There were vast plains, incredible mountain ranges, and natural stone structures everywhere. It felt idyllic, peaceful, and I wondered how it got such a bad rep. Yes, some of the creatures were terrifying, at least the ones I met, but other than that, the world looked perfect.

Metice lived far away from the general population. Traveling from his home was like passing through the countryside. Occasionally, I would see a beast in the distance, too blurry to make out, but I pretended we were just riding past grass grazing cattle. Nothing special about it.

As we neared the more populated areas, the horses slowed, and I could see in more detail. So much for pretending like this was normal. That's when the fear returned. Above us, creatures with massive, webbed wings flew in targeting circles.

In the distance I saw monsters of all sorts. Some were large, threatening and running on all fours, while others stood bipedal with human-like silhouettes. They were still too blurred by movement for me to make out anything specific. Afraid their eyesight would be better than mine, I lowered the curtain just enough so I could look out with one eye. If they recognized me as human, what would they do to me? I didn't want them to know I was in the ride with Metice, but there were a few when we passed whose eyes turned towards us, and I felt like they were looking right at me.

Just before we stopped, Metice woke up, like an internal alarm pulled him from his sleep. He stretched his arms and side eyed me.

"You didn't rest." He rolled his neck. "I can tell by your energy. You're exhausted."

"How could I?" I pointed to the window. "I'm in a new world, and you expect me to sleep on the first outing?"

"We're here now, so you won't have a chance for a while. Let's go." Metice exited his side and came around to mine to open the door. "Don't complain to me if you have trouble standing later."

"What are you doing?" I looked past him to the busy market I could see in the distance behind him. How did he expect me to go in there? There were all sorts of demons walking the streets. "I can't go in there!"

"I told you I have to make a stop, and you have to come with me. I can't leave you here," he insisted. "It's not safe for you here."

"Aren't you afraid someone will see me? Remember, demon enemies trying to attack the human to get back at you?" I pointed over his shoulder. "What if they're in there?"

"Yeah, I thought of that." He stepped away and reappeared with a cloak in his hand. It was a heavy and ugly yellow, with brown stains all over the rough fabric.

"You expect me to wear that?" I gagged. "Are you serious?"

"Well, if you want to survive." He looked over his shoulder. "Or I could just leave you here, and we can take our chances that no one will find you alone, unprotected."

"That thing smells terrible." Like hell horse shit, honestly.

"And so do most of the demons in there. We have to hide the fact that you're human."

"I can't believe this." I held my hand out. "Fine. Give it here."

Cloaked in the cover of stink, I stepped out of the carriage, and from the moment my foot hit the ground, I felt more vulnerable than I ever had. We were still far from the entrance, but there were a few demons passing us, some flying above our head, all headed to the same place.

"Breathe. It's going to be okay." He closed the door behind me. "We'll be in and out of here in no time."

"I like that you're so confident." My heart raced, the distant sounds from the market already overwhelming. "But the last thing I want to do while wearing this thing is breathe."

"Let's go." Metice led the way.

"You know, I thought it would be a lot hotter here." A cool breeze brushed across my exposed cheeks, and I pulled the hood down further to hide my face.

"Because you believe the cartoonist depictions of our world." He stopped and pointed to the distant grass covered hills. "Hell is a masterpiece of beauty. The air is without pollution, the trees are all fruitful. Anyone can live off the land without concern of poison or punishment. You humans don't know what you're missing out on."

"I don't know about all that, but yeah, every description I've heard of hell was a tapestry of literal fire, brimstone, and monsters that will leave you with nightmares. I've seen some of the monsters in passing. They didn't look that bad."

"That's because you weren't up close." His deep chuckle worried me. "Trust me, some of the beings here, one look in the eye, and you'll never sleep again. There are places like you've described. Every world has its scary bits, but most of the Bane is beautiful and welcoming."

"You don't look so bad," I admitted. Neither did the demonic woman who visited him, but I wasn't going to say that aloud.

"I guess I'm one of the lucky ones. Think of the ones who visited you on Earth." He looked back at me. "You just make sure to keep it in your pants. This isn't the place for horn holding."

"You ain't that fine," I snipped. "And I thought it was a damn dream. I told you that. I'm not about to jump on you in the middle of hell."

"Oh. I get it. That's why you've been staying away from me." He slowed until we were side by side then lowered his head to whisper in my ear. "I suppose that type of activity is meant just for Earth. Maybe in your bedroom? Or maybe you prefer the dining room table. I'm pretty sure we busted it up, though."

"You know, every time I start to think that you might be halfway decent, you open your mouth and prove me wrong." I shoved him away from me.

"I'm just doing the best I can to make sure you don't fall in love with me." He straightened. "You know, I read some of those books of yours. Call it curiosity, but I wanted to know what the draw was. There's also been an uptick in women who are doing these spells and rituals lately. I mean, we've always had the issue, but it's gotten a lot worse, and now I see why."

"Do you?"

"It's those books you read. They're nothing but porn. Your authors write these stories of monsters coming and fucking the senses out of these women, and you all just gobble it up dreaming of the day it happens to you. The problem is, most of the demons being summoned aren't the type to want to drive a woman crazy in bed. I mean, they'll drive you crazy alright, and then after days or even weeks of torture, they'll probably eat your face." He looked at me. "You got lucky with me."

"I'll have to thank the universe for that. Wait, you read the books?" I couldn't help myself. I laughed at the thought of this massive demon reading Earth smut. "How many books did it take you to come to that conclusion? It sounds like you read quite a few of them. Don't tell me you were enjoying them."

"It's called scientific research," he reasoned. "How could I properly assess the situation if I didn't get an adequate amount of data for the experiment?"

I laughed." Just tell me how many books you read. I promise I won't tell anyone."

"That's not important." He avoided the question.

"Some great researcher you are. You won't even share your data sources." I pointed at him. "How do you expect me to trust your findings?"

"The point is, you human women really need to stop being so reckless. There are plenty of men on Earth. Can they really be so bad that you're all turning to other worlds for the hope of love?"

"What do you think?" I scoffed. "The last guy I went out with left shit stains on my front seat. So yeah, it's that bad."

Metice stopped in front of me and turned to look me in the eye, his face tight with the laughter he held back. "He did what?"

"Yeah, literal shit stains on my front seat. So you'll have to excuse me if I thought maybe a mystical magical man created by a spell would be better than dealing with that ever again."

Metice's face looked like it would explode. His cheeks tightened, and his lips were pressed so tightly together, it looked painful.

"You're going to hurt yourself." I shook my head at his ridiculous expression. "It's fine, you can laugh."

He burst into laughter, and I thought he would hurt himself. The sound brought the attention of three passing wide-faced demons while he doubled over, smacking his knee and holding his sides. Two of them pointed at Metice, grunting in a language I didn't know, while the other looked at me. I waited for those ice blue eyes to turn away from me. They were slender beings, smaller them me with bodies like standing geckos. If they suspected anything about me, I doubted they'd want to face the demon I traveled with.

When the three continued without engaging, I returned my attention to Metice, who still had the nerve to be laughing. I had a sense he hadn't laughed that hard probably ever. Glad my misery could bring someone joy.

"I'm sorry, but that's just too good. I'm going to have to remember that and tell this to the others. You know, one of my guys has been called to your world at least six times! He needs to know this is what he's up against."

"Now that you know, maybe you can start an agency leasing out the demon broods for the horny women of Earth," I joked.

"You know that's not a half bad idea." He scratched his chin, as if he really thought the idea was a good one.

"I wasn't being serious." I slapped his shoulder. "That's disgusting."

"Disgusting? Look, joke or not, it might be a good business venture." He caught his breath. "The women are already calling the demons there. I could make sure they get a good one. It would do wonders for book sales. Maybe that screenplay of yours can be a part of this."

"Please. Stop." I pinched the bridge of my nose in part to stop the budding headache.

"Fine, fine. We'll talk about it later." He placed a hand on my shoulder.

"Can we go now?" I wanted to get whatever this was over with so I could take the stink cloak off.

"Yes. When we get in there, stay close to me." Metice straightened as we got closer to the entrance of the market. "Rembile isn't a place for a human. It's barely a place for demons."

"So why are you bringing me here?" I asked. "If it's so dangerous, shouldn't I be waiting for you somewhere else?"

"It's part of the bargain for the witch who's going to help us. There is an herb we need. It's a key ingredient, and it has to be as fresh as possible. Unfortunately, this is the closest place to her den where I can get it. We'll be in and out; just stay close."

And just like that, my nerves returned. The closer we got to the entrance, the more my stomach hurt, and the closer I got to him. I was a second from climbing his back and making him carry me when I heard the first sounds of demonic voices. They were making deals, arguing, and there were even sounds of laughter. Honestly, it was like any other market I had ever been to, just with the genuine threat that something might take a bite out of me.

When we reached the gate, we were a couple nearly fused at the hip. Each step he took, I took only slightly quicker because his legs were longer. At first, I thought everyone was looking at me when we crossed under the arch bearing the name of the market. It was like every creature there, both those with two eyes and those with twelve, turned to us. I pulled the stinky cloak closer around me, making sure to shield my face as much as possible. The thought was stronger with each step. I was a human and a market full of demons. How was this my life?

"They're all looking at me," I whispered. "This isn't working."

"They aren't looking at you." His voice was steady, like the steps that carried him forward.

"How could you know that?" I wanted to look at him, but I didn't. I kept my eyes on the ground and avoided potentially having the hood fall from my face.

"Relax, you're fine," he spoke calmly and kept moving forward.

I could have rebutted, but he was right. When I checked the creatures around us, those strange beings who looked as different from each other as the human who walked among them, they weren't looking at me. They looked right over the small and unthreatening visitor to the large demon next to her. I clutched the hood tight around my face and risked looking at him.

Metice no longer looked like the gentler version of himself. His horns were sprouting from his head, bigger than I had ever seen. They twisted up into spiral points above his head and glowed a soft red. The angles of his face had sharpened, and his cheekbones rose into high ridges. His eyes glowed with a purple hue. His body expanded, and it was like with each step forward he got larger.

I stumbled after looking at him and almost fell on my face. Metice's hand wrapped around my arm and kept me upright.

"Watch it." he said, eyes forward, not missing a step.

I struggled to regain my footing and keep up with him. Again, no one looked at me. He had their attention, not me. I could tell they were terrified of him. Good. Maybe it meant they wouldn't bother us. We could get in and out no problem.

At least, I hoped that's what it meant.

The market looked like an OSHA report waiting to happen. The open storefronts were like broken boxes stacked into dangerous towers. Each structure looked like with one strong breeze, it would fall over, and yet these demonic beings big and small went in and out of the buildings with no problem. They were scaling the sides of them, flying in and out through windows, and hopping from the top floors down to the ground with no issue.

I looked around and kept an eye on the ones I could see, the demons who steered clear of us. Some were large and threatening, while others were small and kind of cute. There was one in particular that ran up to me. It was blue all over, with huge cartoonish eyes, and it reminded me of something like a cross between a sheepdog and a baby alligator. It whimpered at my feet and wagged his tail in front of me.

"It's kind of cute." I leaned down to get a better look, but Metice grabbed my shoulder and pulled me back. "What is it?"

"It's called a denati. Yes, it's cute, but it's also annoying. The moment you give that thing any type of attention, it will never leave you alone. Don't touch it."

"I wasn't going to touch it. Do I look like the type of girl who walks into hell touching demons?" I didn't have to look at him to know the smug smile was spreading across his face. "Forget I said it."

After a few more minutes of walking over broken pavement, around bins of trash, and avoiding clusters of ugly demons, Metice came to a stop in front of a shop with tattered green drapes hanging in front of the door.

"Stay here." He pointed to the space next to the door where a raggedy little stool sat. "I'll be right back."

"What?" I looked where he pointed. "What do you mean *stay here*? You can't expect me to stay out here alone."

"It will only be a minute," he answered. "You'll survive."

"I can't stay here by myself." I looked around. "What if something happens? One of these things might try to snatch me up."

"Has anyone even looked at you this entire time? Just stay put, and you will be fine."

"Why can't I come?" I grabbed his arm to stop him from leaving. "I'm serious. Why?"

"The owner is weird about new people." He shrugged.

"What kind of person runs a store and gets weird about having new people come in?" I stomped my foot. "That makes no sense!"

"Not a person." He tapped the side of my head with his finger. "Remember, you're not home anymore. Stop using traits of humanity to talk about demons. Things don't work the same here."

"Fine. Just..." I looked around and found the area we were in was actually pretty empty. "Hurry up."

"So proud of you, brave girl." He patted my head like I was an obedient pet, and I wanted to punch him in the side, but I knew it would hurt my hand if I did.

At first, it was fine. I waited patiently for him to return, and though he said he would be in and out, it took longer than I would have liked. And then, as I stood there waiting for this brooding demon man to return to my side and protect me from any unwanted threats, something appeared. If I were on Earth, I would have thought it was just a little old lady, someone who probably skipped too many visits to their chiropractor. She was hunched over, with long grey threads of hair hanging in front of her face and wide eyes that were sunken into her skull. She stood across the path and watched me intently. So much for being hidden.

When it looked like she might approach me, I abandoned the sense that told me to stay put, and I moved. Yes, I knew I shouldn't have done it. It was the one avoidable thing that happens in all those stories. It was how the main character ended up in danger, but the last thing I wanted was that woman touching me or realizing there was an unaccompanied human in her world. I moved to the side of the building, just far enough that I was out of her line of sight, but close enough that when Metice came out of the store, he would be able to find me.

And of course, just as I felt mildly comfortable again, a crowd of demons came out of nowhere. They grunted and cheered as they marched by me, and while I tried to stick close to the building to get out of their way, I got swept up into the crowd and pushed further and further away from the storefront. I fought to get back to my position, but then a huge wall of a demon who smelled like a mixture of chocolate chip cookies and broccoli lifted me from the ground. He tossed me in the air like a beach ball at a rave, and his cheers muffled out the sound of my own screams.

"Put me down!" I yelled, but the crowd wasn't concerned with my pleas. I had no idea what they were celebrating, but I didn't want to be a part of it. A few minutes later, the big demon dropped me. I stumbled forward and pressed my back against the wall of another haphazardly built building. I had no idea where I was.

"Fuck." I scanned the area. "Fuck. Fuck. Fuck! How do I get back?"

The best thing I could think to do was walk opposite the general direction I knew they carried me, but it didn't help. The longer I walked, the more lost I became as I realized the place was more a maze than anything. There was no structure to the way the market was built, no grid system to follow. Each turn led to another collection of splitting pathways.

"How the hell does anyone find their way around this place?" I muttered as I pulled the hood down around my face and hoped I still smelled as bad as I did when I first arrived. My nose had adjusted to the smell, so I could no longer tell.

Moving nervously through the twisted streets, I got that gut feeling, the one that said something was watching me. If I didn't get back to Metice soon enough, I would be in some real trouble. So, I kept stumbling forward, trying my best to remember which way I'd came. Then, I heard the growl: a deep, guttural sound that came from behind me. I turned around to find the goofiest looking beast I could have imagined.

It looked like a miniature zebra, but it had short thick legs, and a belly that hung to the ground. Sharps spikes that matched the pointed teeth in its mouth lined its back. Its face looked smushed, creating a permanent grin. Goofy looking or not, the thing could definitely kill me if given the chance. It wasn't far from me, but it sniffed the air, and its eyes locked on me. It sneered. Whatever it was, it knew I wasn't supposed to be there. This thing knew I was human. There was no need to wait for it to attack first—I turned and ran.

I clutched the cloak, making sure it didn't fall off me. The last thing I needed was something else realizing I was human in a world full of demons. I turned two corners, looking back over my shoulder once, only to find the thing was still coming. I kept running, kept pushing forward. It was big, ugly, but apparently, it wasn't that fast. Its belly dragged across the ground, slowing it down.

Turning another sharp corner, I skid to a halt, recognizing the little blue demon dog. It ran up to me, frantically sniffed me, then bit the bottom of the cloak. At first, I shooed it away, but then I realized it was pulling me in a specific direction. Knowing I had little time before the overweight demon caught up to me, I followed it.

It led me into a nook just to the left, pushed me back against the wall, then turned and pointed its ass at the entrance. A cloud of rainbow mist shot from its ass and filled the space with the scent of apricots.

"What?" I gawked then slapped my hand over my mouth as the fat demon zebra ran by the opening. The aroma from my little friend's ass threw it off. It turned in circles, trying to catch my scent again, then took off running in the wrong direction.

Once it was safe, the little blue demon dog bit the bottom of my cloak again and dragged me out of the opening. I didn't know what to do at first, but it looked at me and pointed his nose to the right of us with a whimper.

"Do you know where he is?" I had to give this thing credit. It was clearly smart and wanted to help me out.

It nodded and whimpered again, jutting its nose in the same direction.

"Please don't lead me into a worse situation." I pulled the cloak tighter around me and followed its lead.

A few minutes later, I ran right into the angry demon.

"I told you to stay put. Are you okay?" He grabbed me, pushing the hood aside so he could see my face. "What happened? Are you hurt?"

"A hoard of happy demons carried me off and dropped me on my ass," I explained. "I'm a little embarrassed, but I'm not hurt."

"Are you sure?" He double-checked my appearance.

"Yes." I smiled. "Look at you, genuinely concerned about me."

"I," he started, but my new little pal whimpered at my feet. He looked down and pointed at it. "What is that?"

"What?" I looked down.

"Why do you have that? I told you not to touch it."

"I didn't touch it. It helped me find my way back." I took a step away from the little blue guy, but he scurried closer to me. "Um..."

"Great," Metice waved his hand as he fussed and turned to walk away from me, calling back to me over his shoulder. "I'm not feeding it or cleaning up after it. You wanted it, it's yours. Let's go."

8
Date with a witch

"I should name it." I looked down at the blue beast resting by my feet. Metice was right: I was stuck with it. It followed us out of the market and jumped into the carriage as soon as Metice opened the door. "Is it a boy or a girl?"

"Does it matter?" He looked down. "Why would you want to name it?"

"It saved my life," I reasoned. "Come on, if it's going to be with us, it should have a name."

"It's a boy," Metice said, then looked out the window.

"Really? How can you tell?" There were no discernible markings, and the last thing I wanted to do was look between its legs, knowing it could fart mist in my face.

"You're alive." He huffed. "The females aren't friendly. She wouldn't have led you back to me. She would have killed you."

"Oh, well, I'm glad this little guy found me instead. I think I'll name him Piko."

"Piko?" Metice's nose twitched, like the name had a stench to it.

"Yeah, it's cute, don't you think?" I leaned down to look into those large blue eyes. "What do you think? Do you like that name?"

Piko made a yipping sound and then curled up to sit on top of my feet.

"Piko it is," Metice muttered.

"How big will he get?" I reached down to scratch behind Piko's floppy blue ear.

"Not much bigger than this. I mean, there could be instances where he might expand, but the females are typically larger than the males."

"Expand?" I shrugged. I hoped he didn't grow too much. He was cute the way he was. "Thinking of expanding, what was that back there?"

"What do you mean?" He lifted the curtain with his finger to look out the window.

"Don't play coy. How did you do that in the market? You looked different and you were larger than normal." Metice continued avoiding eye contact.

"I told you I can grow." He turned and winked at me. "That doesn't only apply to your favorite part of me."

"So you can change any part of your body? Is that as big as you get? Can you do other things?" The thoughts spilled from my mouth as fast as my brain could produce them.

"You have too many questions, woman." He shook his head. "Besides, none of that matters if we get this done. My body and it's modifications won't be a concern for you."

"Fine, keep your secrets." I rolled my eyes and settled into my seat.

With the heat from the newly-named Piko on my feet accompanied by his soft purring, my own exhaustion surfaced. I barely slept the night before and was wide awake for our first trip. Partner that with running from the fat demon zebra, and I could barely keep my eyes open.

I watched Metice, who was lost in his own thoughts, staring out of the window again. There were things I wanted to say, questions I wanted to ask, but my brain wouldn't allow it. That was the thing about pushing yourself beyond your limits. Once you were there, it was nothing else you could do but rest.

My eyes fluttered against the sunlight, and I slowly drift away to a dreamworld filled with fat demon zebras trying to take a bite out of my ass. I would have given anything for it to be another unsettling sex dream.

I woke up to the smell of apricots. My head rested on Metice's shoulder and the wild succession of heartbeats coming from his chest drummed in my ear. My first conscious thought was that I was happy to be with him, despite knowing it meant I was in hell. Thoughts of us together invaded my mind and produced butterflies in my stomach—butterflies that died the moment I looked up and saw the disgusted look on Metice's face.

"Your Piko just shitted in my carriage." He pointed to the floor across from us beneath the opposite bench seating.

"What?" I looked down and sure enough, there was a fresh pile of rainbow-colored poop on the floor. It swirled like the sweet dessert atop a perfectly formed ice cream cone. "Oh no."

"You're cleaning that up, not me," Metice fussed. "Anyway, we're here."

"Oh." I straightened and looked out the window to see we were sitting in the middle of nothing, just a vast expansion of valley.

"You were making a lot of noise in your sleep. Have an interesting dream?" Metice asked.

"Yeah, I dreamed that there was a monster chasing me through that market," I answered him as I turned my attention to Piko, who nuzzled my leg.

"A monster?" Metice stiffened, like he could defend me from my unconscious mind. "What kind of monster?"

"Yeah. An ugly thing. Fat. Zebra-like with spikes all over its body. It was disgusting," I explained. "Nearly got me, but I woke up."

"You dreamt about a Cabaraga?"

"You know what that thing is?" I turned to face him.

"A Cabaraga—at least that's what it sounds like you're describing." He thought about the creature for a moment before continuing. "They're like guard dogs for shop owners."

"Oh." My face warmed as his eyes narrowed.

"You saw one, didn't you?" He looked at me like a parent ready to scold a disobedient child.

"Yes." I dropped my eyes. "Back at the market. It chased me."

"What? And you're just now telling me this?"

"It wasn't a big deal. Piko saved me. Look, I got away and made it back to you." I tried to justify my omission. "There was no need to worry you about it."

"Do you know how dangerous that could have been? What if it was a tracker?" He chastised me, and it actually made me feel worse.

"A what?"

"A tracker. There are some demons here who can lay a mark on its prey, and wherever you go, it can find you." He sighed. "Rayna, you're in a world you don't understand with beings who have abilities unlike anything you can fathom. You must be more careful."

"A tracker." The reality set in: he was right. I didn't know what I was up against. It never crossed my mind that something like that could happen. "I'm sorry."

"Don't apologize. Just don't do that again." He looked away from me and out of the window. "If something like that happens, please tell me. You said you were okay. Why would you lie?"

"Metice, I didn't lie about that. I am okay." I placed my hand on his knee. "Okay? I'm really sorry."

"Right just, don't do that again," he repeated before he got out the carriage.

A moment later, he opened my door.

"Piko stays here." Metice pointed to the little blue demon. "No unannounced guests."

My new pet looked up with sad eyes and whimpered.

"I said stay," Metice spoke to him and not me.

I climbed out of the carriage but turned to comfort Piko. "It's okay, I'll be right back. Don't worry."

Stepping outside the carriage revealed the hills on the side where Metice sat. As far as the eye could see, there was a mixture of small and large formations. Where we stopped, there was a quick path that led to the mouth of a large cave set in the side of one of the larger formations.

"That's where we're going." He pointed to the opening.

"Somehow, I knew that." My stomach groaned, and it wasn't because I was hungry.

"Don't be nervous. Just follow my lead."

"The witch who's supposed to help us is living in that cave, and you're telling me not to be nervous?" I pointed to the opening. "Only creepy shit happens in caves."

"Yes, you need to be calm, because if she realizes you're nervous, she'll use the energy against you. I'm not saying it will be easy to do, but I will be by your side, and we'll make it out of this."

"You know, you give me whiplash sometimes." I huffed as I put one hand on my hip and shielded my eyes from the sun with the other, looking up at him.

"What do you mean?" His eyes squinted in confusion.

"Sometimes, you can be a real jerk, and then other times, you're nice to me. You say things about being by my side and making it out together," I explained.

"I say what works in the moment." He shut the door to the carriage, and it felt like a dismissal of my vulnerability.

"Well, there's the jerk side again. Thanks." I sucked my teeth. *That's what I get for being open with him.*

"Come on, let's go. We need to get this over with before the sun goes down."

"Something happens when the sun goes down?" I glanced up at the sky again.

"Yeah, the real demons come out." He walked toward the cave. "We'll want to be out of here by then."

"Excuse me, real demons?" I jogged to catch up with his quick pace. "What does that mean? *Real* demons?"

"Did you think what you saw back there at the market was the real deal? Those are the day dwellers. They're the nice demons, definitely not the ones you have to worry about in this place. It's the ones who wait until the sun goes down so they can do their dirty deeds without being seen you have to worry about," he explained. "I would prefer not to have to fight them off to keep you safe."

"Shit," I cursed.

"Yeah, so let's get this done now." He looked back at me. "Keep up, human."

"Hilarious."

The walk from the carriage to the cave wasn't that far. I'd barely broken a sweat by the time we made it to the entrance. He looked at me once, and I nodded, confirming I was okay to continue. Then, we went inside.

And it was just a cave. Nothing magical happened when we walked through the entrance, though I hoped it would. I hoped the appearance was a façade, and once we entered, we would be inside a lavish mountain side resort with top amenities. We were not.

The cave was massive, dark, and smelled like onions. Metice took the lead down the short tunnel that led to the larger cavern. In the center of the space was a large pool of water that glowed and moved with circular ripples, though nothing visibly disturbed its surface. To the left of the pool were makeshift racks that held different jars and containers. Behind it was what looked like a doorway to another part of the cave we would never be able to see.

On the right, sitting in a massive clawfoot chair, was a woman. I want to say she was hideous, but I'd be a lying ass hater if I did. The woman was drop dead gorgeous. Her deep brown skin glowed with the same magic as the water. Her head slowly turned to us beneath the gilded head piece she wore and revealed eyes that glowed a soft shade of pink.

Welcoming us, she stood and towered even above Metice. Her curvy form walked over to us, breasts bouncing with each step beneath the sheer black fabric that hung draped across her body. Intricate tattoos covered every inch of her skin, some converting their form as she walked. A kitten became a tiger, and then it shifted to a lion taking up more space on her torso as the other inked depictions moved out of its way.

"Likosa," Metice said her name.

"You actually came. I didn't think you would." She stopped in front of us. "Your reputation has taken some deadly hits. Rumors have it, the once great Metice is now something of a coward."

"Just because I choose to stay out of the shitshow doesn't mean I'm afraid of it." He cleared up her misconception. "I gave my word. I'm here."

"I was shocked that you reached out. Must be something really important to make you take such a risk."

"It is," he said simply. I expected him to look at me, but he didn't. He remained focused on Likosa.

"I see." She held her hand out palm up, glowing the same shade of pink as her eyes. "The bargain."

He pulled a small bag from his pocket and handed it to her.

She opened it and took out a spider shaped herb. Likosa held the herb in front of her face, sniffed it, then licked it.

"Perfect." She grinned. "I accept."

"What are you going to do with that?" Metice asked as she tucked the herb back in the bag.

"I don't believe your bargain included me answering any questions for you." She dropped her head and glared at him through her long lashes. "Would you like to modify our terms?

"Not at all." Metice shook his head. "So, are we good?"

"Yes." She looked around him, finally acknowledging my presence. "This her?"

"Yes." He stepped aside and gestured for me to move forward.

"Hmm." She looked me up and down. "Cute."

"How long is this going to take?" Metice asked abruptly. I pulled my eyes from the woman and looked at him. He looked almost jealous.

Is he into her? Does it bother him that she's giving me attention?

"You in a rush?" She reached out and drew her finger across his cheek. "It's been so long since I saw you. I'd think you want to stay awhile."

Watching her touch him did something to me. I clenched my fists at my sides to keep from telling her to keep her hands off him. He said I had to keep my cool, and I tried, but Likosa caught it.

"Ooh." Those pink eyes snapped to me. "Looks like your human doesn't like when I touch you."

She locked eyes with me, leaned into him, and kissed his cheek as my insides boiled.

"Damn." She took a step back. "Settle down, pretty one. I won't bite him."

"Likosa, get this over with," Metice ordered.

"Yes, sir." She winked then pointed at me. "You're going to have to get naked."

"Excuse me?" I took a step back from her.

"Don't be afraid." She held her hand out to me. "I need your tits out for this to work."

I looked at Metice and he shrugged, but I had a feeling he knew exactly what was going on.

"You knew about this, didn't you?" I asked him.

"I knew it was a possibility, yes." He nodded.

"I can't believe you."

"Don't tell me you're shy about your body," Likosa chimed in. "There's no reason to be embarrassed. Besides, look at you, your curves, those tits and high ass. Most human women would kill for your body. Trust me, I know firsthand."

"No, I just..." I took a deep breath to calm the building nerves. I also wondered what body Likosa was referring to. Don't get me wrong, I loved my body, but I also had cellulite, love handles, and this weird petal-shaped mole on my hip that randomly appeared. The doctor said it was nothing to worry about, but the thing was ugly.

"It will be fine. A few minutes in the nude, then you're safe to go home. I think it's a good tradeoff." She leaned down to look me in the eye. "Don't you?"

"It's not looking like I have any other choice, so yeah, okay." I stripped and handed my clothes to Metice, shoving them into his chest.

"Bra and panties too," Likosa ordered as she walked over to the pool of water.

"Seriously?" I couldn't believe she needed that much access to my flesh to make her magic work.

"Do you want this to work or not?" She put a hand on one hip and straightened her headpiece with the other. "I'm waiting, cutie."

I took my panties off and gave them to him.

"Let's go." She pointed to the pool. "Into the waters."

With Metice watching my every step, I headed for the pool. The cool ground did nothing to help my nerves. When I passed Likosa by the water's edge, she placed her hands on my shoulders to guide me.

"I promise to be gentle," she whispered in my ear as she ushered me forward.

"What's going to happen?" I asked as we entered the sloping edge of the pool. With each step, we went deeper into the water. The rippling surface moved against my skin, giving a comforting massage.

"Tell me, have you ever been with a woman?" She brushed my hair away from my face.

"A woman?" I shook my head and glanced back at Metice. "No."

"Don't worry, he isn't going anywhere," she reassured me. "So, the thing about what I do is I work with sexual magic. I feed off the subject's energy and use that to fuel my spells."

"The subject meaning," I pointed at my chest. "Me?"

"Yes." She smiled. "I assume your demon thought I would be using him, but for the nature of this spell, it has to be you."

She ran her finger down my spine as we moved deeper into the pool, and it was like electric pulses going from the tip of her fingertip into my body.

"The thing about my magic: I need you to be aroused. So, you may want to do more than just float here. You may want more from me. I just might give you what you want."

She led me to the deepest part of the pool, where my feet no longer touched the bottom. She wrapped her arm around my waist and urged me to lean back.

"Lie back. Don't worry, I got you." Like magic, her clothes dissolved in the water. She was completely naked, the tattoos that covered her flesh dancing frantically as the water moved faster. "Is this what you want?"

"I-" I didn't know what she was asking me until I felt her hands caressing my skin. She no longer held me afloat. The water did the work and formed what felt like a raft of pressure beneath my back to hold me up. Instead, she drew circles with her fingertips across my flesh.

"I'm sorry, but I'm going to need you to give me a clear answer." She looked into my eyes. "Pretty human, is this what you want?"

The word slipped from my lips in a deep moan. "Yes." I was in hell, in a world far from my own. What would it matter if I let her do what she wanted?

Her hands moved over my body like feathers, touching every inch of me. My stomach, hips, breast, neck, even my pussy. She paused, fingers lightly feathering my clit.

"Are you sure?" Likosa lowered her face, and her full lips brushed against mine as she spoke.

"Yes," I whispered my answer through shaky lips, and that was good enough.

Her fingers slipped into my pussy, and she kissed me. My back arched like I was on a bed and not in a pool of water. She moved from my lips, and I gasped as she separated my legs, then kissed my pussy. Full lips pressed against me, and then she whispered something in a language I couldn't understand, and the water engulfed us.

We were below the surface, and though I should have drowned, I didn't. Somehow, when I breathed, my lungs weren't flooded with water. Air found a way through the liquid to me. Despite the odd mechanics of the moment, I couldn't be too worried about the water with her hands still exploring my body and her words, foreign and too fast for comprehension, echoing in my mind.

She kissed me again and her tongue swirled inside my mouth with the unexpectantly sweet taste of the water. When our lips met, there was a whisper at the back of my mind. This time, it came in English: *by the blood*. I heard it twice before the echoes faded, and all I could think of was her touch.

Next thing I knew, my mouth was on her neck, shoulder, and breasts. My hands explored her body just as much as hers did mine. There was no resistance. I wanted this, and with each kiss, each stroke of my fingers, I consented for it to continue.

When I came to orgasm, her large nipple still in my mouth, the water crashed around us, and we lay entangled on the ground at Metice's feet. My breaths were ragged attempts to re-acclimate to the air.

Likosa stood and helped me to my feet, kissed me once more, and fixed my hair.

"Good to go." She smiled at Metice. "She's all yours."

9
Time to go home

"That's it?" Metice stood in front of us, jaw tight and tone tense as I tried to keep the expression of orgasm hidden. "Is it done?"

"Would you like more? Will a blood sacrifice do?" Likosa ran her fingers down my arm, and I pulled away from her touch.

"Nope! Absolutely not." I walked over to Metice, who handed me my clothes and a towel to dry off with. "I'll get dressed, and we'll be right on our way. I'm not sacrificing any of my blood."

While I dressed, the two of them spoke in whispers. I tried to hear what they were saying, but I couldn't. Blame it on my human ears, but whatever they said to each other, they didn't want me to know about. If they did, they wouldn't have been whispering. So instead of trying to eavesdrop, I quickly put my clothes on and headed for the exit, where I waited for him to meet me.

"Does she stay like that all the time?" Likosa returned to her clawfoot throne and watched closely as Metice guided me out of her home.

"How would I possibly know that?" Metice sounded irritated.

How the hell can he be mad at me? He's the one who brought me to her knowing full well what kind of magic she does.

"You sound like you were friends." I gave him a hard side eye. "When we first got here, it looked like the two of you were very familiar with each other."

"Not as familiar as the two of you," he grunted and led the way back to the carriage, walking twice as fast as usual.

"Are you kidding me right now?" I couldn't believe it, but it looked like he was jealous as he marched ahead of me. I was damn near running to keep up with him. "You're the one who brought me here. You already said you knew this was a possibility. It's not my fault you thought she would use you instead of me."

He said nothing else until we made it to the carriage, and then he opened the door and stood back. "Get in."

"Are you seriously going to stay mad at me?" I threw my hands on my hip and refused to get in until he gave me a direct answer.

"Who said I was mad?" He looked down at me.

"So is it jealousy?" What else could it be?

"Why would I be jealous?" He pointed to the open door. "Get in."

"Fine, you're not mad or jealous. Maybe your stomach hurts. Maybe you just need to poop." I hopped in the ride and greeted my new pet, who jumped into my lap. "Did you miss me, boy?"

"Here." I looked back at Metice, who handed me a small gray piece of fabric. "What's that for?"

"I told you I wasn't cleaning that up" he pointed to the colorful mess still on the floor of the carriage.

"Oh." I took the cloth from him and scooped up the poop then handed it back to him.

He stepped aside and pointed to the ground. "I'm not touching that."

I dumped the mess and looked at him, waving the cloth in his face. "You want your hanky back?"

"Just toss it." He stepped further back.

"That's littering." I didn't know if there were waste management laws, but I wasn't about to risk being trapped in hell because someone caught me tossing trash on the ground.

"It's compostable. This isn't Earth. There's no such thing as littering here."

"Hmm, good to know." I dropped the cloth, and he closed the door.

"We're pulling it close." He looked out the window at the rising moon as the hell horses raced us back to his home.

"Do you think something's gonna get us?" I leaned forward to look out the window. "Are we in trouble?"

"I wouldn't rule it out." He lowered the curtain.

"Are you serious?" I shifted in my seat to look at him. "Can these things move any faster? What happens if we get caught out here?"

I shouldn't have asked that damn question, because as soon as I did, the terrifying screech of a monster rang out through the night. I had no idea what it was, but it was close, and my gut said it was coming straight for us—the one time I needed my gut to be wrong. I looked at Metice and saw the same worry and tension on his face. We were in trouble.

"What is that?" I moved to open the window curtain to look out of it, but he gripped my wrist and pulled me back.

"Don't move," he said firmly.

"What's going on?" I asked, but he said nothing. "You're scaring me, Metice."

"Don't worry, just please. Be still."

The carriage slammed to a halt, and the horses screamed, frightened by something. Another screech rang out and this time, it was echoed by at least five others.

The carriage shook as a series of heavy beings dropped to the ground surrounding us. I gripped his arm as shadows were cast across the windows, accompanied by hissing and rattling.

"Meti," a deep voice called out. "I know you're in there. Come out and talk to me."

"I'm going to get out of the carriage," Metice whispered, and I dug my fingers into his arm, afraid to voice my concern because I didn't want whatever was waiting outside to hear me. "You're going to stay inside. Do you understand me? This is not a moment for you to debate me or to go against what I'm telling you. If you come out there, I cannot promise I'll be able to protect you. Please, right now. Stay inside."

The door shut behind him, and it took everything in me not to reach for him and pull him back inside. Sensing my discomfort, Piko jumped into my lap and nuzzled me. His soft whimpers echoed the way I felt inside. Something was out there, something that worried Metice so much, he feared I wouldn't make it out of the interaction alive.

And there was nothing I could do but sit and wait.

Voices spoke in a mixture of languages. Some words I understood, some I didn't. What I did get was that whoever was out there wanted Metice to return to work. What work was he supposed to be doing?

"I'm not doing this with you," Metice said. "I told you I'm not coming back."

The thing responded in a series of clicks and curling letters before it said, "Only so much time."

Metice said something else I didn't understand, and then it started: fighting. Blow after bone crunching blow landed, and something large slammed against the side of the carriage. The damn thing tipped, but luckily, it didn't fall over. I pulled Piko to me and held him tight, hoping it would end soon, and my demon protector would survive whatever was happening outside.

After the fighting stopped, the screeches sounded once again, followed by the batting sounds of heavy wings. And then, there was nothing. The silence lasted too long for comfort. Had they killed him? Just as I worked up the nerve to open the door, it swung open, and a bloodied Metice climbed inside.

"What just happened? Who did this to you?" I questioned him and placed my hands on either side of his face. This was the second time he'd returned to me beaten up. "What did this to you? Are you okay?"

"I'm fine." He grabbed my wrist, and those dark eyes met mine with heart-crushing sadness. "It's okay."

"Metice, you need to tell me what's going on. What keeps doing this to you? These are the same marks you have the other night."

"I told you I had a life before you." The horses started running again, and we jerked back against the forced motion. "One that brought me a lot of trouble, one that I'm trying not to get wrapped up in again."

"And because of me, it's coming back." That was my understanding. His life was fine until I arrived. "Is this because of me?"

"It's not because of you. It's been happening. But now there are people who know about you, and they want to use you against me. If they knew you were here, in this carriage, if they had seen you..." His dark eyes locked onto mine. "I don't think I could have protected you. Not now, not like this."

"Are you ever going to tell me what's really going on?" I asked. "This isn't okay. You can't survive like this for much longer."

"There's no need for that. Soon, you'll be home, protected by Likosa's magic, and my problems won't be yours." He wiped the blood from his lip. "We just need to get you home safely. That's all that matters."

"Are you sure this spell is going to work?" The damn things had found us. What was to say they wouldn't be able to do the same when I was back in my world without him?

"Fortunately, we have proof now that it will. If it didn't, they would have known you were here." He shifted his weight and groaned. "They wouldn't have let you live if they realized you were with me."

"We need to clean up your wounds." I looked at the flesh through his torn shirt. This was worse than the first time. "You're already starting to bruise."

"I'll heal." His head dropped back on the head of the seat, and he pulled me to his side. "Just relax. It's a long ride back to the house."

Metice slept, but I couldn't. I watched him, and yes, his wounds were healing, but it was much slower than the first time. The demon was weakening. What did that mean? Would that thing come back and kill him?

"Get your things," Metice said as we entered his home. "I'll take you home now."

"No," I denied his request as he headed for my room.

"What?" He turned to look at me. "What do you mean, no? We need to get you out of here."

"You're hurt. You need to rest. I can go home tomorrow." I stood firm in my choice.

"Rayna." Metice rubbed his hand over his coarse hair, and I could see the tips of his horns emerge, retract, and emerge again.

"You already said the spell worked," I reminded him as I walked over to him and placed my hand on his chest. The budding horns retreated, and I felt the tension melting away from his body. "That means I'll be safe here one more night. I doubt they will come banging on your door to fight again. Looking at you now, that would kill you. They want you alive. Am I right?"

"Yes, you're right." His eyes slowly slid closed as I moved my hand to his cheek.

Face cradled in my palm, he looked different to me. Sweeter, gentler than before. Something was changing about this man the longer we were together. Yes, he kept that hard exterior, but there were moments when he showed me who he truly was. He leaned into my touch, and his chest rose with a deep breath. He might debate me, but I could tell he was relieved to have me stay with him.

"Then it's settled." I picked up Piko, who sat by my feet. "Rest. I'll pack my things, and you can take me home tomorrow."

"Okay, whatever you want." Metice gave up the debate. We both knew he'd be lying if he continued to fight me about my decision.

"Do you need help cleaning up?" I looked at his exposed skin. The lacerations had already closed, but the bruises and stains of blood were still there.

"No, I'll be okay." He shook his head and looked at his bathroom door. "I'll clean up."

"Good." I put Piko down and headed for the steps. "Let me know if you need me."

Bags packed and fresh out of the shower, I stood at the bookcase and sighed. There was something devastating about not being able to read them, or at least take them with me. I looked at my bags and wondered how many I could fit in them. Maybe he would be able to transport the books with me. Would that be too much?

The knock at the door interrupted my useless calculations. I already had most of the books at home, and with my luck, there would be no time to read them any time soon.

"Yes?" I opened the door to find Metice standing there in grey pajama pants and a matching open robe. "Are you okay?"

"I'm okay." He stood outside the door. "The shower helped."

"What's wrong?" I looked around him. The room behind him was lit with the light of the moon. The light bounced off the floor and cast a soft glow that outlined his body.

"Nothing's wrong," he said simply and then just stood there, awkwardly looking at me. It was like he had a deep dark secret and had found out I knew.

"So why are you here?" Suddenly, I felt self-conscious. *Why is he looking at me like that?*

"You said to let you know if I needed you." Metice entered the room and headed for my bed. He pulled the covers back and sat.

"What's going on?" I slowly crossed the room. "Are you okay?"

"I'm okay. This may feel off putting and I'll understand if you say no. Rayna, after today, I want nothing but the comfort of your presence. Just lay with me, please." There was something vulnerable in his tone, something I never expected from him.

"Okay." I joined him in the bed.

There was nothing to say. I had no witty comebacks or comments about him wanting to be in my bed. Metice's body healed, but I could feel it: something inside him was hurting. If being with me could help, I would give him that.

Metice pulled the covers over us, and we lay together in silence. There was nothing to talk about. He pulled me into his side and rubbed my shoulder before nuzzling his head against the top of my bonnet-covered hair. It didn't take long until he was softly snoring. Piko sat on the floor at the foot of the bed, also snoring. Between the two of them, it wasn't long before I was knocked out as well.

I woke alone in my bed, the aroma of fresh food filling the air. Metice sat at the table outside my room.

"I repaired the table," he announced as I exited the room. "I thought it would be nice to have one more meal together before you go."

"Thank you." I joined him at the table. "Did you sleep okay?"

"Better than I have in years, yes." He sipped from a cup of what looked like tea and smelled like honey. "Thank you for allowing me to sleep in your bed."

"Oh, um..." I didn't know what to say. It wasn't like I was going to kick him out. "No problem. I'm glad you were able to rest."

"I thought you might want to try another local meal." He pointed to the food on the table. "All safe for human consumption. Fruits and a treat we call sinulo."

"Sinulo?" I looked at the plate of what looked like soupy scrambled eggs with swirls of brown, green, and purple.

"It's like a sweet egg. It's delicious, trust me." He pointed to the plate with pride, and I wondered if he'd made the meal himself.

I sat down and took a spoon full of the colorful substance. Looking at him first, I popped the bite into my mouth, and I might not have gagged on his dick, but there was no way I was keeping that shit down. The sour taste hit the back of my throat, and I spit it right back out and into his face.

"Oh shit, I'm so sorry!" I smacked my hand over my mouth.

"I take it you don't like it?" He picked up a napkin and wiped the food from his face.

"I'm sorry, but no. That tastes..." I paused. "Actually, let me keep my thoughts to myself."

"Well, I tried." he shrugged. "Ready to go home?"

"Actually, yes I am." I placed the plate on the floor, and Piko ran to it and cleared it in seconds. At least it wouldn't be wasted. "I mean, thank you for taking care of me, but I miss my things, and I'm sure work is piling up. That's if I haven't been fired from my contracts. I've been here for a week now, right? By your math, that means nearly two months away from home. No way I'm going to be able to excuse that sort of absence easily."

"You're worried about work?" Metice frowned, as if the concept was foreign to him.

"I'm human. I have bills to pay." I reminded him that I didn't belong in his world. At home, my bills were on autopay, but there was still so much I needed to handle. I also worried about my friends. Keri must have been losing her shit.

"Right." He stood. "Let's get you home."

Bags in hand, Metice did his thing. The room tensed with energy, and my vision faded. Gone was the mountainside home in hell. When my sight returned, I was standing in the moonlight space in my bedroom.

"Oh God, what is that smell?" I gagged and ran to the window to open it. As the fresh air poured in, I scanned the room and found the half-eaten bowl of broccoli cheddar soup on the table. "Dammit! It's going to take forever to get that smell out of here."

"I bet sinolu tastes a whole lot better than whatever that is," Metice joked. "Why does it smell so bad?"

"How long have I been gone?" I looked at him as I found a plastic bag and dropped the fuzz-covered dish inside. "In Earth terms?"

"You were right before. It's been just under two months since I took you away," Metice confirmed, and a little part of me died inside. I'd hoped he'd say I overestimated my timeline, but two months had gone by. A quick look out the window showed the changing season. The canopy of trees in my backyard had begun their colorful shift as summer gave way to the cooler autumn days.

"Exactly. Well, that explains this. It's fine; a few bottles of room spray, and it should be okay." I paused and considered the landmine that must have been waiting for me in my refrigerator. *All those poor leftovers.*

I tossed the bag aside and went on the hunt for the spray. Of course, because I hadn't been in my own room in weeks, that damn ugly ass table got in my way. I slammed my foot against it and went flying. Metice caught me, but we both fell on the bed. I face planted into his chest and knocked the wind out of him.

"Maybe it's just on Earth where you're this clumsy. Is it the added gravity?" He wrapped his arm around my waist as the laughter shook his body.

"Shut up." I slapped his chest and then realized we were in my bed. "Um."

"Don't worry. The next time I have you, you won't be able to claim it was a dream or blame it on intoxication." He laughed at my expression and rolled me off his chest and onto the bed before standing. "I'll get going now. I'll keep an eye on you for a few days, make sure the spell really worked and you're okay."

"Thank you." I stood from the bed, straightening myself and headed for the cabinet, remembering that was the last place I had the spray. "Wait, what about Piko?"

"What about it?" he asked.

"Him!" I corrected Metice as I retrieved the spray and popped the cap open. "He'll miss me. You have to take care of him."

"You can't be serious." He folded his arms over his chest. "What do you expect me to do about that?"

"Metice," I mimicked him and crossed my arms over my chest. There was no way he could toss that little guy out. "He saved my life. He deserves to be cared for. If I could bring him here, I would."

"Okay, I'll bring him to you." He looked around the room. "Maybe he can eat your disgusting leftovers for you."

"That's not funny." I gave him my best 'I'm so disappointed in you' glare.

"Fine." he grumbled. "I'll make sure the little nuisance survives. Enjoy your life demon free."

"Don't pretend you aren't happy," I teased him. "Now you'll have a friend in hell, someone to keep you company now that I'm gone."

"Yeah, right." Metice walked over to me and put his hand on my shoulder. He gently pushed me and followed each of my steps with his own until my back was pressed against the wall. The joking was long over.

"What are you doing?" I pressed my hand against his chest. "Whatever you're thinking is going to happen here isn't. Not with my room smelling like ass."

"I'm not seducing you. I'm giving you a warning." He lowered his face to mine. "Rayna, stay out of trouble."

"What?" I laughed nervously. "Why wouldn't I?"

"I'll be watching you." His hand slipped around my waist. He pulled me to him, crushing my hand between our bodies as his heart raced beneath my palm. Those dark eyes grew darker, and his voice dropped at least two octaves when he spoke again. "Keep yourself safe, or I'll take you back to hell. I can't promise that I'll let you come back next time."

"Let me?" His words did two things to me. They terrified me... and they turned me on. *Dammit girl, get it together.*

"You heard me." He kissed me, and that talented tongue of his danced in my mouth and made my head swim in a cloud of arousal. Then, mid-kiss, he vanished.

"Right, definitely not trying to seduce me." I fanned myself then gagged at from the fresh wave of spoiled broccoli air.

Four months later, winter had rolled into my city, and I was on another date. It took a while for me to get there though, and still I sat across the table from a man who should have been able to hold my undivided attention and I couldn't have cared less. He was great on paper, but my brain worked overtime comparing him to a horny demon with his rotating team member.

For the first month, I waited for Metice to return. He didn't. I buried myself in my work. It took a lot to repair the broken relationships and a couple of my clients never called me back. I couldn't blame them. I also had to explain myself to Keri.

"Where the hell have you been? You call me one night talking about being in hell, then completely ghost me?" Keri burst into my house two days after I returned home.

"I'm sorry." What else could I say? It wasn't like she would believe the truth.

"Where did you go?" She frowned at the lingering smell of broccoli. *Why did it take so long for that stank to go away?*

"I needed to get away, Keri," I explained as best as I could without bringing up demons again. "I felt like I was losing my mind, seeing demons and shit and clearly, I needed help with that. So, I found it."

"You could have told me." She smacked my arm. "You had me ready to round up the girls. I put in a police report and everything!"

"You did what?"

"Girl what did you expect? I called your mom, your dad, hell, I even found that crazy aunt of yours on Facebook. She preached to me for two hours about how your soul was where it was supposed to be!"

"She said what?" I couldn't help wondering if my aunt knew more than we gave her credit for but refused to go down that rabbit hole. "Keri, I'm okay. I'm sorry I ghosted out. I won't do that again."

"You better not." She hugged me. "Rayna, you're my sister. You can't do that to me."

Keri refused to leave my side for two days after that. When she was forced to go back to work, she called me in between meetings and video chatted with me on her drives home. I appreciated her, not only because it made me feel loved, but also because whenever I wasn't buried in work or trying to repair the relationships I'd shattered with my absence, my thoughts returned to him.

I started to question myself. Maybe I had made it all up. Maybe Keri was right to be worried about my sanity. I spent night after night waiting for a demon to appear in my bedroom. I worried if he was hurt, if the unseen monster who'd beat him up had finally finished the job. I couldn't get him out of my mind, and it was so bad that eventually, even work couldn't keep my thoughts from him.

The second month, I returned to therapy. For reasons I hadn't unpacked yet, I didn't give my therapist all the details. I told her I had a mental break, but that was all. Things got tough, and I just needed a reset. She could tell I was holding back, but the thing about a good therapist was that they let you get to the truth on your own time.

Two months later, and I was sitting across the table from my fifth date in two weeks, feeling hopeless. This guy, like the two before him, seemed really nice, but my gut told me not to get my hopes up. The two previous, though we connected on many levels, completely ghosted me. I wondered if it was my fault. Sure, a demon preoccupied my thoughts, but I still managed to appear mostly normal on the dates.

With both, the first date went great. I waited for a call, a text, a damn carrier pigeon, anything to let me know they were interested. It never came.

The last guy, a doctor named Dennis, I'd actually run into after our date. Walking through the pharmacy, hands full of overnight pads because they were on sale, and I run into the man who ghosted me! I might have tried to say something witty, spark up a conversation to find out what went wrong, but he didn't give me the chance. The man ran away! He bolted like he'd just seen a damn ghost.

The date ended, and Chris, a radio personality with an upcoming deal for his own television show, sounded excited about the future.

"I had a great time with you." We were standing outside the restaurant when he pulled my hand into his. "It was great meeting you in person finally."

"You too." I smiled. "Get home safely."

The valet pulled up with my car. Chris paid for me and tipped the driver before putting me in the car. I was three blocks away when I realized I had left my scarf in the restaurant and chose to double back. That would have been the third one lost since the temperature dropped. Christmas music played over the radio and just as the singer proclaimed she wanted "you" for the holiday, I pulled up to see Chris looking terrified as a tall, dark figure spoke to him.

"What the hell?" I gripped the steering wheel and squinted to make sure I was seeing things clearly.

Chris stepped away, face pale, and I squinted, trying to see who the guy was. What the hell was this man wrapped up in? I couldn't get involved with someone who had thugs chasing him down. I waited at the end of the street to see if I could catch a look at him.

He turned around, and when I saw his face, my mind raced to put the pieces of the puzzle together as the doctor's frightened expression flashed in my mind. Purplish black skin, horns retracted. Metice. No fucking wonder none of my dates were calling me again. How many times had he done this?

I pulled the car forward and stopped next to him. Rolling down the window, I called out, "Get in."

"Rayna?" He clearly hadn't expected to see me. This time, it was Metice who looked like he'd seen the walking dead.

"I don't want to hear it. Get in!" I hit the button on the door handle, and the click of the locks disengaging sounded.

10
Sabotage

Metice climbed into the car after the attendant returned to his post and gave the two of us a suspicious stare. He clearly recognized me from moments before when I'd picked up my car.

"Is everything okay?" He lumbered over.

"It's fine," Metice muttered as he got into the car.

Too irritated by his presence, I put the car in drive and took off, forgetting all about my scarf. I grumbled a string of complaints to myself, refusing to speak to him. Whenever I felt my blood pressure rising, I slapped my hand on the steering wheel. I did it so many times, my palm felt sore. The demon sat next to me, unbothered by my outbursts as we dove together in silence, not a word spoken until we pulled into my garage.

"Are you fucking kidding me?" The second the car was parked, I jumped out and ran around to his side, swinging his door open.

"Rayna." He leaned forward, and I swear, the ancestors claimed my hand, because I couldn't remember deciding to slap him, but that's exactly what I did. Then, I cursed my foolishness, because my hand was already burning.

Metice gripped the door and gritted his teeth. "What was that for?"

"That was for me putting two and two together and finding your demonic ass scaring off my dates. Why would you do that?" I shoved my finger in his face. "Here I was, thinking something was wrong with me, and the entire time, you're chasing off the few good men still on Earth? Is there something wrong with your brain? Did you suffer a head injury I don't know about?"

"Am I allowed to speak, or are you going to slap me again?" He rubbed his jaw. "Damn, that actually stings."

"I'm not sure. Let's try it and find out." I threw my hands on my hips and waited for him to speak again.

"I-"

"I don't want to hear it!" I threw my hand up in his face, turned, and went into the house.

"You can't be that upset." Metice entered behind me as I entered the code to stop the alarm from sounding.

"Don't tell me how upset I can be when you've been sneaking around my back and ruining my already struggling dating life."

"Ruining?" he laughed. "Are you really upset to be missing out on that guy? I thought you had higher standards than that."

"Excuse me?"

"He spent the entire date talking about himself and hardly noticed you hadn't responded. How many questions did he ask you about yourself? I'll wait while you count."

"I-" I stomped my foot. "What is your point?"

"My point is that he didn't even care enough to notice when you left your scarf." Metice opened the black peacoat he wore and pulled out my scarf. "Now, tell me why you would be upset about not hearing from a man who could be so careless with you?"

"That should be for me to decide, not you." I removed my coat and placed it on the table in the foyer. "What are you doing here, anyway? It's been months."

"It has," he agreed.

"You said I would have a demon-free life." I reminded him.

"I didn't lie about that. I had no intention of being a part of your life again. You came back and saw me."

"No intention of being a part of my life, and yet you're making decisions about who I should and shouldn't date?" I pulled my fresh braids from the heavy top bun and sighed at the relief. I would have never attempted the style so soon after getting the braids done, but the cool winter air helped ease the pain. "How can you call this demon free after doing what you did?"

"Hmm." He smiled and reached out to touch the braids that fell around my face. "I like your hair like that."

"Metice." I slapped his hand away. "Answer my question."

"Rayna." He dropped his voice into his chest and stretched the syllables of my name. It was something he'd started when I was in his home, and it drove me crazy—not that I told him that.

"Don't do that. Don't say my name like that." I moved away from him. "Just answer the question."

"How did I say your name?" He followed me down the hall. "Tell me."

"It doesn't matter." I avoided the question and turned, flipping the switch to light the living room as I headed further into my home.

"You're upset, and rightfully so," he announced, as if I needed his approval.

"I didn't ask you if I was right to be upset. Why are you back here? Did something happen? Was there a demon here?"

"No, there wasn't. The spell worked." He alleviated my growing concern. "Everything is fine."

"Okay, so what am I missing then?"

"I-" he hesitated.

"What?" I snapped. "Drop the act. You're not this damn shy."

"I missed you, okay?" he admitted then watched as the shock colored my face.

"You missed me?" I repeated his words to him. "Did I hear that correctly?"

"Is that so hard to believe?" he asked. "Or are you used to the human men who don't tell you such things?"

"I'm ignoring that comment for now, because I'm still stuck on the part where you miss me."

"For you, it's been a few months. For me, it's just a few weeks. I checked on you the first few days, like I said I would. Then, I waited for you to call out to me, for you to need me. Days went by, and nothing. I couldn't take it anymore. So I came back, and when I get here, I find you on a date with a guy who looks like an armpit." He grunted. "I get it. For you, it's been long enough to move on, but for me, it's a punch to the gut to see you here with someone else."

"An armpit?" I thought about who he could have meant. "Jericho?"

"Yes." He grunted. "How could you even consider being with someone like that?"

"Wait. Were you jealous?" I snorted, not because I thought it was funny, but because sometimes, when my nerves got the best of me, my brain's solution for release was laughter. I immediately regretted it when his brow furrowed.

"Jealous? No. Embarrassed is more like it."

"You were embarrassed? Why?"

"For you. Why would you even be seen in public with him?"

"I can't believe this. You have the nerve to do what you did and then lecture me about the men I chose to spend my time with." I paused. "Wait. What was wrong with the doctor?"

"Could you not smell his breath? It damn near knocked me over." He waved his hand in front of his nose. "Almost passed out when I talked to him."

"What did you say to them?" I ignored the childish comment. The doctor's breath was fine; Metice was being an asshole.

"Honestly, it didn't take much. A light threat, and they were gone." He shrugged. "See, you should choose better. A better man would have at least told you what happened. A good man wouldn't have allowed empty threats to stop him from being with you."

"This is unbelievable." There I was, standing in my home, listening to a demon I once thought I made up tell me about how I had to choose better men, as if women didn't hear that shit enough. "What do you want me to do?"

"I'm not sure what you mean."

"You just admitted to sabotaging me. Is this something you plan to keep doing?"

"If you keep dating losers, yes." He stood in the hall, jacket open, staring at me like he hadn't just confessed to being a stalker.

"And the alternative is what? Stay single forever? Date a demon from another world?" I threw my hands up. "Give me a break."

"How is it that someone who is so impressive, someone with so much life under your belt, deals with such ridiculous men?" His brow furrowed as he tried to understand the logic behind my situation. "Why do you put yourself through that?"

"What else would you have me do, Metice?" I asked. "Look, I'm sure it's easy for you to sit there looking how you do. You're obviously a desired demon from your world. You're probably used to having the best of the best throw themselves at you, but it's different here. It's different for me. The dating landscape is not what it used to be."

I threw my hands up, already frustrated with the topic, but continued.

"Throw on top of that toxic recipe that I'm a black woman in the world that tells me every damn day that no matter how impressive I am, I'm unwanted. If I step outside of my race, I'm a traitor to my people. But then I'm finding more and more often that the black men, the men who should want me, who should uplift me, don't. Not the way I am. They're stuck on having women be submissive, but they give us nothing to submit to.

"They taught us to be successful, to strive for greatness and build something for ourselves. I did what they said, checked all the boxes. Successful in my field, check. Money and a beautiful home, check. Hobbies and talents, check. You see that as a great thing, but guess what? To a lot of men, it's all a red flag. Don't get me wrong, it's not just black men. We get it from every side.

"So many of them feel threatened by a woman who has her own. You know, I was on a date with the guy who told me I should pay since I was so successful. Then he went on and on about how he didn't even understand why I was dating. I had everything; I didn't need a man.

"It's crazy to think that achieving my dreams and being good at what I do is held against me. And now, every time I log onto a social media app, all I see are people saying if you haven't had a relationship or snagged a man by now, you might as well give up, because the current and future generations are all but lost for."

"And after all that, you still try the date. Why?" he asked, genuine concern coloring his face.

"Metice, I don't want to believe it. There has to be something out there, right? Someone who wants what I want. Like, all of this wasn't for nothing. I know there are men out there who still want love and appreciate a good woman. I know there are men who aren't threatened by their partner's success. It's just harder to find them. Just gotta dig through the muck of men fighting to hold on to a relationship type that no longer has a place in our world."

"I guess that makes sense if you didn't date, you wouldn't be sitting here talking to me now." He shook his head. "I don't want you dating these men. You shouldn't be putting yourself at risk for such morons."

"Wait, is that what you want?" I dropped my hands to my side. "Do you want to date me?"

"No," he muttered after a long pause.

"Stop lying. You hesitated." I pointed at him and then started singing as I teased him. "You *like* me, don't *you*? You want to *date* me. You want to be my *boyfriend*, don't you?"

"You need to eat." He ignored my question.

"What?" I dropped my hand. "I just got back from dinner."

"You went to dinner, but you didn't eat," he corrected me. "He ordered for you without asking your opinion. You didn't like it. I know that because you moved the food around, then stared off into space while he rattled on. You didn't eat. Rayna, you need to eat."

"Don't change the topic," I fussed. "You're trying to distract me with food, but I know the truth now."

He walked around me, picking up my coat from the table and heading for the living room. I watched him ignore me, open the closet, and hang up both our coats, securing my scarf with my coat. Then, still ignoring me, he headed for the kitchen.

"What are you doing?" I followed him.

"Making sure you eat." He pointed to the bar stool by the island. "Sit and hush."

"Excuse me?" I rolled my neck. "Don't order me around in my own home."

"I know you like to talk, but can you just not right now?" He pinched the bridge of his nose.

"You better be glad you're making me dinner, or I would kick your ass out." I snapped my fingers in his face.

"Right." He chuckled.

"Do you even know what you're doing? Can you cook human food?"

"You agreed to be quiet."

"Fine." I threw my hands up and watched as the demon moved around my kitchen. "You sure you know what you're doing? I don't want my house to burn down."

I expected him to be a clumsy mess in the kitchen. The entire time I was in his home, I didn't see him cook. I didn't even spend time in the small kitchen he had. Whenever we did eat, he went out for food. But he surprised me. Metice moved around the kitchen like a trained chef, only speaking to me when there was something he needed that he couldn't find.

Thirty minutes later, he sat a plate of tacos and rice in front of me and stepped back.

"Try it." He nodded.

"If I die…" I frowned, pretending like the look and smell of the food didn't make my mouth water.

"Don't be dramatic." Metice picked up a taco from the plate and held it to my lips. "Take a bite."

I scrutinized the chopped steak inside, looked up into his dark eyes, and then sunk my teeth into the tortilla. Damn it if it wasn't the best damn taco I ever had. My eyes rolled to the back of my head, and my legs bounced hidden by the counter.

"What do you think?" he asked.

"It's alright." I said and took another bite. "Is there more?"

"Why would you want more if it's just alright?" He fed me the last bite, and I licked the juice from his fingertips.

"Hush and make me another taco." I grinned around the bite. "How did you learn to make this?"

"I told you I come to other worlds to study," he explained as he served me another taco. "While I'm there, I immerse myself in the cultures and learn as much as I can."

"When did you learn to make tacos?"

"Recently."

"Oh?" My eyes widened as I scooped up a spoonful of rice.

"You're always going to that taco place by the pond. Why you would continue to go there after being attacked there confuses me," he admitted. *So he had done more than just watch me on my dates. This man is obsessed!*

"It's my favorite." I should have been alarmed by his admission that he'd known my habits, but I felt comforted. All that time I thought he'd forgotten about me, he hadn't.

"Well, these can be your favorite now." He placed another taco on my plate. "Are you done being mad?"

"No." I shook my head and put a spoonful of rice in my mouth.

"Have another taco." He pointed to the food in front of me. "Maybe that will help."

I did. In fact, I had three more before the button on my pants threatened to pop. Instead of embarrassing myself, I pushed away from the table and refused the next offered bite.

"I'm stuffed. Oh man, I can't eat anymore." I waved my hands in surrender. "Make sure you put that up so I can eat it tomorrow."

"You're making me do the dishes as well?"

"I didn't ask you to cook." I shrugged.

"No wonder you're single," he fussed but started cleaning.

"Are you going back now?" I asked, watching him closely. He was doing a good job, so there was no need for me to pick at him, though it would have been fun.

"Do you want me to?" He looked over his shoulder at me.

I hesitated, but there was something I wanted to tell him, something I had to say. "You know, I got real close to convincing myself I made you up."

"What?" He dried the last dish with the towel before placing it on the drying rack.

"I expected you to come back at least once. You didn't." I nodded. "Those first few days, every little sound scared the hell out of me. I figured it was either something coming to kill me, or you coming to make sure I was okay."

"I didn't know you expected me to come." He walked around the table to sit next to me by the counter. "That wasn't the plan."

"I know it wasn't, but it really broke me to think I could be so delusional," I admitted. "Even went back to therapy."

"Did it help?" The humor drained from his voice.

"Let's just say it did." I shrugged and dropped my eyes to my hands.

"It was hard for me too." He placed his hand on my knee. "All I had was that damn denati to remember you by."

"Piko!" I gasped. "Oh, is he okay? Are you taking care of him like you said you would?"

"Yes, the thing is fine. Finally got him to go outside to drop his rainbow shits." He grumbled. "Disgusting little thing."

"At least they smell good." I nudged him in the side with my elbow.

"To you, maybe." The corner of his lips lifted into a quick smile. "The stuff was everywhere. I ruined a few pairs of shoes stepping in it."

"But you're still taking care of him, so you must like him." I teased.

"What if I did come back to see you?" He looked me in the eye, changing the subject.

"Metice." My heart raced. That question opened a door to something dangerous.

"It's strange, yes, but it's better than what you're doing now," he reasoned.

"Dating a demon from another world is better?" I shook my head. "How do you come to that conclusion?"

"You're already my soulmate." He gripped the edge of my seat and pulled me closer to him. "It's not much more than that."

"Where is this coming from?" I asked. "You were so against even knowing me before."

"I told you. I missed you," he said.

"It's more than that. Maybe you don't want to tell me, and that's okay, because I can't date you, Metice. I can't do that to myself."

"I understand. It was a long shot." His shoulders dropped. "Can you at least let me visit?"

"Metice."

"I'm not asking for much. I just," he pulled my hand into his, "Rayna, I want to know the person I'm tied to. I still haven't found a solution to this. It doesn't seem like you can feel me, but I feel you, every emotion you've gone through. Do you know how hard it was to stay away in the beginning? I felt your sadness, your confusion, even your anger. I wanted to fix that, but I couldn't. So excuse me, but I want to know you. I don't want you to feel those things again."

"Do you think this is a good idea?" I couldn't deny that little spark of excitement that started in my stomach. Could I have him in my life? Would it work? I knew damn well it wasn't smart, but did that matter? I missed him. The only way I'd been able to deal with those feelings was to tell myself he hadn't existed at all, but I knew it wasn't true.

"Do you want me to lie so you'll agree?" He grunted. "I'll do it."

"That's not helpful."

"Look, it won't be easy, but this is what I want." He paused. "If you don't, I'll respect that."

"Will you leave my dates alone?" I raised a brow at him.

"I cannot promise that." He shook his head. "If you're going to date a human, they need to be worthy of you."

"Damn it, Metice." I slapped his shoulder, and he grabbed my wrist, then pulled me into him.

"Yes, Rayna?" He looked into my eyes, and when I didn't answer, he kissed me.

Those full lips pressed against mine and erased all sense left in my head. Any doubt I had about his existence melted, disappeared, and I felt myself falling into the abyss of poor decisions. I let the fall happen.

My lips moved against his as I accepted the taste of his lips. He pulled me into his lap and held me while we continued kissing.

"Does that mean you want me to come back?"

"You better." I nodded. "This is such a bad idea."

"Yeah, it is." Metice stood with me still in his arms and carried me to the bedroom.

II
Commitment?

When he left, my brain went into hyperdrive, worrying I wouldn't see him again. Would it be another four months before the demon made an appearance in my life? Of course, I busied myself with work and other hobbies and even made some progress on the painting I'd been slowly working on for months. It was a strange landscape I didn't recognize, but the image came to me clear as day.

Three days later, when the overthinking started, I felt it: that familiar tension in the air announcing his return. He popped in as I was searching for something to watch to distract myself from work. He'd clearly made a detour, because he stood in front of me, a frown on his face, holding bags full of groceries.

"What is this?" I placed the remote control on the couch beside me.

"This is me making sure you have proper food in your home," he fussed. "Do you know how difficult it was to make those tacos? You shop like a child."

"Well, damn. Welcome back." I stood. "You could appear with a friendly greeting, you know."

"I could, but then that wouldn't be me, now would it?" He winked. "You want to help me with these?"

I tossed his response back in his face. "I'm sure you remember where everything is."

And that's how it went. He stayed away for no longer than a week at a time. Then, Metice would show up fussing about something. We'd have our witty banter, and he would reward me by cooking enough food to last while he was away. It was nice, pretending like we were a normal couple. We talked about everything, learning more and more about each other.

We didn't have actual dates, but we had activities. I had him doing everything from painting to watching movies and playing card games.

"What are you painting?" He pointed to the painting sitting in the corner of my living room, still half-finished.

"I'm not really sure," I answered. "It's a landscape that's been in my head, and I'm just trying to get it out."

"You're really talented."

"Years of school and working helps." I grabbed a glass of wine from the table. "I've been creating since I was a child. Made my name doing independent works and showing in galleries before I started working with corporate clients. I don't take for granted the life I've been able to lead because of my art. Not many can do that."

"That's very impressive." He grabbed my hand and pulled it to his lips. "What wonders you do with these hands?"

"Tell me about your life." I sat next to him on the couch and sipped a glass of wine on his fifth visit. "You already know so much about me, Metice. I want to know more about you. I know it's limited, but tell me what you can."

"What would you like to know?" He glanced at the movie we'd been mostly ignoring.

"Where are you originally from?"

"I'm from the Bane." He used the true name of his world.

"I mean, I know you are now, but where did you originally come from before you became a demon?"

"I've always been a demon, Rayna." He looked me in the eye.

"Oh?" His answer shocked me. "I'd always assumed there were no demons born, only made, like a punishment."

"Human lore. Yes, it's true, some demons are made. They live a life somewhere else, and then by forces I cannot explain to you, they are recruited to our world," he spoke and pulled my feet into his hands. I realized it was a coping mechanism for him. Whenever the conversations got too deep, Metice would rub my feet. I had no complaints about it. "But that's not true of every demon. We are born, some living their entire lives in the Bane."

"How was it for you? Growing up there?" I leaned forward. "What was your family like?"

"If you want me to paint you a pretty picture of my upbringing, I can't." He focused on his task and kneaded the arch of my foot. The pressure felt so good, my eyes rolled back into my head. "I grew up alone mostly and had no family. But I was strong, one of the few to be born in the world for a millennium. They thought it was no longer possible for a while. Something happened, and suddenly, there were no more natural births. Demons found new ways to make life, like taking it from other worlds."

"Shouldn't they have treated you better than everyone else?" I asked. "Weren't you like the golden boy?"

"Why would you think that?"

"You were born there," I reasoned. "I'd think that would make you special when people were trying to do that. Is that why everyone is after you now?"

"That's not how it works. Born or not, I wasn't from a prominent family. I knew from a young age that if I wanted a good life, I would have to work my way up," he answered. "It strengthened me. Am I more resilient? Yes. But if anything, more people resent me for it than not. In my world, I'm a minority. Things have shifted. More are being born again. It takes the edge off."

"Did you work your way up, or find another way?" I took another sip of wine. "It didn't seem like you were living a life of poverty. Your home is carved into the side of a mountain. On Earth, that means you have money and power."

"Damn near to the top until I stopped." He nodded.

"Stopped?" I asked. "Why did you stop?"

"I realized I didn't want to be at the top. You get to a certain point, and you recognize how little it all matters. Success doesn't mean what you think it does." He sighed. "One day, I woke up and it hit me, I had spent centuries trying to prove myself to demons who didn't give a damn about me. They only cared about what I could do for them, and I realized I no longer wanted to do that job. Damn the status it gave me."

"And you still can't tell me what that job is?"

"No, I can't."

"One day, you will." I pulled my foot from his hand. "I'm your soulmate. You can't keep the secret forever."

"Sure," he hesitated. "About that."

"What?" I reached for the bottle of wine to refill my cup, but he grabbed my arm and pulled my attention back to him.

He cleared his throat before speaking. "I may be closer to finding a solution to dissolve the bond between us."

"Oh?" I tensed and tightened my grip on the glass so much, I feared it may break.

"Is something wrong?" He looked at my hand.

"I didn't think you were still looking." I turned from him and focused on the muted screen depicting a group of wolves in battle.

"I told you I would." He reached for his own glass. "I know it took a lot longer than I thought, but I keep my word. Problem is, I don't have as many allies as I once did."

"Right." I honestly hadn't thought of separating our bond in weeks. It didn't feel necessary. Despite his lack of humanity, Metice had become one of my favorite people, and I wasn't sure I wanted to end that. If our bond broke, what reason would he have for coming back? "How do we fix it?"

"I'm not sure yet. I have a lead on someone who might know, but-" He paused.

"But what?" That damn tinge of hope raised in my gut. Maybe he would say he didn't want to do it.

"It will be dangerous." Metice's words crushed that budding hope like an ant beneath a boot. "From my research, the process is difficult and painful."

"Painful? Is that for you or me?" I asked. Call me selfish, but I figured a centuries old demon had a higher pain tolerance than I ever would.

"Both of us." He sipped his drink. "If it were just me, I would have done it already, but I wanted to give you a heads up so you know what to expect."

"Do you still want to do it?" I asked. "Knowing that it will be painful and dangerous?"

"It's the safest thing for you," he answered.

"But the spell worked. They can't find me," I rebutted.

"They know about you. They know if they find you and hurt you, it will hurt me. That is motivation enough for them to keep trying." He rubbed his hand over his face. "The unknowing downfall of becoming top in the business. Once you reach it, no one will let you go."

"Hmm." There I was, sitting next to a being I'd just found out had never been anything but a demon. My head spun with thoughts and budding emotions. Was the idea of his humanity that important to me? Did I want to sever our bond? Was I willing to deal with any demonic downfall if we didn't? And what the hell had he been through to make the other demons want to hurt him so badly? Maybe he wasn't innocent just because I wanted him to be.

"Are you okay?" he asked. "You look like your mind is somewhere else."

"Yeah, sorry. You've given me a lot to think about," I admitted.

"I understand. I should go." He stood. "There are things I need to take care of. You take your time to think. I'll be back, okay?"

"Okay." I nodded, and he vanished.

He was gone for a week. Seven days of thinking about what he said. Seven days of worrying that the demons who hated him had finally gotten to him. Could I deal with that worry for the rest of my life? That's what it would be if I chose to remain bonded to him, constant concern that he'd been hurt or that they'd finally found a way to get to me.

When I hit day seven, I realized I'd need to get food or I'd starve. Metice had taken the role of grocery delivery man, and I stood in front of an empty refrigerator with my stomach growling. I'd just stepped inside my home after a quick trip to the grocery store when I felt the familiar tension of his return.

"Rayna." Metice appeared in the kitchen behind me.

The petty part of my brain wanted to ignore him, but then I smelled it: the sweet scent of apricots. I turned to find the demon standing in my home holding the little blue pet I'd convinced him to care for.

"Piko!" I screamed, holding my hands out. The damn thing went crazy.

He jumped from Metice's arms, shot across the kitchen, knocked over every chair, and darted down the hall towards the stairs. Metice ran after him, and I prayed he wouldn't completely destroy my home.

"Piko!" I ran after the two and flinched every time I heard something smash to the floor. "Please stop! It's okay, boy."

When I caught up to them, Metice had Piko blocked into the corner of my bedroom. The ugly little table that I hated so much was smashed on the floor. The shattered pieces looked far more beautiful than when they were whole.

"Is he okay?" I asked, standing behind Metice.

"He's fine. Just shocked by the transition." He lowered his voice. "Come on, buddy, calm down."

Piko whimpered, and then his enormous eyes locked onto me. That silly little face grinned, and he bolted across the room, through Metice's legs, and jumped into my arms. The impact knocked me backward and into the armchair next to my desk as he licked my face and chirped.

"I think he recognizes me." I laughed, then pushed Piko back. "Okay, I like you and all, but no licking my face. I don't get down like that."

Piko nuzzled his face into my neck.

"He's missed you. I didn't think he would after all this time." Metice sat on the edge of the bed and watched me reconnect with my pet.

"Why did you bring him here?"

"Since I started coming to spend time with you, I think he can smell you on me. He started acting depressed, pooping everywhere. I figured I'd give this a shot."

"I'm glad you brought him." I paused. "Wait, will this get you in trouble? Are there rules against this sort of thing?"

"There are, but I'm not new to bending rules."

"That is a line said often before shit hits the fan." I shook my head. "You've just jinxed us."

It took an hour to get Piko to calm down, but it wasn't until after he was fed that he fell asleep. His little snoring called out from the hallway floor where he passed out.

"Do you want more?" Metice asked as I finished my last bite of pasta. "There is still some in the pot."

"No, thank you." I leaned back and rubbed my belly with a large smile spread across my face. "That was more than enough."

"Good." He nodded. "Glad to see you put some real food in your home."

"I had to." I pointed to the fridge. "My meal services stopped unexpectantly, and I had nothing else to eat. Did you expect me to starve until you came back?"

"Meal services?" He stood from the kitchen table and removed my plate from in front of me. "Is that what I am to you?"

"Maybe," I winked. "Maybe a little more than that."

After watching his ass in the tight black pants he wore, I cleared the thoughts from my mind. I was supposed to be upset with him for being missing in action for so long. A pair of firm cheeks couldn't be enough to distract me from my disappointment. Instead of watching him, I grabbed my open soda and headed for the couch. Shortly after, he joined me.

"Did you think about things?" Metice asked as he sat next to me. We'd avoided the talk since he got there, but time was up.

"How could I not?" I put the remote down, having found nothing even remotely interesting to watch. Because what the hell could compete with what we needed to discuss? "I had a week to do nothing but think about things."

"And what did you decide?"

I took a sip from my drink and wished I'd chosen something stronger.

"Metice..." I turned to him, prepared to tell him how it would be a terrible idea to be together. Despite the way I felt when I was around him, I knew a long-distance relationship with a demon from another world was a bad idea. And the way I'd worried about him the last week wasn't healthy. It consumed every moment of my life, and I couldn't put myself through that.

Before I could get any of that out, he interrupted me with three words that made all that seem so unimportant.

"I want you." Those dark eyes locked onto mine, and his words erased everything else in the world.

"Metice, this is a bad idea." I clung to reason.

"Is it?" He pulled me into his lap and pressed his lips to my neck.

"That's not fair." I feigned resistance, putting my hand against his chest. "We need to talk about this."

"What is there to talk about?" His fingers made quick work of the little gold buttons on my top before he peeled the shirt away.

"You said there might be a way to break the bond between us." How the hell was I supposed to hold this conversation with him when he was so determined to distract me?

"Yes, I did say that." His lips made a trail past my collarbone and to my breast.

"I-" If I had thoughts in my head, they disappeared when his tongue flicked against my nipple, shortly followed by his teeth teasing the sensitive flesh. "Metice, please."

"Okay." He pulled back, lifted me from his lap, and sat me on the couch next to him. "Let's talk."

"I still don't think it's smart for us to pursue this. I mean, this is nice. Your visits, the food, the talking. It's all nice, but how long can we realistically keep this up? How far can a relationship go when you're not from my world and I'm not from yours?"

"A lot of heavy questions." He nodded. "Is this how you do your dates? All the questions of the future laid out in one swift blow?"

"Come on, that's not fair." I pulled my shirt back on. "You left me for a week. Of course, I came up with a laundry list of things to discuss."

"True." He leaned forward, putting his elbows on his knees and sighed. "I've had the same questions while away from you. In that time, I came up with very few viable answers as to how we make this work. All I know is that I want to try. Don't you?"

"Yes, but..."

"But what?"

"They already have me on the psych watch list as it is." I chuckled, but there was nothing funny about it. "I don't know if I want to put myself through this."

"If this is too much for you, I will leave, Rayna." Metice turned to me, the soft light from the television illuminating half his face. "I'm not that selfish, at least not with you. I won't hurt you like that."

"The smart thing for me to do right now would be to tell you to go, sever the bond and go our separate ways." I chewed on my lip.

"But..." He waited for me to finish the thought.

"There's this thing about knowing the smart thing to do and then actually doing it." I sighed. "The smart thing doesn't always feel like the right thing."

"Isn't it funny how that works?" The grin spread across his face before he shifted his weight and pulled me back into his arms. "Let's be foolish together, Rayna."

My name on his lips was all I needed to convince myself. Call me dumb, but that was enough. His deep voice wrapped around the letters of my name and pulled me into submission. And just like that, his hands returned to my body, slipping beneath my bra to tease my nipple.

He grabbed my arm and guided me to stand in front of him before he leaned back on the couch to look at me.

"Strip for me, Rayna," he directed me.

A soft shiver ran across my flesh. There weren't many men who could direct me sexually, but something about Metice made me want to give in. With his eyes watching me intensely, I slowly removed the layers of fabric that hid my flesh. My top, my bra, and the leggings all hit the floor, leaving me standing in front of him in just my panties.

"Let me see that pretty pussy." He turned me around and smacked my ass. "Bend over and grab your ankles."

I bent over and wrapped my hands around my ankles, looking through my spread legs. I could see the hungry grin on his face.

He slid my panties to the side and slowly slipped two fingers into me before his tongue found my clit.

"Hold that ass open." He pulled my hands back to grip my ass, and his tongue moved from my pussy to my asshole.

"Oh God!" I cried out, and that got me a slap on the ass. "Fuck, sorry," I laughed.

"You'll learn," he growled before he bit my cheek.

Bent over, I could see his dick growing, strangled by the fabric of his pants.

"I want to see you," I moaned. "Take your dick out."

He slipped his hand into his pants and slowly revealed his full length, then I watched as he stroked himself with long, deliberate passes up and down his shaft. I reached back and tried to help, but he slapped my hand away.

"Don't touch. Just watch," he said as he continued stroking himself and devouring me, drinking my juices as I came.

Before the orgasm ended, he stood and slipped his dick inside me, holding me in place as he expanded against my tightness. I pushed back on him, urging him to fuck me. He complied, grabbing my forearms and controlling my motions. He had me on my toes as he pounded into me, one hand gripping both arms behind my back, the other smacking either side of my ass.

"Oh, she's ready for me," he growled and flipped me around until I was on the couch, bent over, where he continued to fuck me from behind until I came and collapsed on my stomach.

I could hear his admiration, soft moans as he rubbed my ass while I rested. I wanted him. All I could think about was tasting his dick. I turned on him and pushed him back on the couch, dropping my eyes to his dick dripping with my orgasm.

"You want to taste me, don't you?" He grabbed my face and rubbed his thumb across my lips. "Tell me you want my dick in your mouth, Rayna."

"Yes." I licked my lips and lowered myself until I was eye to eye with the tip. "I want to suck that beautiful dick."

"Open that pretty mouth," he said, and I did.

He rubbed the tip of his dick against my lips, and my mouth watered.

"Stick your tongue out," he said, and again, I did as he wanted.

Metice rubbed the thick head across my tongue, and it vibrated against my lips. That was it. I couldn't hold back. I pulled him into my mouth, sucking and running my tongue in spirals as I did.

"Fuck!" he called out and wrapped his hands in my hair, softly tugging the two-day old braid out. "Mmm, suck it!"

I continued until I felt him tense. "I'm about to come," he announced, and I slowed.

This wasn't over. I needed him to last longer. Slowly, I pulled him from my mouth and climbed onto his lap. I rocked my hips, rubbing my pussy lips up and down his shaft until the tension left his body. Then, I lifted my hips and slid him inside of me, pausing just as he was buried to the hilt.

We kissed, and he massaged my back as my hands ran the length of his horns. Though I couldn't explain why, his horns turned me on. The more I stroked them, the wetter I became. Though I didn't move, my walls pulsated around him, and he revved in response.

He pulled me back just enough to put my titty in his mouth.

"You like that, huh?" I asked as he teased my nipple with his teeth.

"What can I say?" He smiled around my nipple. "I'm a breast man, and your tits are so beautiful."

When he switched to the other side, I started bouncing my ass on his dick. His hands gripped my hips and aided my efforts as his hips lifted beneath me. We stayed like that, tit in mouth, dick riding, until we both came.

Metice then carried me upstairs while still inside me, and I won't lie, I was afraid he would drop my big ass, but he didn't. He easily took the stairs, opened my bedroom, and laid me on the bed. By the time my back hit the mattress, he was ready to go again.

This time was different, sweeter. Metice nuzzled his face into my hair and neck as his weight pressed down on me. He slowly slipped in and out of me, letting me savor every inch of him. The kisses were deeper, the touches more intentional.

"You're so damn beautiful," he whispered in my ear as he continued. "I can't believe you're mine."

And I came, over and over again.

When he finished, I lay there exhausted, catching my breath. Buck naked, he stood, covered me with the sheet, and headed for the bathroom. I lay there in disconnected bliss as he drew me a bath, popping his head out only once for instructions on how to put the back pillow in the tub. I heard him curse at least four times while trying to get the suction cups to take.

When the bath was full. He returned to me, picked me up from the bed, and took me to the tub. He didn't join me. He let me soak and sat next to me, quietly washing my body. Then—I almost lost it when he did this—he detangled and twisted my hair! I couldn't believe it. This man, no, this *demon*, was gently combing my hair and putting in near-perfect two-strand twists while I soaked in a lavender-scented tub. It was too good to be true, but I didn't fight it.

Just as the water chilled, he helped me from the tub, dried my body off, and wrapped me in a towel to carry me back to the bed. I'd never had such care, and after the sex we had, the aggression, it felt nice to know he was capable of being so gentle with me.

He turned me into my bed and, when he was sure I was comfortable, headed to take a shower. By the time he returned, I was already drifting off to sleep. The heat of his body, the soft purr of his breath, was all I needed. A moment later, head on his chest and his hand on my ass, I passed out.

When I woke, he was gone, but breakfast was on the table: a bowl of fruit, scrambled eggs, and toast. I made myself a cup of coffee and checked my phone.

I had one missed call from my mother and a message in the group chat talking about getting together.

"Yeah, I'll fall for that again," I muttered and put the phone down.

I felt the surge, that feeling of tension that announced a visitor from another world.

"Couldn't stay away, huh?" I turned around, and the cup crashed against the floor, sending hot coffee everywhere.

It wasn't Metice.

12

Crazy Ex-Girlfriends

"Son of a bitch!" I hopped back from the splash and rubbed my leg where the hot liquid touched me. I was definitely going to have a blister after that.

"Guess I'm not who you were expecting?" The green giant stood in my kitchen wearing brown leather head to toe and watching me with a smirk on her face. "I should have expected as much. It's not as if I come here as much as some other demons."

"What are you doing here?" I backed away from her. "How did you find me?"

Metice said the spell worked, and as far as I knew, it had. There had been no demons knocking on my door and no threats to my life. At least, none he had told me about.

"Funny thing about that." She walked over to the table where my prepared breakfast waited. She pulled the chair out, sat down, and the bitch actually started eating my food! "I couldn't find you. I tried, but whatever Metice did, it worked. I wasn't the only one looking for you. One minute, we could track you, and the next... nothing. We knew it was magic, because for the love of all that is hellish, we couldn't remember where we'd come before. So, I had to switch gears, and instead of looking for you, I watched him. It didn't take too long before a little demon told me my dear friend was slipping away quite often. Now, I wondered where he could be going. Why was he slipping into other worlds when he wasn't working anymore?"

"Working?" This was the second time she dropped a hint about Metice's past. *This bitch is doing this to get under my skin.*

"Oh, I guess he hasn't told you about all that. His job." She dangled that information out there and took pleasure in knowing she knew more about him than I did. "It's not like he would want you to know about how he was responsible for going to new worlds and bringing souls back to ours. No? Probably not."

"What are you talking about?" I frowned. She had to be messing with me, but it wasn't like I knew all that much about Metice. What he'd told me had barely scratched the surface.

"I really shouldn't say more." She shrugged. "Not my secrets to reveal. I should let him tell you all that."

"What do you want?" I wasn't about to let her ass mess with my mind. That's exactly what she wanted. I'd seen mean girls operate. Tactic one: install doubt and fuck up the target's confidence.

"I want you to leave him alone," she said flat out, eyes narrowing at me. "It's simple, really. You stay away, and you never have to see me again."

"Let me guess: Metice was more than just a friend?" I scoffed and felt a small part of myself die as the fresh scent of coffee filled my nose. Dammit, and I was out of that dark roast too.

"Oh, we have a smart one!" She sarcastically clapped her hands. "Makes my job so much easier. I really hate having to over explain things. But you know, some people just don't seem to get it the first time."

"I never thought I'd have to deal with a crazy ex-girlfriend from hell." I shook my head and reached for the paper towel. "You must really be insecure to come all the way to another world to try to intimidate me."

"Ex-fiancée, to put it in human terms," she corrected me. "But I'm sure he didn't tell you that part, either."

"Excuse me?" The towels I'd ripped from the roll fell to the floor, soaking up the coffee, and my heart broke. What the hell did she mean she was his ex-fiancée?

"Metice was to be bonded to me. Or, in your human terms, we were supposed to get married." She popped another piece of my food into her mouth and frowned as if it wasn't appetizing. "That was until he turned soft. I wish I knew what happened to him, but he woke up one day, and he just wasn't the same Meti anymore."

"I have no idea what you're talking about, but it's time for you to go." I pointed to the door she hadn't used to enter my home.

"I can't do that." She shook her head 'no' and wagged her finger at me. "Not until you give me your word that you will leave him alone. That is, after all, my reason for coming here, and I would hate to waste the trip, you know?"

"I can't do that." I shook my head. Even if I wanted to, it wasn't that simple. Metice and I had a bond between us stronger than any verbal commitment we could make to each other.

"Don't you value your pathetic human life at all?" She leaned back in the chair and crossed her arms over her chest. "You know I could crush you, right? What about that little blue nuisance? Your pet you left behind in hell. It would be a shame if something happened to him."

"Are you seriously threatening my dog?" I laughed and straightened the robe I'd wrapped around myself. "What is it with villains and going after dogs? Did your mother not hug you enough as a child?"

"Pets are easy targets, and you humans are all so emotionally driven." She chuckled and straightened her collar. "I will never understand why you get so emotionally attached to things you really should be eating. Imagine how great a poodle tastes roasted with a good chili sauce."

"You're disgusting."

"And you're going to lose your life if you don't leave Metice alone, as I asked. I won't ask again."

"Get out of my home," I demanded again.

"No." She looked around. "Maybe I'll hang out until he gets back."

"This is absolutely insane."

"Is it?" She pointed to the floor. "You might want to clean up that mess before it stains your pretty floors."

"You know what? You're right." I nodded. "But I don't think this paper towel is going to work."

Carefully, I moved around the counter to the drawer where the kitchen towel hung, but instead of grabbing it, I pulled the butcher's knife from the drawer and held it out towards the intruder.

"Oh girl, no." She bared her teeth and growled as two tentacles sprouted from her back like whips. "That was the wrong move, and here I thought you were smarter than that."

The demoness, whose name was still unknown to me, stalked towards me. Her tentacles whipped out in every direction and destroyed my kitchen. The bar stool went flying toward my head, and I ducked just in time to miss it. I hopped up, hoping to run away, but the other extension slammed into my chest, knocking me against the refrigerator.

The custom magnet with the picture of me and my best friend fell and shattered on the floor. I didn't have time to worry about it, because I looked up to see her booted foot coming for my chest. I rolled out of the way, but she caught my robe with her hand and pulled me backward, slamming me to the floor instead.

The shards of the magnet dug into the back of my arm.

The knife was still in my hand, and I took the one opportunity to use it. I pushed it upward into her stomach as she kneeled over me, but it did nothing. The blade bent against her tough body, doing no damage at all. Great.

"You really are a dumb bitch." Her maniacal laughter rang out like a sick anime character.

She started punching me in the face, her fist crashing into my cheek, eye, and chin. After the fourth punch and my pointless struggles, I tasted my own blood. My heart raced with a mixture of anger and fear.

"No," I cried after the fifth punch made crushing contact with my jawline. Before the sixth could land, I lifted my hand to her chest, hoping to just push her off.

I did a lot more than that.

My insides heated quickly, like an electric kettle with two drops of water in it. In a flash, it felt like I had the worst fever of my life. Sweat formed on my brow as my mouth dried out. Then came the rush of adrenaline accompanied by a foreign sensation. A surge or power gushed through me—from where, I had no idea—but I was grateful for it, because it shot the bitch off me. She didn't go far, but she stumbled back until she fell onto her ass and her tentacles retracted from the shock.

"What the hell was that?" I looked at my own hands, then common sense kicked in, and I decided to save the questions for later. I quickly got to my feet and backed away from her.

"Oh, you're not just a normal human, are you?" she grinned. "It looks like Metice has more secrets than I thought. I think I need to take you back to my world."

"Excuse me?" I wiped the blood from my lip. "I'm not going anywhere with you."

"I wasn't giving you the choice." She jumped to her feet and charged at me.

Her arms reached out to grab me, but instead, I grabbed her wrist. The plan was to give her another shock like the one before, and once again, my plan didn't mean shit, because instead of blasting her away from me, I felt that same tension, the one that usually announced the arrival of my demon companion.

The world turned fuzzy, and my vision blurred. When I blinked, the look on her face matched the fear I felt. Because we were no longer in my kitchen. We were hanging in the air, and when I looked down, I saw the depths of a massive canyon. The cool breeze felt great until the slap of reality hit, and I realized just how terrible our position was.

"Oh shit!" I screamed and let her go.

"You stupid-" She clawed at me, but I slapped her hands away.

And then, the bitch fell.

I hung in the air, watching her for a second. Maybe I had the power to fly. That was my last thought before gravity grabbed hold of my dumb ass too.

13

BDSM? Really?

The strong rush of air passing across my ears ended with a loud and painful slam to the ground. I expected to have a quick moment of consciousness at the bottom of the canyon before I passed out, but when I opened my eyes, I was looking at the arched entrance to my home. As if the shards of magnets in my arms and the blows to my face weren't enough to ruin my damn day, landing in my front yard, bloodied and dressed in a bathrobe, sure was.

Don't get me wrong. I was happy to be alive, but when the pain shot up from my ass through my spine and into my shoulders, I questioned if death wouldn't have been a better option. I laid there, splayed out, eyes drifting to the sky. The cool breeze brushed across my body and gave a weird sense of relief to the pain.

"Are you okay?" the shaky voice of an elderly woman called out. "Do you need help?"

I looked up to see my nosy neighbor, Mrs. Green, staring at me from her front porch. Great, the entire neighborhood would hear about this shit now.

"I'm fine!" I called out and scrambled to get up from the ground, pulling the robe tighter around me as I rushed for the door. Thank God for keyless entry. If she got any closer, those prescription goggles she wore would kick in, and she'd see just how not okay I was. I mean, how the hell was I supposed to explain being outside in the middle of winter in my damn underwear?

The door slammed shut behind me just as Mrs. Green stepped off her porch. I looked through the peephole and watched her throw her hands up in the air and return to her chair. No juicy gossip for her to spread today.

"I can't believe this shit." I looked at my dirty hands and thought about the power that surged through them earlier. "So, that just happened. That was real."

And suddenly, I couldn't breathe. My house felt too small, like the walls would fold in and crush me. I opened the robe and grabbed the magazine off the entry table to fan myself.

"How is any of this possible? And what the hell did she mean about Metice?" My mind ran as I spoke the questions aloud to no one.

I stumbled into the house, ass hurting more with each step, and looked at the disaster that was my kitchen. The bitch had made more of a mess than I thought. The table sat top down, legs up, food splattered all over the ceiling and wall. All those pretty counter trinkets I'd bought for the aesthetic more than their function were smashed across the floor.

"Not my coffee maker!" I cried out when I found my top-of-the-line machine broken in half. "Evil ass bitch!"

As I carefully picked up the pieces of the two-hundred-dollar machine, I felt it. The tension. That feeling that once excited me but no longer had the same effect.

"Not this bitch again." I turned around, holding the broken appliance in my hand. If I needed to use it as a weapon, I would.

"What happened here?" Metice appeared.

"*Now* you arrive!" I dropped the pieces and laughed. "That crazy bitch was in here kicking my ass all up and down my kitchen, and you were nowhere to be found."

"Rayna, what happened?" Metice waved his hand in front of my face to get me to focus. "Who was here?"

"What happened?" I turned over a chair and sat down, grimacing at the pain that shot up my spine. "I think I broke my ass."

"What?" He moved toward me but stopped when I held my hand out to him.

"Your crazy ex-girlfriend showed up here." I pointed at him. "Just a friend, my ass! What's her name?"

"Who?" He clearly wasn't listening to me. He kept looking at my dirty robe and scarred knees.

"The big green bitch. You know who, Metice. Don't play with me." My frustration grew, and for a moment, I felt that heat in my gut again, but it quickly dissipated.

"Olian was here?"

"Olian?" I sucked my teeth. "That's her name? Well, yeah. Olian was here, and she came to tell me to stay the hell away from you, the man she was supposed to be marrying until I came along. I mean, damn, I know you wanted to keep your secrets, but this is something you definitely should have told me! *Oh, by the way, I have a psycho ex that might try to take your head off with her fucking tentacles!*"

"Calm down please." He took another step toward me, but I held my hand up again to stop him.

"Don't tell me to calm down after I was just attacked in my own damn home and found out that I apparently have some freaky ass powers I haven't even had three seconds to stop and process."

"Rayna, I'm trying my best to follow you, but you're losing me."

"How difficult is it to follow?" I cocked my head to the side. "You left. She came. She told me to stay away from you or she would kill me. Then, she attacked me. We fought. Well, more like she demon kicked my ass, and then somehow, I blasted her big ass up off me." I pointed to the floor, where it all happened. "Then she came for me again, talking about how she was going to drag me back to hell. But when I tried to blast her again, something else happened."

"What happened?" he asked, but there was something strange to his voice, that slight rise in expectation. It was as if he already knew what I would say but wanted me to be the one to say it first.

"I'm still trying to wrap my mind around that." I stood carefully, using the edge of the knocked-over table as support. "We were here, and then we weren't. Then I dropped her, and I fell too, but I landed in my yard. We weren't over my yard, though. We were over a canyon somewhere. It was enormous, so deep that I couldn't even see the bottom."

"Oh shit." He took a step back this time, and his expression said everything. Metice had just received confirmation of what I assumed was another secret he'd held from me.

"Oh shit is right." I paused, then turned my finger back on him. "You knew, didn't you? She said you were keeping a secret. Am I the secret? Are my powers the secret? What else have you hidden from me? What else do you know that I don't?"

"Can we pause? Let's clean up this mess and get you dressed. Then, we can talk." Metice tried to deflect, but it only told me my assumptions were right.

"And that means everything she said is true, and you definitely know a lot more about me and all this shit than you told me before." I turned and headed for the stairs. "Fine. You clean this up. I'm going to go process everything that happened and hope when I see you again, I don't want to kill you—not that it seems possible. I mean, I tried to stab that green ho, and nothing happened. Are all demons knife-proof?"

Metice said nothing else as I continued talking and headed up the stairs. With the pain I was in, all I could manage was a quick shower. I chose a summer dress instead of weather appropriate wear, as it was the easiest thing to put on. I contemplated going back downstairs, but that felt like too much work. The pain was setting in, and all I wanted was my bed—the same bed where I slept next to that lying ass demon the night before. I propped my pillows under my stomach and laid ass up across the center of the bed.

"Rayna?" Metice's deep voice pulled me from the nap I'd slipped into.

"Yes?" I groaned as the pain returned with my consciousness. "What do you want?"

"Are you okay?" he spoke from behind, but his shadow stretched across the wall in front of me.

"Do I look okay to you?" I groaned and shifted my weight to adjust the pillow beneath my belly. "My back hurts, my arm is cut up, and I'm pretty sure I broke my damn ass when I fell from the sky!"

"Let me help you." He tried to help me maneuver, but I smacked his hand away.

"Don't touch me." I scooted across the bed away from him.

"Why are you being so difficult?" He reached for me again but stopped when I pulled away from him.

"I'm not being difficult just because I don't want your hands on me. Why have you kept so many secrets from me?"

"I told you there were things you shouldn't know." He straightened and watched as I continued to adjust myself without his help.

"And that's fine when it's all your shit, but it wasn't, was it? You knew things about me, things that could put my life at risk, and you kept me in the dark. Tell me how the hell you think that's fair?" I finally found a comfortable position with my back against the headboard. "And what the hell did your ex mean about the job you walked away from? You went to other worlds to take people to hell? You said you studied those worlds, not that you were kidnapping innocent beings."

"It's not that simple." He sat in the chair across from the foot of the bed, giving me the space I clearly wanted. "And I did study the worlds when I went."

"Give me a break!" I shook my head. "If it's not that simple, explain it to me so I understand. No more secrets. No more pretending to protect me from the truth."

"Where should I start?" he asked.

"The most important part." My heart raced in my chest. I wanted to know the answers, but then again, I didn't. I knew his answers could change the way I looked at him. "Why were you taking people from their homes?"

"Well, first, let's get something straight. None of the people I took were innocent. They knew what would happen to them," he explained. "They were magical beings, and by your standards, they were all evil. Each one of them made deals with who they thought was the devil. They made bargains, promising their souls to someone they didn't know for temporary power, and they got that power. And when it was time for them to pay up, it was my job to go and retrieve them. When I took them to my home, it wasn't an arbitrary kidnapping. It was picking up people who had a debt to pay and making sure they paid it."

"So you're like the errand boy for the devil?" My stomach twisted with a mixture of disgust and pity.

"I was, yes. That was my job. I got an assignment, was told my target, and I went and retrieved them." He said the tasks as if they meant nothing to him.

"And one day, you decided you no longer wanted to do it anymore?" I watched him closely for any semblance of regret for what he'd done.

"Exactly. I had a change of heart," he explained. "I didn't want to do the job anymore because it didn't feel the same. It was no longer just a job, so I had to walk away."

"Why?" I leaned forward. "What changed? Why did you walk away?"

Metice took a deep breath and looked at me. I could see the internal conflict playing out in his eyes. He didn't want to tell me, but he had to. How else could we move on from this? How else could I ever trust him again?

"I landed on a world devoid of water. I'm still not sure how the natives survive, but they do. My landing was rough, and I'm still not sure what happened. I blacked out, and when I woke, there was this old hag, my target, dragging me back to her home." He sighed. "She knew why I was there, and yet, still she helped me. If it wasn't for her help, I wouldn't have survived. She waited for me to be better; she didn't run like most do."

"She wasn't afraid of you?"

"No, she said she saw me coming years before I ever arrived." He paused, choosing his words. "And then she told me something about myself, something about my future that I wouldn't be able to run from. Those words changed everything. There was no way I could move forward the way I had been, not knowing the truth."

"What did she tell you?" I wanted to know. What could have been so significant that it would change his very pursuit in life?

"I don't know that I want to tell you that part." He rubbed the back of his neck like he was burning from his own embarrassment.

"More secrets, Metice? Tell me what she told you. What could it have been to make you turn your back on everything you worked so hard for? What happened to your fiancée, and the life you wanted so much before you met her?"

"She told me who my soulmate would be and made it so I would feel them when they were ready for me. At first, it felt like she put a curse on me. When she told me more about the person, about who they would be and what they would be capable of, I realized this person was a lot like the ones I was tasked with bringing back to my world, and it felt like a punishment for what I'd done." He rubbed his face, taking a deep breath before continuing. "For years, I carried that thought and felt this ridiculous guilt because how could my soul mate be the type of person who would make a deal with evil? Despite how much I wanted it to be a lie, it wasn't. I knew that because I felt you, and it happened long before you did that spell."

"What do you mean, you felt me?" I'm not gonna lie, that made me uncomfortable. Had he known about me since I was a child? Had he been waiting in the shadows for me?

"It was a few years ago. I have no idea what caused it, but I woke up one day, and I could feel you. Didn't do anything about it, though. I could have sought you out, tried to learn more about you, but that just felt wrong. Instead, I ignored the feeling and found any and everything to take my mind off you. What I could tell was that you were here on Earth, which meant you were human. And I thought, hey, she's human. She won't live that long. I can bear this. It'll go away. But then you did that spell, and I literally couldn't stay away any longer."

"So, you were sitting in hell knowing that I'm your soulmate and waiting for me to die?" I went from creeped out to irritated. Here I was, trying to find my love on Earth, and the man who was meant for me was ignoring my existence.

"When you say it like that, it sounds really bad." He chuckled.

"Because it is really fucking bad." I threw a pillow at him. "There's nothing funny about it."

"Okay. Yeah, maybe it is." He caught the pillow and placed it at the foot of the bed. "But I'm a demon, and you're a human. A magical one. I couldn't risk it."

"And what about your fiancée?" I moved the focus to the other question I had. "When did you end things with her, because she's acting like it just happened?"

"Shortly after I first felt your presence," he answered. "I knew you were human and there was no path of us being together, not that I was hoping for one. Maybe I could have gone on with my life as usual and tried to commit myself to her, but it wouldn't have worked. There's this thing about demons and becoming one with each other. It's not just signing some forms and having a ceremony. When we become one, it is a literal action. Our souls intertwine on a level that I don't believe humans are capable of understanding."

"And you walked away from her?" Suddenly, I felt cold, like the window had opened and allowed the winter breeze inside. Olian had a broken heart. That's why she wanted to kill me. What was that saying about a woman scorned? She wouldn't give up.

"Two days before our ceremony was supposed to happen." He sighed. "She would have known everything as soon as the process was over. She would have known that my soul belonged to someone else, not her. No matter the process, she would have always felt that void. Knowing her, she would have gone after you. I thought I was protecting you by ending it.

"And here I am anyway." I leaned my head back on the headboard. "Well, no wonder the bitch is trying to kill me."

"Yeah, I know. I should have cut it off as soon as the witch told me what she saw in my future, but I couldn't. Like I said, I didn't want to believe it was true," he admitted. "Besides, I'd worked hard to get where I was, and I still had a long way to go. I didn't want to give that up over some supposed vision of a soulmate I didn't know."

"Wait." The chill I felt before stopped as my sluggish brain caught up with Metice's story. There was something far more important there that I'd overlooked. "You said the witch told you I was like the people you were taking to hell. What does that mean?"

"I wasn't sure what it meant until I felt you. I did some digging on the energy signature. Every magical bloodline has a unique one. I'd never encountered yours before, and I couldn't find out much without seeking you out. All I knew was somewhere in your bloodline, there were powerful beings who had magical abilities, people who could do things that defied the logic of your world. I'm not even sure they were originally from Earth, but again, I don't know exactly who or what they were. I tried researching, but I came up with nothing." He paused, scrutinizing me with a furrowed brow. "But with your skills teleporting across worlds and apparently concentrating energy through your hands strong enough to knock over Olian, I'm thinking at the very least that you have some form of psychic powers."

"Okay, let's just gloss over the fact that you alluded that I may be a descendent of aliens." I waved my hands in front of my face, as if clearing a whiteboard with too much scribbled data. There was no way I was about to unpack all that. "Is there a way to figure this out now? I mean, is there a blood test, something you can do to tell me what I am?"

"Yes, there are ways." He nodded. "There are always ways to finding the truth, but maybe not ways you'd like."

"Right. Okay." I held my hand up while I gathered myself. I wanted to curse, scream, and fight him, but my ass was already sore, so I used my words instead. "Metice, I'm still trying to understand why you wouldn't have told me all of this before now. Okay, maybe leave out the crazy ex-girlfriend, because that's really your personal shit, but all these details about me? My bloodline, my potentially alien lineage, my apparent power? How could you know something like that and not tell me? I know you said you didn't want it to be true, but come on. That's a lame excuse and a copout."

"I wish I could say that I had a better reason, but I didn't. I wanted you to be able to go back to your regular life, without all this." He looked me in the eyes and held my attention. "You have to believe me."

"Why?" I didn't believe him. He didn't want to leave me alone or send me back to an uninterrupted human life. My ass would still be perfectly intact if that were true.

"What do you mean, why?"

"Why did you want me to go back to my regular life?" I clarified. "Which, by the way, I don't believe, since you came here to interfere with my regular life, reintroducing all the shit you claim you wanted to keep me away from. The only reason Olian found me is because she had her minions track you. She told me that while she was here."

"Because I know what my world does to humans. I've seen it time and time again. Being connected to the dark energy of the Bane destroys the human soul. I was born there, Rayna. I am the energy of my world, just like you're the energy of yours. With you being tied to me, a demon, a being of the dark, it could really be bad for you, Rayna."

"Well, doesn't that just hit the 'man making decisions for a woman without taking her opinion into account at all' nail on the head?" I threw another pillow at him, which he caught and held. "Did you think saying that would make me feel better about all this?"

"It wasn't my intention to discount your opinion." His jaw tightened.

"But that's what you did." I pointed at him. "And don't look at me like you're frustrated. You're not the one who's been lied to. I'm the one whose life is constantly being turned upside down by this. I should know what I'm up against."

"You're right." He stood. "I'm sorry, Rayna."

"And I guess I should take your apology and forgive you?"

"No, make me work for your forgiveness. I've broken your trust. That's a big deal," he said with a straight face, and I had to keep my jaw from dropping. That wasn't what I expected him to say. "Let me earn your trust back, please. Let me help you."

"Help me?" I kept my tight-lipped expression. "How exactly do you think you can help me now? Can you reverse time? Can you change the mind of the demoness who wants my head?"

"I cannot do either of those things, but I can help your body." He pointed to my butt, pressed against the pillow behind me. "That will take a long time for your human body to heal. Something tells me we're going to need you in better condition, and soon. Stay here. I'll return soon with something to heal your wounds."

"Yeah, right okay." I waved him off. "Do what you gotta do."

The tension set in, and a moment later, he was gone, and I was hobbling my ass from my bed to my car. Yes, I should have stayed put. Yes, this was a cliché move for me to do, but everything about our meeting had been like a playbook drafted from one of the many fantasy novels that lined my pewter painted shelves. So, if I wanted the shit to play out the right way, I had to play my role, right? Well, that's what I told myself anyway, and that's what I did. I took my thirty-almost-seven-year-old brain and overrode it with the mindset of a seventeen-year-old with no bills or business credit hanging over her head. We do what we must for the plot!

It took me ten minutes to get my pants on, and another thirty to get my hair in a bun and my hoodie over my head, and that was all I could manage. It didn't matter; I wasn't going anywhere where my looks would matter.

Much later than it should have been, I stood leaning against the doorframe, waving at the camera above Keri's door.

"Rayna?" The door swung open, and the scent of warm cinnamon flooded my senses. "What are you doing here?"

"Can't a girl just drop by her bestie's house to see what's up?" I tried to keep the sound of pain from my voice, but even standing there had every fiber of my body screaming out.

"Maybe, but since I haven't heard from you in weeks, the last thing I would expect is an in-person visit." Keri, however, did not keep the hurt from her voice. After my return and her overbearing visits for the first month, things went back to normal. She went back to work and her boyfriend bubble, and I turned my focus to trying to save my career and finding a viable man to date to distract myself from the demon I really wanted.

"Yeah, well, here I am." I threw my hand up. "Are you going to let me in or leave me standing out here in the cold?"

"I guess I don't want you to freeze to death. If you do that, then I can't shit talk you for disappearing again." She stuck her tongue out at me and then stepped aside, waving me forward. "Come in."

"Thank you." I straightened, took a step forward, and the expressions of pain I held back had to have colored every inch of my face, because Keri freaked out.

"What happened to you? Are you hurt? Why are you moving like that?" She closed the door behind me and then fluttered her hands around my body, as if she could energetically heal my wounds. "Is your face busted up? Did you get into a fight?"

Her questions came with each step I took into her home and down the short hall to her couch, where I finally sat before answering. I figured once I sat down, she couldn't cart my ass out of her house to the emergency room.

"I'm fine, Keri." I winced as I adjusted the pillow behind my back. "Just had a little fall. You know how it is when it's winter here. People fall left and right."

"Yeah, when it's icy outside. We haven't even had our first real snow yet." Keri crossed her arms. "You need to go to the hospital and let a doctor look at you. You may have broken something."

"I'm fine." I waved off her concerns and shifted my ass until I found a position that was least painful.

"Where did it happen?" There was the lawyer side of her brain kicking in. I always knew when Keri started searching for a case by her narrowed eyes and the way her left hand twitched, ready to take notes. "Tell me. Was it at home, at an establishment? Have you been out on any new dates? Don't tell me one of those weird ass men had something to do with this. I will call the girls, and we'll find his ass."

"Look, I'm fine. It was just a minor fall." I wasn't technically lying. "I'll go and see a doctor, but can we just chill for a bit?"

"Rayna." She sat across from me in the armchair. "I don't know. If your mama knew about this, she'd be cursing my ass out for not forcing you to go right now."

"Please, Keri." I rolled my eyes. She knew damn well my mom wasn't that overbearing. If nothing else, she'd be mad I didn't make an appointment with my own doctor. My mother was no fan of emergency rooms.

"Wait, what's really going on?" She paused, leaning back as she narrowed her eyes. "Something is different about you."

"I don't know what you mean."

"You're in pain, yes, but you got that glow about you and…" She stood and crossed the room to get in my face. "Your skin is clear! You always have acne, and you said that for the women in your family, your skin is all irritated unless you're having sex! You're having sex, aren't you? Is that how you hurt your ass? Was this a rough sex injury? Wait, you're into that BDSM stuff?"

"Okay, you're going off the deep end." I laughed at her. "BDSM? Really?"

"Well then, what is it? And tell me the truth, Rayna." Keri was so close to me, I could smell the chocolate coming from her breath and see the traces of the sweet treat still on her tongue.

"You wouldn't believe me if I tried to tell you. I just didn't want to be alone." I dropped my shoulders. "I wish this was easier. If you really want to know, I need you to listen without judgement. The shit is going to sound crazy. You're going to want to tell me to call my therapist. I get it. But right now, I just want to be a woman dishing crazy drama to her friend. I want my friend to ignore how outlandish this shit sounds, pour me a glass of wine, and let me vent. Can you do that?"

"Why wouldn't I believe you?" She leaned back from me and scanned my full body, like the secrets were tattooed on my flesh.

"Keri, can you do that?" It probably wasn't a great idea to drink in my condition, but it made no difference to me. I told myself the wine would ease the pain. It might have also thinned out my blood and caused my injuries to worsen, but apparently, I was magical, so maybe things worked differently for me.

"Yes, of course." She straightened. "Getting the wine now!"

I spent the next several hours sipping wine and telling Keri every detail I could remember, from the first time I met Metice, to multiple demon attacks, to being dragged to hell, to banging a demoness and fighting his crazy ex. Every juicy detail, and my friend hung on every word. Before the wine kicked in, she looked concerned but kept her comments to herself. By her fourth glass, she was shouting jokes about my lesbian lover and asking if I would ever see her again.

"So that's what your life has been?" she asked as she emptied another bottle of wine into her cup. "A demon with a rotating dick."

"Everything I've told you, and that's what you're hung up on?"

"Well, hell, aren't you? I mean, you can call him whenever you want, right? Then he shows up and takes care of you?" She waggled her brows and then dropped her eyes to the glass in her hand. "I wish my man would come when I commanded."

"Is everything okay with you two?" That comment caught my attention. I hadn't talked to Keri in a while, and I figured she was still happy in her new love, but it sounded like I wasn't the only one with a troublesome man on my hands.

"Yeah, it's fine. Just out of the honeymoon stage." She held her glass to her lips but put it down without drinking. "We had our first fight, but it was nothing. Still a little tense, but we'll be okay."

"Do you want to talk about it?" It would be good to talk about someone else for a change. Metice said how he didn't think Keri was a good friend to me, but the same could be said about me. I got lost in my new world—granted, what I dealt with was a lot more of a mind fuck, but still. I cared about Keri and wanted her to be okay.

"Actually, no." She saw my face drop and quickly added, "It's just that, he's the one, Rayna. This is my guy, and I don't want to be airing out our dirty laundry every time I get with my girls. You know how it is when you constantly listen to your friend complain about a man and then they end up getting married? Everyone rolling their eyes as the bride strolls down the aisle. I don't want that."

We caught each other's eyes and blurted out at the same time, "Tricia!"

Keri fell out laughing, and if it still didn't hurt so much, I would have been laughing just as hard. Our former friend had all but landed her ass in jail messing with a guy she swore she would never see again. Five years later they were married with three kids and headed for divorce.

"Look, I get that." I raised my glass to her. "But if something serious happens, you tell me. I'm not playing that shit."

"You can call your demon to handle it for me." She winked while lifting her own glass.

"Hell, if I can figure out my magic, I'll teleport his ass to the desert and leave him there. I don't need a man to fight my battles." After about a minute of miming superwoman poses, Keri's face turned serious, and I swallowed the knot that quickly formed in my throat.

"Do you really believe all this is real?" She raised her hand to stop me. "I'm not going to tell you to call your therapist, and I won't tell anyone else, but I have to know, for me. So I can support you in the best way. Is this something you think is really happening to you?"

I thought about how to answer her. I could've lied and said it was all an elaborate creation of my imagination, but I didn't want to. It was selfish of me. I didn't want to be in the shit by myself anymore. Could I really drag my best friend into it with me?

"I-"

Bang!

We both jumped and turned our heads to the front door as the blue painted wood shook, something pounding against the outside of it.

"What the hell?" Keri stood, ready to defend her home, but before she could reach for the box I knew held her little pink bestie, the door flew in off the hinges.

Standing in the doorway, clothes singed and hair missing from half her head, was the big green demoness bitch.

14

The Bitch is back

"What the actual fuck?" Keri screamed and jumped from her seat. "Rayna, what is that?"

"That would be the ex-girlfriend." I kept my cool while my friend freaked out. One of us had to be thinking clearly. Besides, I was already hurting and needed to reserve my energy for when shit really got real. "You believe me now?"

"Son of a bitch." Keri pressed her hand against her forehead. "Demons are real. I'm too drunk for this shit."

"I suggest you sober up real fast." I shifted in my seat.

"You stupid human bitch!" Olian called out from the entrance. "Did you think I wouldn't find you again?"

"You made it back." I carefully stood, trying to hide any sign of my pain. "Did you have a pleasant trip?"

"Ray, maybe we shouldn't taunt the demon woman." Keri slowly moved to the box that held her friend. It didn't matter what she did; Olian's attention was locked on me as her hands gripped the doorframe.

"You think you can do that to me?" Olian screamed, and wood from the frame splintered in her hands. "Do you know who I am?"

"Metice's ex." I nodded. "He filled me in. Look, I'm sorry about what happened between you two, but that had nothing to do with me. I didn't even know him when he broke up with you."

"I am so much more than my attachment to some man," Olian screamed as her eyes darkened to a fiery orange.

"And yet, here you are, stalking me because of an attachment to some man." I pointed out the irony in her statement.

"Rayna." Keri still moved towards the box but warned me to ease up.

"It's fine, Keri." I waved her off and kept my eyes trained on the demoness. "This is how Olian and I talk to each other. Just a bit of healthy banter, right?"

"Oh, look, the human found her confidence. Isn't that cute? One little magic trick, and you think you can take me?" She flexed, and the skin on her arms rippled with energy as the tentacle sprouted from her back. The veining across her skin moved to accommodate the expanding muscles beneath. "Prove it."

Olian ran forward, and I held my hand out, hoping the magic that had knocked her on her ass the first time would work. Of course, it didn't. I stood there holding my hand out to her, focusing on energy, because that was the only piece of instruction I could remember. The magical girlies just focused on what they wanted the power to do, and it did it. Now, though, it looked like I was just standing there, waiting for a high five. Instead of a blast of power from my hand, three shots rang out. *Pop, pop, pop.* Three holes appeared in the demoness' chest.

Olian stopped and looked at her chest, yellow blood spilling from the fresh wounds. She looked at Keri. "You stupid bitch."

I looked to my right to find Keri standing there, her pink Glock 19 affectionately named Poppiana pointed at the demon's chest.

"Take that, demon ho!" She jutted the gun forward.

Olian reached for Keri like she would attack. Then she choked, and the same yellow blood spilled from her lips. Her eyes rolled back into her head, and she fell forward. Her skull cracked against the hardwood floor, the sound echoing down the hall.

"Is she dead?" Keri leaned forward, peering down at the demoness. "I mean, did I just kill a demon? I didn't think bullets were strong enough for that. Shit, they didn't work in Constantine."

"I don't know. Damn, I thought dropping her from the sky would have killed her, but it clearly didn't."

"Yeah, okay. We need to get out of here." Keri grabbed my bag and hers, then pulled her keys from her pocket. "On second thought, we can take your car. I just got mine detailed."

"Seriously?" I followed her as she carefully tiptoed around the fallen demon.

"Hey, these are your demons," Keri whispered. "I'm already going to have to deal with cleaning this up. How the hell do you get demon blood out of teakwood floors?"

"Hell if I know." I made it past Olian's body. "Let's just get out of here in case she wakes up."

"Still think it was a bad idea for me to get a gun?" Keri waved the weapon before stuffing it into her bag.

"Now is not the time to debate gun laws." I shook my head as we headed for the car.

My body hurt terribly badly, but I moved as quickly as I could. There was no way I was taking my time to avoid further injury, because that would mean giving the demon the chance to regenerate and catch up to us. Keri took the wheel, and I sat in the passenger seat as she peeled off down the street, tires squealing.

"What the hell do we do now?" Keri gripped the steering wheel and adjusted her collar. "I really shouldn't be driving right now."

"I don't know." I glanced over my shoulder, afraid Olian had somehow healed that quickly and was chasing after us. When I saw nothing, some of the tension eased, and I felt my jaw unclench. There was no threat, only the passing of busy homes and trees dusted with the fresh snow that fell as we drove. "She shouldn't have been able to get back here. I didn't see that happening, and Metice isn't here. He says he can feel me, sense when I'm in danger. This is the second time she has attacked me, and *nothing*. He's nowhere to be found. Something must be wrong."

"Maybe she found some way to block it. I mean, you said he had that one witch work her magic to block you from other demons. What if there's some spell at play that doesn't tell him when you're a danger? At least, not when she's there." Keri offered what sounded like a totally plausible reason, considering everything that had happened.

"Is that the lawyer side of your brain kicking in?" I asked. "How the hell are you so calm right now?"

"Hey, I told you half of what I do is playing detective to figure out what's really going on behind the story people give me." She laughed. "You think criminals tell the truth to their lawyers?"

"I just got to figure out somewhere safe to go. I can't go back home. Not yet." I looked out the window. "She's been there. If she's looking for me again, that's the logical place for her to go next."

"I think you better figure that out real quick." Keri adjusted the rear-view mirror. "We got company."

"What?" I asked.

"Something's coming up behind us quick, and I don't think that thing is a fucking car."

I turned in my seat to look out the back window and damn near shit myself. Running behind us was a thing that looked like a demonic transformer. It ran on all fours, with massive talons that destroyed the concrete beneath it. The thing was the size of my car, with a yellow body and a blue spine and neck that reached down with a snarling face. Its beady red eyes and sharp teeth were a threat to what would happen if it caught us.

Luckily, the thing wasn't accustomed to running on ice. The fresh snow on the road caused it to slip, and it slammed into a parked car as the sharp hook that stuck out from its forearm ripped through the door.

"What the hell is that?" I couldn't take my eyes off the thing.

"You're asking me? I'm not the one familiar with demons, you are," Keri yelled. "Hang on."

Keri whipped the car across two lanes and pulled onto the interstate, because that's what you do when a monster is chasing you—you get on the expressway! I wasn't sure what shocked me more: the monster chasing us, knocking unsuspecting drivers around the road, or Keri's driving skills.

"The snow is coming down fast." I looked out the window. It was like the clouds were just dumping out clumps of snow. There had barely been any at all when I arrived at Keri's house, and now, you couldn't even see the ground.

"What are the odds one of your demon buddies can control the weather?"

"God, I hope not."

She weaved in and out of cars with ease and put a sizeable distance between us and the thing behind us. For a second, I thought we would outrun it, but of course, two seconds after I had the thought that we might actually survive this encounter, another one of the jacked beasts dropped in front of us. Just as we were hitting a turn beneath an overpass, it hit the road less than a hundred feet in front of us.

Keri tried to maneuver around it, but with us already turning at a high speed on an icy road, that spelled disaster. Keri's scream rang out as everything spun around us. The crunching sound of metal against pavement broke what composure I had as the car flipped I didn't know how many times. My leg twisted beneath me, the bone snapping as the force pulled my body in different directions. I cried out, but a moment later, my head slammed against the door, and everything went black.

"Ray? Ray? Are you okay?" Keri nudged my shoulder.

Her voice registered first, then the touch of her hand, then the pain in my leg. The car was upside down. I was on the ceiling. Keri was hanging from her seat, still strapped in.

"Ow!" I groaned. "Son of a bitch."

"Are you okay?"

"I'm alive. Does that count?"

"We have to get out of here." She pulled at her seatbelt. "I'm stuck. Can you reach my bag? I have a knife."

I tried to reach for the bag in the back of the car by the rear window, but unfortunately, my leg wasn't the only thing broken. The moment I moved my arm, the pain shot up into my shoulder. I looked down to see the bone sticking out the side of my arm.

"Fuck!" The hyperventilating started immediately.

"Ray," Keri spoke calmly. "Breathe. You're going to be okay. I know it hurts, but we have to get out of here."

"Keri, I'm so sorry." Tears ran down my face. "I shouldn't have come to you. I shouldn't have pulled you into this."

"Not the time, Ray," Keri said. "Breathe. You need to get the knife."

"You're right, okay." I took a deep breath, and with my good leg, scooted myself across the ceiling of the car. It was a slow and painful process, but I made it.

Just as I touched the bag and slid it to Keri, we heard it: sharp talons crunching against the ground. Our time was up. Keri hurried to get the knife out of her bag and worked on the seatbelt. She dropped to the ceiling when I caught the first glimpse of the monster outside.

"Dammit," Keri said, scooting toward me. She pulled Poppiana out of her bag. "Let's hope this works just as well on their asses."

We would have exactly six seconds to find out, because one of the things took that moment to rip the car in half. I watched as the bottom half of my car went flying and flinched at the ground shaking crash that rang out when it landed.

The snow fell in our faces as one beast became three. Two others stepped into view beside the original, and they were just as terrifying. Their heavy growls were echoed by their clawed fists pounding against the ground, like they were cheering for their own success. Whoever sent them would be proud.

And then my bold bestie started firing. Shots rang out and bullets bounced off their targets, but only one landed in the eye of the demonic creature, who fell over. If only she could do that exact thing two more times. She aimed the gun at the next one, but it was too late. In defense of its falling creature, it backhanded my friend, and her limp body went sliding across the snow-covered grass.

"Keri! No!" I called out, but there was nothing I could do.

Yelling pulled their attention back to me, and I could only hope that would save my friend's life. The monsters surrounded me, growling and making a yipping sound that hurt my ears. I covered my ears but screamed out when the damn thing clawed my legs. Its grip wrapped around both my legs and crushed my already shattered bones.

I screamed, more from the pain than the fear, as the familiar tension of the shift wrapped around me. Everything went fuzzy, this time lasting longer than it had before. But when my vision cleared and I regained consciousness, I knew without a doubt that I was back in hell.

15

First Death

Pain coursed through my body like lightning strikes. Unrelenting pulses of red-hot fire threatened to knock me back out. I gritted my teeth, refusing to pass out. Instead, I sat with my back against the rigid wall and stared through the prison bars at the demon mutts who'd dragged me back to hell. They were smaller, tamer, and looked like puppies.

It was all a show, though, because every time I moved or even breathed too hard, they would turn on me. Their bodies expanded and contracted in a matter of seconds. The first few times, it terrified me, but with the pain and blood loss, their threatening show was more annoying than anything.

For the first few hours, I was alone with the dogs. Or at least, it felt like hours. Then, a group of demons entered the room, and I froze, expecting them to acknowledge my presence and threaten me. Instead, they acted as if I didn't exist, and it made me feel like I was losing my mind. Still, I wasn't dumb enough to open my mouth and call attention to myself. Instead, I watched them and wished they were speaking in a language I knew.

There were five, three female and two male, and I could only tell that not by their faces or distinctive voices, but by their bodies. They seemed overly pronounced. The females' breasts were the size of basketballs, and the males' dicks hung carefree like elephant trunks between their legs.

Their guttural clicks and deep foreign words turned from conversational to seductive. Soon, the air filled with musk as these demons became aroused, and I sat there, wondering how they could get hot and bothered while I lay bloodied and dying just a few feet away.

I averted my eyes, staring at the pool of my blood on the stone floor. I was not about to sit there and watch demons fuck. That would not be the last thing I saw before I died.

The heavy door opened again. I could hear it, but I couldn't see anything beyond the fuzzy edges of my vision. Just eight bulky metal bars separated me from a room furnished with six large sofas in different colors and fabrics, what looked like a bar stocked with drinks, and no visible windows, though there was the soft glow of moonlight coming from somewhere. There was a painting on the wall, a figure I couldn't get my eyes to focus on long enough to decipher.

More voices flooded the room, and then there was one I knew. A female—no, a petty and jealous ass bitch. Olian.

"Ah, you're still awake?" She walked into view. "I thought you'd be down and out by now, but you really are a strong one, aren't you?"

I said nothing as she sat in the chair provided by another demon, a male with dark orange flesh and muscles fit for show. She petted his arm as she sat, and I swear, he blushed.

Olian wore a sheer red gown that had so little fabric, it barely counted as clothing. Her breast and hips threatened to rip right through it when she sat, but the split in the front saved it from disaster.

"Well, I'm glad you're awake, Rayna," Olian tossed the braids that hung from half her head over her shoulder. "I wanted to have a little fun with you before I end your pathetic life. I thought about keeping you alive, using your power for my gain, but he will come for you. The spell hides your location, but Metice is smart enough to figure out where you are."

I stared at her, not a word spoken. She was playing a game, and I wouldn't take part in it, though it annoyed me to look at her and find she was quickly healing from what happened. Her singed hair on the left side of her head had grown out, now braided down into a half mohawk. The holes in her chest were gone, just a few faint scars where they once were, but she looked weak, and her green skin looked less like vibrant treetops and more like one of those sickly zombie corpses in old horror movies. She wasn't fully recovered, but it wouldn't be long until she was.

"Oh, you're so annoying." She slapped the arm of the chair when she realized I wouldn't cry and plead for my life. That was clearly what she wanted. "I tried to be nice about it, but then your friend had to go and shoot me. You should be glad I'm not going to make her pay for that. Fine. How about we demons give you a little show before you go?"

Olian parted her legs, and I saw her big green pussy head on. I looked away from the pocket with the full carpet, opting to stare at the dog's ass instead.

"You will look at me." She snapped her fingers, and her orange demon helper opened the bars that separated me from them.

I didn't have the energy to fight him when he grabbed my head, turning me to look at her. I closed my eyes, but he pried them open and hissed in my ear, the sharp, snake-like sound a threat to keep them open.

In front of me, Olian lowered her fingers to what looked like a normal pussy, lips, clit, hole, the usual... but as she rubbed her clit, normal went out the damn window. Her lips parted, and three tentacles matching the ones that sprouted from her back before reached out of her pussy. I flinched, moving back, but the orange demon pushed me forward.

Olian moaned as her tentacles, green and moving like vines, reached out to me. I squirmed, trying to avoid those nasty things, but I couldn't. The wet pussy arm slid across my face and lips, and there was no holding it back: I vomited right into the bitch's pussy! I gagged as I stared at the chunks dripping from her inner thigh.

Olian screamed. She said no words, just opened her mouth and emitted a screech before she hopped up from the seat and smacked me so hard, I lost sight for longer than was probably safe. When my vision cleared again, the orange demon finished tying me to the wall. He used what felt like a metal clamp, locking my head in place so I couldn't turn away from the show in front of me.

Then, he followed Olian out of the room.

"I need to clean myself. Now! Make sure they have everything perfect!" she screamed as the door slammed shut behind her.

Though I could feel myself dying, I still found humor in what had just happened. Yes, it was gross as fuck, and if I survived, I would have nightmares about it, but in that moment, losing blood and going numb to the stabbing pain of broken bones, I chuckled then coughed, attracting the attention of the dogs, who seemed completely unphased by the impending orgy.

This was why the big orange goof tied me up, so I could see the group of demons who were licking, touching, and doing so many more graphic things than I could ever have come up with in my head. Some had wings, others had additional arms. One impressive demon had two dicks and fucked two others at the same time. I guess having dual tools made up for the ugly face.

Their moans increased, and so did the smell of their sex. It wasn't like human sex; it had a dirty, metallic layer to it. I was grateful that my sense of smell was failing me too. How long would it be until I lost everything? How long would it be until there was nothing left of me? Olian said Metice would come, but Keri was right. She'd done something to block him from being able to sense me. How long until he tracked me down? Would I even survive?

I tried to do the math, the time on Earth to the time in the Bane. A few hours there was a day in my world. Was Keri okay? Did she survive the crash? What about all those people, those innocent lives caught in the tidal wave of my insanity? It was a selfish thing to think, but I found a moment of peace in knowing that Keri knew the truth. She knew I wasn't insane. Even if I never saw her again, she could stop worrying that her best friend was a nutcase. Yes, being dragged to hell and murdered by demons was much better than being labeled psychotic.

There it was. The blurred edges of my vision closed in. I could hardly see the fuck fest in front of me, could barely hear the grotesque sounds of their moaning. Just a little while longer, and I would be gone. Instead of trying to decipher the different body parts revealed in front of me, I thought of Metice. His face, his voice, his touch. I called to those gentler moments we'd shared, in his home and in mine. I let the memory of him comfort me. Funny, because I was still pissed at him, but in the final moments of my life, being angry seemed far less important than thinking of the good.

He was the good I could reach with my mind—everything else, things further back, my mother's laugh, my cousin's jokes, my father's days of old, they all seemed so far out of reach. But Metice was there. Fresh, strong, comfortable.

The final sounds of my heartbeat thumped in my ears as the icy chill in my limbs reached for my core. I held on to him. It was all I could do to keep my fading mind busy with thoughts of him to fend off the fear of what would follow.

In those moments, those spaces between my slowing heartbeats, something changed.

The faded images shifted from soft, seductive movements with moments of aggressive thrusting to chaotic energy. I tried to clear my thoughts to gather what happened, but I couldn't. There were muffled screams battling for my attention, and something hit my face—a rock, maybe, then more. Like rubble. Then, there were splashes of something wet across my skin, the sense so dull, I barely registered it.

Something heavy and wet fell next to me as the muffled sounds of fear continued.

Then, it appeared. Towering above my limp body was a massive form that reached out to me.

Why was it here? Was this death? Is that what happened when your life ended? Those tales of the Grim Reaper must have been true. It didn't even dawn on me to fight for my life. I accepted this enormous being lifting me from the ground and carrying me away.

The heat of what I thought was the sun, a brief sigh of relief, touched my face before I died.

16

The choice is not yours

METICE

I didn't have many friends left in hell, that much was true. The ones I *did* have were reluctant to help me. They didn't want any targets on their back. I couldn't blame them for it; I knew what walking away from the establishment would do. It wasn't like I was the first to quit the job, but I *was* the first to quit the job and dump the boss's daughter at the same time.

It wasn't the boss who was after me; it was Olian, my jealous ex-girlfriend. Now, because of her, my soulmate was in trouble, and the only person I knew who wouldn't kick my ass for coming to them for help was the witch who fucked her right in front of me.

I entered Likosa's home, carved into the side of a damn hillside. The first entrance where we met her before was empty. This place was mostly for show, though the pool in the center did aid in her elemental practices. I walked around it, avoiding the memories of what I'd seen there, and headed for the door on the opposite side.

Three knocks, and the door swung open, revealing more modern accommodations and letting the fragrance of fresh herbs and flowers flow out to greet me.

"Meti, you're back soon. I was sure that little show of ours would have kept you away from here for a nice, long time." Likosa placed her hand on her hip and intentionally let the sheer pink robe slip from her shoulder, revealing her nipple. "How can I help you?"

"I need your help. It's Rayna." I kept my eyes on her face. With Likosa, any sort of slip up could be taken as an invitation to participate in activities I had no interest in. The goal was to protect the one woman who meant anything to me.

"Hey, no refunds." She shook her finger in my face. "I did the spell, and it worked perfectly. I can't help if she stumbled into some other demonic troubles."

"It's not that. She's injured. I need you to heal her. If she's going to make the journey, we need her at full strength. I don't have time to wait for her to heal at a human rate."

"I see." She stepped aside. "Come in. I guess I can whip up a quick elixir for you, but you will owe me one."

"I'd expect nothing else." There was always a deal to be made. That was how my world worked. Sure, there were other forms of official currency, but most often, those I encountered wanted bargains for favors.

"Good." She pointed to the soft pink seat by the large round pink marble table. "Have a seat."

Everything was done in shades of pink and touches of green. I never asked why she chose the colors; it didn't matter. In all the years I'd known her, I'd only been inside her true home a handful of times.

Likosa wasn't of the Bane; she was from another world. She landed in ours by accident, or so she says, and decided not to leave. My theory was that she was running from something, and it had to be pretty damn dangerous, considering how powerful Likosa was. The woman landed in hell, made a name for herself, and gained the respect of demons all over. She was pretty damn impressive.

"What's wrong with her?" Likosa asked as she moved around the kitchen, opening cabinets and collecting items.

"She fell. I think she has a few fractured bones..." I paused, trying to figure out how to explain everything.

"What is it, Metice? Stop wasting time and tell me." Likosa stopped and looked at me. The cool breeze moved through the kitchen from the open window, and I could have sworn she used it to coax the truth from me. It felt like a gentle hand touching my leg, thigh, arm.

"She used her magic." The air moved around my face and neck like the caress from a woman. "I'm not sure if that has some effect on her or not."

"Tapped into those psychic abilities, huh?" Likosa poked her lips out and nodded her head, an expression I'd come to know meant she was impressed by someone.

"You knew?" The breeze ended, and I shook my head clear of its effect.

"Of course, I did. There is something else, though, something I can't quite figure out. It's been driving me batty." She paused and leaned her hip against the counter. "I was looking into it, and I came close, but I don't think you'll like what I found."

"What?" My heart pounded in my chest, but I had to keep calm. How could things get any worse? Rayna was already in danger because of me. "What did you find?"

"The story of the witch who healed you. You remember her?" She placed the items down on the counter and looked at me.

"Yes, of course." I nodded. "What about her?"

"You're going to have to take Rayna to her."

"I'm sorry, what?" I choked at the thought. "Why would I do that?"

"She's the one who can help you and the girl much more than I can."

"She's a soul tied to the energy of the Bane," I reminded her. "It's not like I can just walk in there and talk to her."

"Of course you can. You're you." She winked.

"This just got a lot more complicated than I thought."

"You were going to tie your souls together for good, right? Make it so you can stay together?"

"I-"

"If you do that, Metice, she must reach her full potential, or you will lose her forever."

"That is a choice I'll make with her." Rayna was already pissed off at me for keeping things from her. I promised I would earn her trust back. Making that kind of decision without her wouldn't help my case.

"That is a choice, that will be taken from you." She reached into a drawer and pulled out a box wrapped in ribbon. "Here, this is what you need."

"You knew I'd be back?"

"Of course I did, child." She sighed and fixed her robe, tightening the belt around her waist. "I'd think you'd stop doubting my abilities by now."

"Thank you for your help." I nodded. "I will repay you."

"Of course you will." She ushered me to the door. "Hurry up and get back to that lovely woman of yours."

I had to leave Likosa's home entirely before I could perform the shift that would take me from my world to Rayna's. It was Likosa's rule, and I wouldn't break it: I couldn't open a shift in her home. It made her vulnerable. To what, I didn't know, but I needed her on my side, and I wouldn't do anything to risk losing the friendship.

I'd already been gone longer than I wanted to. The woman was hardheaded and not likely to have actually stayed put like I asked.

The sky darkened overhead as the day shifted into night, and I moved across planes. This was why I was so valuable to the people who wanted me. I could step in and out of worlds without the use of any technology. It was a gift I was born with. I'd known nothing of my family before me, just that I had a gift that was rare in our world. Because of that, there were plenty of demons willing to pay top price to have me skip through realms collecting things for them.

That's what I did until I couldn't anymore.

Her home smelled like vanilla. The scent welcomed me with each arrival, like walking into the hands of a masseuse. My tension melted away, despite knowing we were far from having all our problems solved. Unfortunately, this visit didn't bring the same lasting relief.

The sweet smell of vanilla still welcomed me, but the moment I stepped foot into her home, I felt the absence of her. With Rayna, her heartbeat was my beacon, calling me to her, but the house was silent.

"Of course," I muttered as I looked around the empty bedroom. "Why would she leave?"

Instead of letting my anger drive me, I tapped into the connection I shared with my soulmate. There was a time when the feeling of her annoyed me, but now, I looked forward to it. It came in handy when the woman refused to comply to a simple request.

"Come on," I muttered as I worked to find the frequency in my mind. The invisible thread was more like a signal, a pulse that connected us. Usually, it took just a few moments to find the soft hum in my head, but this time, I couldn't feel her.

"Dammit, Rayna. Where are you?"

Her laptop sat open on the desk near her bed. I opened the desk drawer to find the small pink notebook where she wrote her passwords—like that was the epitome of security.

After entering what I assumed was the name of a childhood pet, the welcome screen lit up. It took just a few minutes to find her friend's information, the one who suggested she seek therapy when she told her about me.

The easier thing to do would have been to call her, but that would have been too simple, and it wouldn't give me the opportunity to provide a little proof for Rayna's story. Her friend needed to see me, to know I was real, for Rayna's sake. With everything going on, she needed her friend to be in her corner. I wasn't sure what the woman could do, but it sounded like her emotional support was important to my soulmate.

Minutes later, I stood outside her friend's house. The door to the brick home was knocked off the hinges, and the smell of something terrible lingered in the air—blood, and not the human variety. Several police vehicles were parked outside as officers moved around the space, conducting their investigation. I kept a safe distance so as not to call any unnecessary attention to myself while I listened in.

"The homeowner is at St. John's Hospital. She was in a nasty accident. The call about the house came an hour after they checked her in. We came here to find the boyfriend, door knocked off the hinges," one short officer reported to another, who had a belly the size of a small cauldron.

"Is it a domestic case?" the rotund officer spoke, a cigarette between his lips.

"No. He arrived just before we did." The short officer checked his notes. "Neighbor called it in, and his alibi checks out. He was at a game with friends. The kid looks devastated."

"Then why isn't he at the hospital?" the round one asked. "And hey, it's not like we've never seen an abuser show regret for his actions. It could be a show."

"The family doesn't want him there." The short one frowned.

"And you're sure he has nothing to do with it?" It was like the guy wanted the man to go down for a crime he definitely didn't commit.

"Positive." The man nodded. "In any case, it looks like she'll survive. They say she's pretty banged up. The friend who was with her is still missing. A woman, it looks like."

"Alright, find out all you can. Something about this isn't sitting right with me," the big guy ordered before wobbling to his own car and driving away.

St. John's Hospital. I had to go find *the friend*.

The hospital was busy, but it was easy enough to find her friend. The smell of demon blood was still on her. When I arrived, there were doctors in her room, giving reports of fractures and other injuries that would take months to heal. She was lucky to be alive.

I waited for them to leave before slipping into the room and closing the door behind me.

"Who are you?" Keri tensed in the bed.

"My name is Metice, I am-"

"The demon," Keri finished my thought. "Well, I'll be damned. You are real."

"You know about me?"

"Yes, Rayna told me everything about you and your world." She winced from the pain as she adjusted in the small bed. "Why are you here?"

"You don't find anything about my presence alarming?" I thought it would take much more time to convince her of my existence, but she seemed unusually accepting.

"After what I saw, hell, you're like a bunny rabbit." She scoffed. "Those damn things that got us, they were terrifying. You can at least pass for human."

"Where is she?" I asked. "Where's Rayna? The officer said your friend was missing."

"Are you going to take care of her?" She looked me in the eye like it was a challenge, the quiet beeps from the machine behind her bed like a timer counting down to her explosion.

"Of course I am." I nodded. "Tell me where she is so I can take care of her."

"No, I mean really take care of her." Keri's voice was strained with emotions I couldn't comprehend. "Don't play with her heart. I know my friend. That girl will find the smallest detail to toss a man to the side. Do you know she once stopped dating a man because he said she had birthing hips? Petty, right? So for her to be holding on to you so tightly now, it means something."

"I'm not sure what to say to that." That was the truth. "I will protect her and care for her the best I can. I promise you that."

"She's in this, you know that, right? She isn't going back to her normal life." Keri held my gaze. "Your world belongs to her. You're smart enough to know even if you break the bond, she will never be safe. She will never be free of what knowing you has uncovered in her life."

"Is this really the time?" Her words felt like echoes of Likosa's, and once again, I felt like I would choke on the implication. Rayna couldn't walk away from any of this, no matter how much I thought it was the best choice for her.

"Considering time moves a lot slower where you're from, I think you can take a couple minutes to listen to me here," Keri challenged.

"She really told you everything, didn't she?"

"She told me enough." She glanced down, and her eyes lingered on my crotch before she lifted her slow gaze and winked at me.

"Really?" I turned away. Human women were worse than the demon ones. "I need to know where she is."

"Take care of my friend, or I will find a way to come to hell and deal with you," she warned me.

"You human women are insane." I laughed.

"We sure are. The men made us that way." Keri relaxed finally.

"Where is she?" I asked. "I can't help her from here, and I know she's in trouble."

"Two big ass demon things, yellow and blue monsters, they chased us down." Her voice softened as the rising emotions choked her. "I killed one, but it wasn't enough. They knocked me out, and when I woke up, she was gone."

"Dammit, Olian." I cursed the name of the one who owned the trackers, demon dogs with a hellish tech upgrade. When they activated, they became large and terrifying beasts who would do anything their owner commanded. Any other time, they looked like an average mutt.

"Your ex?" Keri asked.

"Yes. Those are her pets. They're trackers. They would have taken Rayna back to her."

"That bitch better not hurt my friend over your dumbass," Keri cursed.

"Thanks." I paused. "You killed one?"

"I shot that jolly green ex of yours in the chest, too. So take my warning to heart, demon boy." she winked.

"Please don't call me that."

"Save my friend, and I won't."

I didn't bother using the door. I knew exactly where I needed to go: back to hell to visit my ex.

17

Care for her

METICE

Olian was a creature of habit. She wanted to torture Rayna and punish me, and that meant taking her to the bricks, a system of tunnel connected rooms in the middle of the wastelands. They were the operation facilities for one of the collectors, a powerful demon who had other demons working for him. In those tunnels were rooms for captors, tortures, and other dark activities. This one belonged to Olian's father.

Olian would be able to tell Rayna and I had been together. She'd smell me on Rayna. Her twisted mind would have definitely come up with some sort of sex play to mix into her torture plans. There was only one place she did that kind of work.

"Are you really going to do this?" the deep voice of Cufio spoke from behind me.

I turned to find the shadow demon, his thin frame radiating with the murky energy. Cufio spent so much time in the shadows, it was hard to distinguish where his body ended and the shadows began.

"Why are you here, Cufio?" I scanned the area to be sure my old friend was alone. "This has nothing to do with you."

"I figured you'd come eventually. News spread fast about Olian bringing your human here. Funny how the rules don't apply to the boss's daughter." Cufio pointed to the system of rooms off in the distance. "Any of us do what she's planning, and we'd lose our necks."

"And you risked coming here. Why?" I asked. "You'd be in just as much trouble if they found out you were here talking to me. What do you want?"

"I want to try to talk some sense into you, Meti. You could fix all this by just coming back." Cufio looked at me, his thick brow furrowed over grey eyes. "They'd take you back. That's all they want, for you to be back on the team. You were the best of us. It was a hard hit to lose you in the field."

"You and I both know that won't fix this." I laughed. "Olian will still try to kill Rayna because of what she means to me. Going back to work for them won't fix that."

"Wow, the human really does mean something to you? I thought they were all insane when they said you cared for her. I figured the Meti I knew could never feel anything for a human." He paused, looking back at the tunnels. "What's the plan here? Are you going to go in there and kill everyone? Then what? There really won't be any turning back from that. What happens next?"

"Don't worry about what happens next. Just stay out of my way," I warned.

When Cufio returned his attention to me, I made a point to show him I meant what I said. My muscles stretched, skin warmed, and horns grew. It wasn't often I revealed my true form. It wasn't as pleasant to look at, but this wasn't a time to care about outward appearances. I could see the fear in his eyes as I changed, the same reaction every time someone saw my true self.

"You know, I wasn't even here today." He threw his hands up and turned to leave. "Take care of yourself, Meti. Some of us still want you to be okay."

As Cufio disappeared back into the haze of shadows, I ran for the room where Olian held Rayna.

She used the same room every time. It was her special quarters, decked out to look like it wasn't sitting in the pits. As I ran, I caught the scent. Olian was there, and so was Rayna. First came that sweet scent of vanilla, and then blood—her blood, and she'd lost a lot of it.

There wasn't any time to deal with doorways or pleasantries. I couldn't waste a moment trying to talk my way inside. They'd drag it out just long enough for me to lose her. Instead, I circled around the poorly guarded building to the wall I knew to be her space. Just as I suspected, sounds of loud and aggressive sex came through the high windows.

"I'm coming, Rayna," I said as I ripped away the final layers of my clothing. If I was going to take on an orgy, I needed my full strength. The clothes wouldn't survive the expansion.

One of the reasons the boss loved me was the hat trick. My dick wasn't the only thing customizable. I drew in the energy of the world around me, the darkness that kept the Bane going, and as I did, my body doubled, then tripled in size. Clenching my fist, I brought razor-like ridges to cover my flesh and create a shield of armor across my body.

When I finished the transition, it took one swing of my fist to knock the entire wall in. I drew back and smashed it in, then watched as the naked demons scattered.

"Metice, you bastard!" Sintk, a bull demon with three dicks, was the only one bold enough to take me head on. He lowered his head, aimed his horns at my chest, and charged me.

I caught him easily by the horn and held him in place. The smell of her blood came to me again, and my eyes followed the trail. There she was: my soulmate, chained to the wall and barely alive. My vision flooded with red.

"I'll make every one of you pay for this."

"Me-" I didn't hear what Sintk had to say. I lifted him in the air by the horn and, in one swift motion, ripped the dirty dicks from his body. When I dropped him, he quickly bled out.

Each demon who dared to approach me died. It didn't matter who they were or what relationship we once shared. All that mattered was her, getting her out of there alive. By the time I reached her, the floor was slick with multi-colored blood.

She lay there, battered and clinging to life behind the heavy bars. Damn searching for a key. I had to get to her. I grabbed the bars and pulled. The metal groaned in protest, but the fight was short lived before they were ripped from their posts. When I tossed them behind me, they flew into the wall and removed the head of a fleeing demoness. An unfortunate casualty of battle.

It didn't matter to me. I would remove the heads of a hundred more if that's what it took. I cared about nothing but her, the hardheaded human woman tied to my world. She was nearly gone. Her chest fluttered with the final breaths of life, and I knew I had to act quickly.

I picked her up from the floor, ripping the chains that held her from the wall, and ran. As I did, I picked up my clothing but didn't stop moving. I had to get far enough away to give her the elixir, but I could already hear them coming.

My chest burned with the fear that I hadn't made it to her in time. It took me too long to get to her, and now, I was losing her.

"Please stay with me," I whispered as I ran, pulling her limp body close to my chest. "I need you to survive this."

Just ahead, a shadow flickered, a sign from an old friend who would put a target on his back if they knew he helped me. Cufio. I let my body shrink but held tightly onto Rayna as we slipped into the shadows and away from the battlefield.

Cufio taught me well to follow his path through the shadows. I had to shrink myself and never step a foot out of bounds. Many were lost trying to follow a shadow demon through their passages. Theirs were the back doors through worlds where the unstable energy waited to snatch people away from their lives. This was the hell the humans knew, eternity trapped in endless suffering, all because you missed a step. If you weren't careful, the ones lost in the dark corridors would pull you in with them.

A moment later, I stepped out of the shadows and into the caverns. This hidden system was one Cufio and I discovered many years prior. We'd stocked it with supplies for such a day as this, when the world turned its back on us.

Cufio wasn't there; I could see the marking of the shadow he used to escape. In another minute, no one would be able to trace him.

"Thank you," I said, though I doubted my friend could hear me.

I carried Rayna to the small cot to the left of the space and carefully laid her there. From the jacket I'd ripped away during my transition, I pulled out the box Likosa gave me and took out the first vial. On it, written in Likosa's hand, was Rayna's name.

When I popped the cork, the clear liquid fizzled and turned golden.

"I hope that was supposed to happen," I muttered. There was no time to find Likosa and ask her. I put the vial to Rayna's lips and poured its contents into her mouth.

"You have to survive this," I spoke to her, unsure if she could hear me. "I know I've been stubborn, but so have you. It's what makes this work between us.

But now is not the time to be stubborn. Stay with me, Rayna. Promise me years of your stubbornness. Please do as I ask. Please fight to stay here."

Rayna's face flushed with warmth. It lasted a moment, but it was enough to convince me the elixir was working. I pulled her hand into mine, but her fingers were cold as ice. If I didn't warm her up, she wouldn't make it. I knew that.

In the center of the hideout was a fire pit, and above it, a small vent to allow smoke to escape through a series of pathways, keeping our location hidden. It seemed my friend had thought ahead. There were fresh cut logs and plenty of kindling. I got the fire going quickly, then lifted the cot with Rayna still on it closer to the fire. It would have been good to get her something more to keep her warm, but to leave her was out of the question, not until I was sure she would be okay in my absence.

"They'll be looking for us, but we're safe here. You don't need to worry about that." I talked to her because it felt strange not to. Pulling her hand back into mine, I continued. "When you're awake, I'll tell you everything, anything you want to know. You were right; I shouldn't have hidden so much from you. It was naïve to think I could protect you from any of this. I won't do that anymore. This is my promise to you. I will support you in this journey and protect you from my enemies. Whatever life you want to lead, I'll be there to guard your dreams and soothe your heart. You deserve that and so much more."

My confessions continued until my eyes grew heavy and my head dropped. Before sleep took over me, I added two logs to the fire. One last look at her, and I saw the color returning to her face, restoring that deep chestnut brown. My last thought before I slept was that I hoped to look into her eyes once more.

When I woke, Rayna had not yet regained consciousness, but she looked better. Her breathing was stronger, and her skin looked warmer.

"You should be okay on your own for a bit." I rubbed her hair, still matted with dirt and blood. "I'll be back soon."

I hoped she wouldn't wake and find herself alone, but I had to get supplies for her.

Back in her house, I gathered things to care for her. In her garage was a large plastic bin that I loaded with jugs of water from her kitchen and canned soups from the pantry. I grabbed her clothing, towels, soaps, and other things to clean her wounds. She had a small bin with first aid items, which I dumped into the larger one.

Before returning to her, I grabbed some bedding, two pillows and a comforter to help keep her warm. I looked around her home again just to make sure there was nothing else she needed.

The painting she was working on sat there, closer to being finished, and as I appreciated the surety of her strokes and admired the transition of colors, I realized this painting, this place from her dreams, was familiar. I'd been there once before, when a witch nursed me back to life and told me of the woman tied to my soul.

"Dammit." This couldn't be a good sign.

Rayna was still sleeping when I returned to her. I poured some of the water into one of the pots we had in the cavern and warmed it over the fire. Then, using the towel and soaps I took from her home, I washed her body of the blood and dirt. The elixir had already healed her injuries, leaving only one scar on her leg where the worst wound was. The others healed without a mark.

I washed and carefully combed her hair before putting it in the twists taught to me by a young girl in South Africa, then covered her hair with the bonnet I grabbed from her bedside. Dressed in fresh clothing and clean of the filth and blood, she looked more like my Rayna.

It was strange to me how much I enjoyed caring for her. She'd given me nothing but trouble, but all I wanted was to make sure she was okay. I looked forward to detangling her hair and washing her skin. The thought of bringing her any form of peace made my chest warm with something unfamiliar to me.

Yip! Yee! Yip!

The sound startled me, and I jumped from my seat next to Rayna. Had someone found us? This place was secure and had been for years. Had they captured my friend and forced him to reveal our secrets?

As I braced, preparing to do all I could to protect her, the sound grew near, and I heard the trumpeting sound of a demon dog's fart. Before his little blue body appeared in the doorway, I smelled the sickly-sweet odor.

Piko.

He crossed the room, and in one leap, landed in my arms.

"Of course you found us." I laughed and patted his head. "Easy boy. Settle down."

He licked my face, and as soon as he saw her, he jumped onto the cot with Rayna. The mutt didn't leave her side for the next two days.

Over the days, I made sure to give her water and kept talking to her as much as possible. Though I wasn't sure if she could hear me, I told her all about my life, laughing at myself because these were things I would have to tell her again.

On the fourth day, something changed. Rayna's body hummed with an energy I'd never felt from her. I stood from my seat as the light, golden like the elixir I gave her, shined beneath her flesh. Two steps into my approach, and that mental connection that was once a gentle frequency became a sharp sting in my mind. Needles punctured the surface of my brain, and my body seized.

My knees cracked against the ground, sending lightning strikes of pain up my thighs and into my gut. Rayna stirred. I fell to all fours, and her eyes opened.

The box, Likosa's gift. I crawled to it, fighting my seizing limbs. It took all my concentration to open the vial with my name written across it.

"Metice?" Her voice was dry as her eyes searched for me.

"I'm so sorry." I closed my eyes and poured the fizzling gold liquid down my throat.

And the world went dark.

I didn't get to look into her eyes.

18

And then comes Marriage.

Rayna

There's a moment when you think your life is done, and you slowly accept it. Then, there's the moment when you realize your life isn't ending, and the pain of your recovery almost makes you wish it would. When my eyes opened to the dirty ceiling of the cave I lay in, all I wished for was anything to give me relief.

My body felt stiff, my bones ached, my throat burned, and every breath I took felt like it was fighting me back. *What happened to me?* The thought repeated in my mind as slow-moving snippets, memories of my past, returned like strokes of a paintbrush, filling in the gaps of an image.

The soft whining at my side drew my eyes to the warm body curled up with me. Piko. His eyes were closed, but he whimpered, and I wondered what he must have been dreaming of. I turned my head just enough to scan the space. This was a cave. Where, I didn't know, but I didn't think it was Earth. There was one small entrance, a fire pit in the center with a dying flame, and then I saw it.

Large feet in leather boots connected to a body on the ground. I carefully shifted to see who the owner of the feet was and panicked when my eyes reached his face.

"Metice?" I tried to get up, but it took much more strength than it should have. He wasn't far, only about a foot from the bed. I could make it to him. I had to.

I rolled out of the bed, knocking Piko over as I did. Instead of crawling to the fallen demon, which would have made the most sense. I stood, took two steps, and then fell forward, right on top of the unconscious demon.

That was all the energy I had, burned up in half a step. I passed out the moment my head hit his chest. I woke to Piko's tongue licking my face, his large, worried eyes darting between me and the one I fell on.

"Dammit." I pushed myself off Metice and sat next to him. "What the hell happened to me?"

Metice groaned next to me, and all I could think to do was pull his head into my lap. It looked like he was sleeping, but I could tell something more was going on. I just didn't know what it was.

"Please wake up." I rubbed his face and felt the stubble along his jaw. "Metice, I don't know what to do. I need you."

His eyes fluttered opened, and he stared up at me, looking at me like he couldn't believe I was real.

"Rayna?" he asked.

"Metice, are you okay? What happened?"

His dark eyes jumped around, trying to focus. The embers from the dying fire crackled as he looked at me. Then, the smile lifted the corner of his lips. "You're awake."

"I am." I nodded and touched his face again. "And so are you."

"Rayna? You're okay." He spoke like he was trying to jolt out of a dream.

"Yes. Are you?" I searched his eyes. Something was different, I just couldn't figure out what it was. "Are you okay?"

Metice sat up and placed his hand on my face. He held it there and then pulled me to him, kissing me gently before wrapping me in his hold. "I'm so glad you're okay."

"Metice, what happened?" I asked, inhaling his scent. It was warm, like a campfire, and made my heart feel whole again.

"What do you remember?" he asked, still holding me, and pressed my head to his chest. "Tell me what you remember, and I'll fill in the rest."

"I was with Keri." I shook my head as jumbled thoughts struggled to settle in my mind. "Then something attacked us. Olian locked me away. Oh my God, I was dying. No, I died. Am I dead?"

"You did not die, but you were close." He ran his hand across my satin-covered head. "I almost lost you, but you're here."

"I..." My throat suddenly felt like I'd swallowed sand, and I coughed to clear the feeling.

"Here." Metice produced a bottle of water from the bin next to the bed. "Drink"

I sipped and eyed the large plastic bin with the moving label still stuck to the side. "Is that from my house?"

"Yes, I had to go there to get things for you," he confirmed. "It was the safest option. Luckily, no one else was there when I went."

"Thank you." I drank more of the water, slowly, because even the first few sips had my stomach shaking.

Scanning the area, I realized just how much Metice had done for me. My clothes were clean despite the chaos, and the bedding on the cot was also mine.

The bin held items from my home, including shampoo. I touched my head and found my hair safely tucked under a bonnet.

"You washed my hair?" I slipped my fingers beneath the band of the bonnet and felt the fresh twists in my hair.

"Yes, I'm sorry. It's just," he paused nervously, "I remember you talking a lot about how hard it was to get your hair to grow after the medication you were on. I'm not sure why, but it felt important to make sure when you woke, you didn't have matted hair."

"Thank you." How could a demon be so gentle? How could he think of things like that?

"I'm the one who should thank you." Metice's response shook me.

"For what?" He looked like a new puzzle to me, and that feeling continued. There was a shift happening in our relationship. I didn't know how to define it yet, but it felt too important to ignore.

"For surviving." He pulled me close to him and kissed my forehead. "I don't know what I would have done if you hadn't."

"You came there for me." I looked up at him. "You saved me."

"Yes." Metice nodded.

"Those demons? What did you do?" I asked and had a moment of regret when I did.

"Do you really want to know the details?" It was like he could sense my hesitation. "I will tell you if you do."

I thought about it. Did I really want to know what he'd gone through to save me? What he'd done to get me out of there? I remembered the feeling of gravel and sprays of something wet on my skin. My imagination filled in details of blood and gore that I didn't want him to confirm.

"No." I shook my head. "I don't want to know."

"You're safe now. You're here with me; that's all that matters." Metice stood and lifted me from the floor to put me back on the cot. "You need to rest, Rayna. Don't overdo it. Your body is still healing."

"What about you?" I asked as he pulled the cover over me.

"I'm fine," he assured me. "I'm a demon. I'm tougher than you, remember?"

"Then explain what happened. Why were you laid out like that?" I pointed to the ground where I found him. "You weren't just sleeping, I know that."

"Likosa gave me an elixir, one for you and one for me. Whatever it did to you, it must have affected our bond. I'm assuming my dose was to account for that," he explained. "Just before you woke, I passed out."

"But you don't know for sure?" I asked. "She didn't fully explain what this stuff does, and you took it anyway?"

"No, unfortunately. I didn't have time to ask questions, but I trust her." Metice grabbed my hand. "Likosa is a friend. She is strange, yes, but she's trustworthy, I promise."

"Okay, but you should still rest. Please." There was no way I'd rest knowing he wasn't. We'd both been through a lot.

"I will." He smiled.

"Why did you choose this dress?" I lifted the soft purple fabric that covered my legs, a dress I'd purchased to wear at a renaissance festival I never attended. It cost so much money, I refused to get rid of it. I thought it would rot away in the back of my closet.

"I thought you would look nice in it, and it seemed easy enough to put on you without disturbing your dress. Was I wrong to choose it?"

"No, it's just, I never got to wear it, and I thought I would never have another reason to."

"Is it for a special occasion?" He scanned my body.

"Something like that, yes." I nodded, but I didn't tell him I was supposed to be portraying bride at the event.

"We can make one. When you're well again." He yawned.

Metice lay on the ground next to the cot. The compact frame wasn't big enough for two, and he promised he would be comfortable, but I couldn't see how he could be. We slept, though, with Piko's soft whimpers echoing around us.

When we woke, I asked if he could go to my home and bring back my mattress. It was heavy, but I couldn't stand seeing him lay on the ground. He did, and we lay together, comforted by each other's touch. Any time it felt like he would move away, I pulled him back to me. It wasn't something I would say aloud, but I was afraid of being in hell, even with Metice next to me.

It took two days, but my appetite finally returned, and Metice made the canned soup he'd taken from my home. I ate and continued to drink the supply of water. Though my wounds healed and my body felt better, there was something deeper that made me feel hollow, some piece of myself that hadn't come back with me after what I thought of as my first death. It was the third day when the fever set in. My body felt like it was on fire, and nothing he did helped.

"Please be okay," he whispered and kissed my forehead.

He stood from the bed, and I groaned, reaching out for him. Piko quickly took his place by my side.

"I'll be back. We can't stay here like this. I need to get you help."

Metice disappeared, leaving me with a worried Piko, who nuzzled my shoulder.

"I'll be okay, Piko. I promise."

Metice returned, and with a worried look, he quickly scooped me up from the bed. "We have to go."

"What?" I clung to the cover that lay over my body, but it fell. Two seconds of the air on my skin, and I was shivering like I'd been standing naked in a snowstorm.

"There is someone you need to meet, someone who can help." Metice pulled me into his chest, and I sighed at the warmth his skin provided. "You won't heal if we don't go now."

Something shifted in the corner, and I blinked several times to make sure my eyes weren't playing tricks on me. The shadow opened! It split in half, and from the center of the opening stepped a demon. He looked more like Metice, nearly human, but I could feel the nervous energy flowing from him.

"You owe me one, Meti." The new guy pointed at Metice, and the fluff of curls on top of his head bounced like punctuation to his words. "Don't forget it."

"I won't. I know." Metice nodded. "Can we go now? Is it safe?"

"Path is clear. Follow me." The man stepped back into the shadows, and Metice moved to follow him.

"What are you doing?" I asked weakly.

"Trust me, Rayna. Please." Metice looked into my eyes.

After searching his gaze, there was no question. I trusted him to take care of me. If this was the path he thought best, I couldn't disagree, not after everything he'd already done to save me.

I nodded, and Metice moved forward. Though his body still warmed me, when the shadows wrapped around us, a new chill spread through me. I kept my eyes closed tightly. Whatever we were walking through, whatever the darkness held, I didn't want to see it. After everything I'd been through, there were some things I still wanted to remain a mystery.

"You can open your eyes," Metice whispered in my ear, and I did. We were no longer in the darkness, but standing in another cavern-like place. Only, this place was different. There was something menacing in the air.

It looked more like the dungeons I expected to find when trapped in hell, like the depictions I saw in fantasy movies. There was red dirt everywhere, immersed in the smell of something burning, like decaying bodies and the exhaust from old cars. I couldn't see much from my position in his arms, but there were disturbing sounds. Moans and groans echoed the ones I heard in the shadows we moved through.

Was this the place the worst of the Bane gathered? Was this the place where souls went to suffer? Their energy, their pain, and their hatred became tangible sources in the air, and for a moment, I feared this was what Metice spent so much time avoiding, the darkness that filled this room. And to save me, he ran back to it?

A rattling chain called my attention to a frail old woman sitting on the ground, dirtied and chained. Though she looked like she was just a few steps from death with her thin frame and matted hair, her energy felt warm and loving. She looked up at Metice and flashed a yellow smile full of rotted teeth.

"You came to see me again. It's been so long. Oh, and a visitor!" She looked at me. "Ah, it's you. You found her. You brought her to me."

"Yes," Metice said. "I'm sorry I haven't come in a while."

"Oh, I heard the rumors. You left the fold. Good for you. I'll survive. I'll pay my time." She waved Metice's concern aside and looked at me. Large eyes covered in grey film found me, and her smile grew wider. "It's so good to see you, child."

"Metice, what's going on?" I asked.

"This is Floushal, the woman who told me about you," Metice explained as he cradled me in his arms. "She is the one who can help you."

"Oh?" I looked at her. "She saved your life."

"Yes, and hopefully, she can save yours. Likosa said I would have to bring you to her. You're not recovering, and I think this is why." He looked at the woman. "Can you help her?"

"Yes, but when I do, you must know you will change," Floushal spoke and reached her boney hand out to me. "I can heal you, but you won't be able to go back to who you were before."

"What does that mean?" I looked down at her. "You're going to change me? How?"

"You come from a powerful bloodline. Your ancestors were originally from a world called Muniko, a world full of beings with wonderful magics and psychic abilities. They shifted through space and time like no other. Unfortunately, some ventured into worlds with terrible beings who sought to use their abilities for evil things." Floushal looked at me like she could see the story she spoke playing out in my eyes. "Some were captured, most were killed, but a few escaped and went to new worlds. You are a child of those who landed in your world. To heal you, I must heal every facet of your being, including your psychic abilities, which I can feel you've tapped into already. I'm not sure what other magics you will develop or what changes will happen after I heal you. There could be some physical ramifications as well. When I do this, it will unlock that side of you fully."

"And if you don't do it?" I asked, not sure if I wanted what she described. I had to know the alternative.

"You will die." She nodded with sad eyes. "The elixir will only keep your body going for so long, but your genetic structure is a unique and delicate balance. It must be repaired entirely, or your body will break down, and you will lose your life."

"Rayna, please." Pain broke through Metice's voice, and his grip tightened. He'd already faced losing me once. Could I put him through that again? "Please don't give up. Whatever happens, I will be there by your side. I promise. I won't let you go through this change alone."

"Do it." Whatever the consequences, death was not an option. I looked at Metice. "You really are stuck with me now, you know that?"

"Do you hear me complaining?" He smiled.

"Likosa gave you a third item, yes?" The old woman held her hand out to Metice, who produced a small box. She opened it and pulled a vial from the box. "Perfect."

"Do you have everything you need?" Metice asked.

"Yes," Floushal confirmed then turned to me. "Can you stand on your own?"

"I think so." I nodded, and Metice carefully placed me on my feet but stayed close enough in case I lost my balance and he needed to catch me.

Floushal pulled a pipe from her shirt, sprinkled what looked like red dirt into it and, with a quick wave of her fingers, the pipe lit. She put it to her mouth and inhaled the smoke. She then opened the vial Metice gave her and quickly blew the red smoke into the vial and sealed it again. The clear liquid turned gold, then blended with the red smoke, creating what looked like glittery blood.

"You must drink it." She handed the vial to Metice. "Half for you, half for her when I tell you to."

She then pulled a golden thread from her mess of hair. Those cold, boney fingers wrapped around my wrist, and she placed my hand into his before tying the thread around our wrists, joining us together. As she did, she recited a spell in a language I didn't understand, but I could feel the weight of her words. My body felt heavier and lighter at the same time, and I felt something else, the spark of a tune in my mind. It was a soft murmur, and then a sharp high-pitched squeal before it settled again. Metice winced. He must have felt it too.

The more she spoke, the tighter the thread became, until it felt like it wasn't just wrapped around my wrist, but my entire body. The pressure was almost suffocating. The invisible threads reached beneath my skin, and I could feel them weaving inside me. They twisted with my veins, threaded through my ribs, and coiled around my heart.

My lungs felt hot, like they were being ripped apart and recreated at the same time. I looked at Metice, and if he felt what I did, he was good at keeping it from his expression. One wince, that was all, while I had tears streaming down my face and gritting my teeth.

Then, I couldn't take it anymore. The pain I felt made my bones feel like brittle glass. I dropped my head back, expecting to scream, but instead, a stream of golden thread exploded from my mouth. My voice was a gargled mess as I cried from the pain. More threads formed, making my throat feel like it would rip apart.

"Drink now." Floushal hit Metice, who looked ready to try to rip the threads from my throat. "You must drink now, or she will die!" she yelled, and when he turned his eyes to her, she continued her spell.

Metice popped the top of the vial. He hesitated for a moment and then poured half the liquid into my mouth. The threads sizzled when they touched the fluid then disappeared, and my throat relaxed, no longer strained by the material.

The elixir was thicker than I imagined, like swallowing raw honey. It coated my mouth and throat, but at least the taste wasn't terrible. It tasted like old grapes, the kind left in the refrigerator for so long, they started to shrivel into soggy raisins. At least it soothed the previous pain caused by those damn threads.

"Drink it now!" Floushal reminded Metice, who looked at me.

Metice downed the rest of the drink but kept his eyes trained on my face.

"And so, it is done." Floushal smiled and placed her hands over our joined wrists, and when she removed her hands, the golden thread was gone.

"Now what?" I looked at my wrist, then at her.

The question mark was the punctuation that invited disaster. The moment I asked, my core burned again, this time centered in my heart. I stumbled away from Metice, who placed his hand on his chest.

"What is this?" Metice choked out his own question, and then, those same threads ripped through his chest. They shot out at me like circuits looking for a connection.

The golden threads waited for a response and found it when my chest opened with the same dramatic display. The threads, what looked like hundreds of them, reached out to his, blending together. Soon, they weren't just individual strings searching for a path of connection. Their deliberate movements created a beautiful woven tapestry made of our essences. She said I would change, and not only could I feel it, but I could see it happening. The very basis of my being shifted, and Metice became a part of me.

The tighter they wove, the closer they pulled us together. When we were chest to chest, they exploded into light that flowed inward and flooded our bodies. The warmth reached all the way down to my toes. I looked into his dark eyes and saw the sun behind them. He was everything, all encompassing, all consuming. He was life.

"Now, you two are one." Floushal clapped, as if she'd just given us the greatest news.

"Meaning?" I looked at Metice, who shrugged. Clearly, I wasn't the only one confused.

"Your souls are bonded forever. Um." She paused, tapping her chin. "Oh, in human terms, you are married."

"Married?" I'm sure if my jaw wasn't connected to my face, it would have been rolling across the floor. "Did you say married? When did I agree to be married? You didn't say I had to be *married* to live."

"It's just a matter of saying." The woman lifted her boney shoulders. "You're alive. Be happy. Look, you're already more vibrant, strength quickly returning to you."

"We don't have time to freak out over this." Metice touched my arm. "We have to go, but you can curse me out as much as you want later."

"You knew this would happen?" I smacked his shoulder. *Was that why he chose this dress? He wanted me to look pretty for our wedding.*

"No," he clarified. "But I know we can't stay here, and knowing you, there is a lot more you want to say. Let's get out of here, and you can lay it on me."

"Fine." I turned to Floushal, who had a twist of joy and disappointment on her face. "I'm sorry for my outburst. Thank you for helping us. Thank you for saving my life."

"Oh, you're so welcome." She smiled. "Metice, do try to come and visit again. I miss our chats."

"I'll do my best." He looked at me. "Time for you to go home. You've spent enough time in hell."

Metice pulled my hand into his and, using his power, we left the old woman behind. He might have intended to take me home, but what his power started, my power finished. I felt it happen mid shift when I took control of the ride. Then, that haze ended, that foggy space between one world and the next. We definitely were not in my home.

We hung in the air again.

"Oh shit. Not again." I braced myself.

And we fell!

19

Training... Duh!

As we dropped, I braced for impact and hoped this time, I wouldn't break my ass entirely. While I screamed like a maniac, Metice reached for me mid-fall and pulled me into him. Maybe he would turn and land with me on top of him, like they did in the movies. Metice was smarter than that. He transported us out of there.

In a blink, we went from falling through the air to laying in a soft field of wild grass. The stuff was like a big pillow, cradling our entangled bodies.

"Are you okay?" Metice rolled over to me.

I lay next to him, chest heaving and mind racing.

"Yes, I think so. Whatever she did didn't fix my asthma, though!" I didn't want to move, just in case there was an injury I wasn't aware of. "What the hell happened?"

"I would say your powers are working." Metice chuckled. "Is that what happened last time with Olian?"

"You mean the falling on my ass? Yes. Is that going to keep happening?" I groaned. "What use is this ability if it just keeps hurting me?"

"No, it won't keep happening. At least, not after you learn to manage it." He rolled over to his side and looked down at me. "Trust me, all of this will get a lot easier soon."

"And you can teach me how?" I perked up. "Your ability is the same, right?"

"Let's hope so." Metice stood and held his hand out to me. "It's similar, but I don't think it's exact."

He pulled me to my feet, and when I looked around at the cotton candy clouds, the strange trees that looked like crazy straws, and what looked like dinosaurs walking in the distance, I realized we weren't on Earth.

"Where are we?" I watched a small bird-like creature flying in the distance. "This isn't my home."

"No, it isn't." Metice nodded. "Think of this as a training ground."

"Oh? I figured we would do that on Earth."

"Yeah, mid fall, I realized it might not be the greatest idea to take you home just yet. We need to make sure you can control yourself. We can do that here. Most of the beings here are animalistic, none intelligent enough to interfere yet."

"This is where you'll train me to jump between worlds?"

"And other things." Metice grinned. "We don't know what else you're capable of just yet. You were able to channel energy and expel it from your hands once."

"Is there some sort of crash course to not landing on your ass every time?" I checked the dress for dirt. "If you weren't there, I'd be laid up again, crying about my tailbone."

"Not that I know of, but we can certainly work on it." He laughed. "And hey, if you hurt your ass, I'll make you feel better."

"Why does it sound like what you have in mind wouldn't actually help my situation?" I rolled my shoulders. "Actually, my body feels great. All the pain I had before is gone. Likosa and Floushal are amazing."

"Yeah, they do good work, but I said I would make you feel better. I didn't say I'd help your ass heal." He leaned back to look behind me, and the grin spread across his face.

"What are you doing?"

"Just checking." He winked. "Looks great."

"Anyway," I rolled my eyes. "What's the plan? Do we train now?"

"You need to rest. I know you may feel good after what she did to you, but I don't want to risk it." He scanned the area. "Just need to find somewhere for us to set up camp."

"Rest? Where exactly do you expect me to rest?" I waved my arms around, gesturing to the massive expanse of shelter-less nature. "I don't see any beds around here, and you still haven't told me what or where this place is."

"Think of it as Earth 2.0. If you could visit your world before humans existed, this is pretty much what you'd find. It's somewhere safe for you, but it will be hard for them to find us," Metice explained. "Mid fall, I figured this was a better option. I've been here and it's...mostly compatible with human life."

"Mostly?" I frowned. "I don't know about this, Metice."

"It's the perfect place for you to practice." He kissed my forehead. "Trust me."

"Do I even need to practice all that much? I'm a quick study. Just give me the Cliffs Notes and I got it. What do I do? Just focus on the location and go?"

"Did the elixir affect your memory?" He tapped my temple with his finger. "You just nearly killed us! And if it were that simple, you wouldn't have accidentally snapped us into the middle of a freefall. Is that what you thought of?"

"Well. No. I didn't." I poked my lips out in thought. I couldn't remember what had been on my mind before we fell. "You thought of all that in the span of a five second fall?"

"I'm quick on my feet, even when my feet aren't under me," he joked.

"Right." My mind wandered as I thought of our situation, and within moments, I was panicking. There I was, in a prehistoric version of Earth with my new demon husband. This for a woman who decided a decade prior that marriage wasn't the goal in life. My heart pounded in my chest, and when I looked at the man beside me, I could see Metice immediately sensed when my mood shifted.

"What is it?" He examined me and pulled my hands over my head like I was a wrinkled shirt he pulled from the closet. "Are you okay?"

"You sure you didn't know we would be married?" I looked at him, hands still over my head like a ragdoll. "I mean, you're so quick-witted. Was there no part of you that thought to keep that from me?"

"Rayna, I know I've hidden things from you in the past, but not this." He dropped my hands and took a careful step back from me. "I told you everything I knew. She told me she could reinforce our bond, yes. Not that it would be anything like the marriage of souls. I didn't know a thing like that was possible with someone who wasn't also a demon. I promise I wouldn't have done that without telling you, and that was honestly much more intense. That light, those threads, that doesn't happen for us."

"Right." My stomach felt like I'd swallowed a sack of rocks. I never wanted to be married, never believed in it, but this was different, right? This wasn't the barbaric practices of Earth rooted in a woman basically being sold to another family. This was something far more important than that, and a hell of a lot more intense. This man was a part of me now. I could feel him inside me, his energy, his upset, dancing through my chest.

"We don't have to act like we're married, if that's what you're worried about." There was something new in his words. Was it the tremble of insecurity? "When we can be sure you will be safe, I'll leave—or we can go back to just getting to know each other. Nothing about us has to change if you don't want it to."

"I guess this is a discussion we can have later." I looked up into those dark eyes. "We have more important things to worry about, and it won't matter if I poof myself into a firepit and die."

"You can be really dark sometimes, you know that?" He reached over and tugged the bonnet that miraculously still hung on my head.

"Says the demon." I winked.

"You need to rest. I'll go get supplies. You stay here." He wagged his finger in my face. "No popping off to places where I won't be able to find you."

"Well, what am I supposed to do until you get back?"

"Enjoy the fresh air and demon free lands." Metice smiled, then he vanished.

With nothing else to do, I sat in the grass and watched the picturesque view. If I had my art supplies with me, I would have started sketching the scene. The animals all looked like abstract forms of the ones on Earth. Their ears and eyes were slightly misplaced, and they all had either too many or too few limbs.

Some glanced at the weird being sitting in the middle of the field, but luckily, none felt too curious. It must have been something Metice did, or at least he'd been there enough to know it was safe.

I sighed, wishing I had my phone. It wasn't like I could make a call, but I'd be able to track the time and maybe play a game or two. I had two more hotels to complete and a garden to take care of. My virtual families were probably so worried about me.

A sweet breeze moved in, carrying what smelled like lavender and geranium. The combination always relaxed me. The soft grass felt like a pillow. I leaned back on the ground, allowing the natural cushion to cup my body. It wasn't long before watching strange cloud formations turned into watching my eyelids.

"Rayna." A warm hand touched my shoulder and gently shook me. "Rayna, wake up."

"Metice?" I opened my eyes to a night sky painted the prettiest shades of purple and indigo. "Oh, wow."

"That happy to see me?" He smiled down at me and held his hand out to help me up.

"No, the sky." I laughed and grabbed his hand, allowing him to pull me to my feet. "But it's nice to see you too. What happened to you?"

"I came back and you were sleep, so I figured I'd let you rest while I got things set up." He stepped aside to let me see what he'd been working on.

Behind him was a full campsite, complete with a luxury tent and campfire. Where towering plants and ancient trees dominated the landscape, creating a prehistoric backdrop, a modern tent setup stood nestled in the clearing, surrounded by dense vegetation. The tent's sleek, streamlined shape contrasted with the rugged beauty of the surrounding scenery, creating a visual juxtaposition that made me ache for my art supplies.

"You did all this?" My hand itched for my paintbrush. I'd have to commit the image to memory so I could recreate it later.

"Well, don't get me wrong, you can handle yourself in most situations, but I don't take you for the outdoors type." He chuckled. "I couldn't see you sleeping in a bag on the ground."

"You're damn right." I laughed. "I love nature, but I really appreciate looking at it through a window."

"You went to Earth to get all this? What about the demons? What if they caught you? Could they have followed you here?" I rattled off all the questions that raced through my mind.

"We're safe, Rayna." He stepped behind me and grabbed my shoulders, slowly massaging them. "I took every precaution. I chose a location far from your home and anywhere they might have searched for us. You can relax."

"I can try." I sighed. "I don't know how easy that will be now that I've slept. My mind is already racing."

"You're still tired. Let's go to bed," he urged. "Once your head hits the pillow, you'll sleep. We can start training tomorrow."

We headed towards the tent when a familiar yipping sounded from inside. A moment later, Piko's head popped out the tan door flap. He yipped again, took off running, and leaped into my arms. Piko licked my face then pouted when I grabbed his mouth.

"No licking in the face." I looked back at Metice. "You went back for him?"

"I couldn't leave him in that cave. Who knows how long the goofball would have sat there?"

"You can admit you like him. I won't tell anyone." I poked his shoulder. "You went back even though it was a risk. You love Piko!"

"I do not." Metice walked ahead of me. "Just didn't want him sitting in that cave and rotting away. You know, they're not the smartest creatures around."

"Right, because you love him!" I called after him.

He was right. The moment my head hit the pillow with his warm body beside me, I was out of it. When I woke the next morning, Metice wasn't beside me, but Piko was. He snored and kicked in his sleep like he was running through his dreams.

I stepped outside the tent to find Metice cooking eggs over a fire.

"Do I want to know where you got the eggs?" I pointed at the pan.

"No," he laughed. "But I swear, they taste just like the ones from Earth."

"I'm sure they do."

"I also got you some protein bars, just in case," he laughed. "How are you feeling?"

"Better. A lot better." The strange call of a bird rang out, and I searched the skies to find the source. There was nothing. When I looked back at Metice, he seemed unbothered.

"Good, because today, we're going to work on your skills." He handed me a plate. "Eat and drink. We have plenty of water. Sorry, no wine."

Despite the weird aftertaste, the eggs were decent and filling. I thought it best to save the protein bars for later. I drank nearly 2 gallons of water and peed, squatting over a yellow bush that scurried away when I was done.

"Oh shit. Sorry!" I called out to the creature that turned and looked at me with beady eyes, like it wanted to run back and take a bite out of my leg. It wouldn't have been anything I didn't deserve.

"Did you just pee on that innocent creature?" Metice teased me.

"I didn't know that thing was alive. I thought it was a bush!"

"I knew you had some strange kinks, woman, but this is too far."

"Oh, shut up!" I threw a rock at him. "You're supposed to be training me, not making fun of me."

"You're right." He clapped his hands and looked toward the cotton clouds. "Let's get to work."

"And what do we do first?" I stretched my hands over my head. "Do I aim for Earth?"

"Absolutely not." Metice pushed my arms down. "You aim for that."

He turned and pointed to a tree with a bright orange trunk.

"The tree?" My heart sank. I thought I would be jumping worlds, and he wanted me to practice walking like a toddler. "That's it?"

"Yes," Metice laughed. "That's it. Go to the tree."

I took one step forward, but Metice grabbed my shoulder to stop me. "Not like that."

"Then how do you expect me to get over there?"

As soon as I asked, he disappeared from my side, and a moment later, he was leaning against the tree and waving at me.

"Oh, like that."

"Yes." Metice reappeared by my side. "Focus on the tree, then imagine yourself next to it. You should feel your energy connecting to the spot you choose. Lean into that energy and imagine yourself crossing it like walking across a bridge."

"That doesn't sound that simple." My unrealistic expectations of a five-minute training sequence that ended with me at an expert level went right out of the damn tent flap.

"I didn't say it was simple, but we start small. Short distances, then we'll gradually increase the range."

"What about my other skills?" The breeze picked up and blew the dress around me.

"We'll work on those later, but right now, this is the most important." He stepped behind me and pinched my ass. "Unless you want to keep falling on those beautiful cheeks of yours."

"Okay, fine." I rolled my eyes, but my face warmed with a blush. *Focus woman!*

Okay, visualize. Can you see yourself next to the tree?"

I closed my eyes. "Yes. I'm standing there, right next to it."

"Open your eyes, Rayna. We don't need your imagination taking over and landing you somewhere dangerous."

I opened my eyes and focused on the spot near the tree. Just as Metice said, the energy connected like a thread through my heart and pulled me to the spot. It opened like a path between myself and the place I wanted to be. I imagined myself walking across the path, then I felt myself moving. Bit by bit, I flowed like rolling on skates across the track.

The next thing I felt was my face slamming against the tree.

"Ow!" I cried out and held my nose.

"Ha ha ha ha!" Metice laughed, doubled over, and smacked his knee.

"Are you seriously laughing at me?" I turned, still holding my throbbing nose. "What kind of husband are you?"

"*Now* you want me to be the doting husband?" He laughed even harder. "I'm sorry, but that was funny. You should have seen yourself!"

"Jerk."

"Okay, I'm sorry." He held his hands up. "I couldn't help it."

"Screw this." I stomped off toward the tent.

"Come on, Rayna, you can't give up that easily." Metice called out. "Maybe I'll go back and tell Keri what you're doing here."

"Excuse me?" I turned on my heel to face him. "Are you threatening me now?"

"She doesn't seem like the type to let you live it down. Keri is a go getter. What would she think of her best friend giving up after one minor slip up?"

"That is low!" I rolled my eyes. Not that I cared that much what anyone thought of me, but he was right: if Keri knew, she'd never let me live it down. I couldn't imagine having both of them making fun of me for it. "Fine!"

I stomped back over to him.

"Good. Let's try again."

"If you laugh at me again, I'm going to hurt you."

"I'm sure you will." He pointed to the tree. "Take your time, visualize."

"Yeah, yeah, yeah." I waved him off with confidence, but inside, I felt shaken. I really didn't want to hit the tree again.

It took ten more tries before I landed safely next to the tree without busting my face or landing on my ass. The third time, I ended up tangled in the rainbow branches, and Metice had to cut me down. He didn't laugh, at least not to my face. After each failed attempt, the demon popped away. I was sure he went somewhere to laugh in safety.

After that, Metice had me try to go a little further each time, and it worked, most of the time. Sometimes, when aiming for a tree, I'd land in a lake. But he was right there—if something went wrong, Metice was there to catch me.

By the end of the fourth day, I was a pro at the short jumps.

"Hey!" I called out to Metice as he stacked wood next to the fire pit.

I was freshly washed from the bucket of water we'd designated for freshening up, and it had me feeling fresh in more ways than one.

"Yes?" He turned around and, in a flash, I was in his arms. "You're really getting a hang of this, aren't you?"

"Better than you thought I'd be, aren't I? I told you I'm a quick study." I wrapped my arms around his neck as he lifted me from the ground.

"That's good, because tomorrow, your lessons get tougher." Metice carried me toward the tent. "Tonight, I'll be gentle."

It was the first time we did more than sleep since our unexpected marriage ceremony. It wasn't that I didn't want to, but it felt different. Metice was no longer just a sexy demon man I was having dangerous fun with. He was my soulmate, my lifeline, my husband. And though I'd decided I didn't want that level of commitment, I felt the weight of what it meant. Being together, in that way, there would be no turning back.

Suddenly, I didn't care about that. I didn't want to turn back. I wanted life with this man, this patient, caring, protective man. And, well, I was also really fucking horny. That's how it always was. The closer I got to my period, the more I wanted to bang.

He carried me to bed and lay with me. His hungry kisses consumed me while his hands peeled the dress from my body. I couldn't explain it, but the way he looked at me had me nervous, like this was the first time he'd ever seen me naked, kissed my flesh, or held me in his arms.

His warm tongue ran across my nipple as his fingers slipped between my legs. He slowly massaged my clit, coaxing me closer to orgasm. I gripped his arm as I prepared to explode, but he stopped just before I hit the peak.

"Why?" I groaned.

"Let me take my time with you." Metice kissed his way from my breast, past my tummy, to my pussy. He kissed my lips, laying gentle pecks between my legs.

His warm breath blew over my clit, and I thought I would lose it. I lifted my hips, thrusting my pussy closer to his face, but he didn't give me want I wanted. Instead, his lips moved to my inner thigh, kissing me until he turned me over onto my stomach.

"On your knees," he said, and I did what he wanted.

Then, he gave me what I wanted.

With my ass up, face down, Metice had his favorite meal. I moaned into the pillow and gripped the sheets as he finally allowed my first release. Even after I came, he continued drinking every drop of my orgasm before I turned to him.

He laid on the bed, and I climbed on top. It was in my nature to go fast, but Metice wanted a different speed. When I moved my hips, rocking quickly and racing to the next orgasm, he grabbed me. His hands gripped my hips, and he slowed me down.

"Rayna, please, let me enjoy you." Metice controlled my pace, restricting me until I fell into the sensual flow he desired. His dick pulsed inside me while he looked into my eyes. "You're mine, and I want to take my time with what's mine. I want to savor you, learn you, be everything you need me to be. Please, let me take my time with you."

He reached up, grabbed the back of my neck, and pulled me to kiss him.

"Fuck, I'm gonna come." Metice gritted his teeth to fight the orgasm before he flipped me on my back and took control. "Not yet. Damn, you feel so good."

He remained on top, kissed me softly, and slow-stroked my soul away until we both hit the limit.

Sweat glistened on his skin as he cried out in orgasm and bit down onto my shoulder. I held his head, pressing his face into me. The pain felt so damn good, and each time that night, when our bodies tangled in passion, he did it the same, slow and steady, enjoying every single moment.

20

A Total Natural

The next day, Metice made Piko a part of our training. The small blue creature looked at me with worried eyes as the demon scooped him up from the ground. He yipped and reached his stubby little arms out for me.

"What are you doing?" I reached for Piko, but Metice pulled him away from me.

"I'm starting the next phase of your training," he explained. "You have mastered getting to places you can see, but now, we need to extend your reach."

"Extend my reach?" In the distance were orange mountain tops. "Like over there?"

"Not exactly. I need you to focus on Piko." He held the creature up to me. "You can feel his energy now, right? With him in view, you can create the thread between you."

"Yes." I nodded.

"Great." Metice disappeared, and when he returned, he had a devious grin on his face. Piko wasn't with him. "Go get Piko."

"What?" I panicked. For all I knew, some dinosaur looking creature could be having my pet for a snack. "Where did you take him? What did you do to him?"

"That's for you to figure out. He's safe, don't worry. Focus on that energy signature. Once you've encountered a new signature, you store it in an internal library you can tap into any time you want. Search your library and find Piko."

"I-" My mind raced. "How?"

"I can't tell you that. It's different for everyone. For me, I visualize a library, but for others, it may not work the same."

"We couldn't have practiced that before you took my pet away?" I slapped him on the arm. "Why would you do that?"

"Now, what would motivate you in that scenario?" He rubbed his chin. "You got this. Just focus. Piko is waiting for you."

I closed my eyes and tried to visualize a library like Metice said, but all I got was a bookstore full of smut. How was I supposed to do this?

"It's not working," I huffed. "My library is broken."

"It has to be something unique to you." Metice rubbed my shoulders. "I picture a library because I've always been a collector of knowledge. Each book on my mental shelf holds not only an energy signature, but all the knowledge I've collected about a place, thing, or person. Find something that connects to you on that level."

"Right, okay." I took a deep breath, closed my eyes, and focused. The first thing that came to mind was my paintings. Each stroke captured the essence of my subject. I mentally painted a picture of Piko in my mind, and soon, I saw the thread between us. I didn't know where it ended, but I was sure it would take me to him.

When I opened my eyes, I stood on a small hill overlooking a pink pond. Piko sat chewing on a piece of meat Metice left him with, so concerned with the meal, he hardly noticed me.

"See, you did it." Metice appeared beside me.

"Not that he seems to care." I pointed at Piko, who tore into the meat happily.

"Now, don't take it personally. I'm sure he's happy to see you, but that meat is fantastic," Metice bragged. "I used a new rub on it, and I think I've perfected my blend."

"Right." I clapped. "Now what?"

"Now, you do it again." Metice held his hands up. "This time, you find me."

I spent the rest of the day chasing Metice's signature around this new world, each time coming across a place that was more unreal than the last. It was something out of a children's book, and I loved every moment—so much so that I started making up rhymes for the places we saw.

"Are you going to write them down?" Metice worked on our meal for the night. I was quickly getting used to having a man who cooked, because I, for one, hated doing it!

"What?" I sipped my water. "What do you mean?"

"The little rhymes you've been creating. What will you do with them?" He held his finger up. "Rivers run blue, and puffballs scurry. I capture this moment before it's time to hurry."

I couldn't believe he remembered the rhyme but assumed it was just another fact in his mental library. "I hadn't thought about it. Maybe."

"Better than the smut you were writing before," he joked.

"Hilarious." I rolled my eyes. "I always wanted to be a writer, but painting and other forms of art came more naturally to me. To me, it's so much easier to tell a story with the stroke of a paintbrush than by stringing a series of words together."

"Interesting perspective." Metice watched me. "I'd love to see you paint someday. Peacefully, without worry of danger."

"Yeah?"

"Of course. That's why we're here. Once you can handle your own, you will return to your normal life. No one will mess with you."

"That's sounds like wishful thinking," I laughed. "You and I both know that the life I had before meeting you is long gone. I doubt I could even reclaim my clients now. How long have I been away from Earth?"

"A few weeks." He nodded. "Might be difficult to explain another extended disappearance."

"Maybe I will turn my adventures into books. I could do children's books. At least this way, when I'm home, I can still afford to live."

"Or," he started, but kept the thought to himself. "Never mind."

"What is it?" I poked him. "Tell me now."

"Maybe you don't have to go back to Earth," Metice offered.

"What?" The nervous laugh caught in my throat. The idea of not going home led me to thoughts of where I would be if I didn't, and those imaginings all involved the demon who sat across from me.

"We're bonded now. Maybe your life can look different when this is done."

"You imagine me living in hell with you?" It might have been better to tiptoe around the question, but I chose the more direct option.

"Living in hell? No." Metice shook his head. "But I imagine you exploring the universe with me. I can't see you going back to being just another human toiling around on Earth, not after everything you've been through."

"Oh." I hadn't thought of that. This new power would open me up to new worlds.

"You know now, your body will acclimate to just about any world. You can see and experience things even your amazing imagination couldn't concoct."

"That's something to think about." I stared up at the night sky.

"It's nothing we have to discuss now. That's why I said never mind. I know you're uneasy about this metaphysical marriage between us." He handed me another bottle of water. "Drink as much as you can. Tomorrow, we'll go a little further. It's best if you're properly hydrated. Eliminates cramping."

A day later, and we stood in a world that smelled like strawberry bubblegum. There wasn't much to see. The ground was a great expanse of grey mulch, with yellow fuzz balls covering nearly every inch.

"What is this place?" I frowned. "It smells sweet, but it looks like death."

"We call it a dekoti." Metice sighed. "This is dekoti 768. Sad to see it this way now."

"What's a dekoti?" The word felt foreign to my mouth, but the meaning settled in my stomach like bad milk.

"A world that was once vibrant with life and is now a shell of itself. Some ecological disaster happened and wiped out everything that once lived here. Funny enough, we've classified your Earth as a dekoti world many times, but life keeps finding its way there," he explained. "You know, there are scholars on other worlds studying your home? They hope to be able to use whatever phenomenon happens there to be able to save and restore worlds like this one."

"So it's true, all the theories of what Earth has gone through?" I'd watched enough natured documentaries that spectated about the many ecological disasters our world had survived, but it was something different to have it confirmed.

"Absolutely." Metice nodded. "It's a resilient place. I think it will even survive you humans."

"I always questioned if science was right. I'd love to pretend to be offended by what you said, but humans *are* the ecological disaster. It's nice to think there's a chance it will recover when we're gone." I smiled. "Why are we here?"

"You're right: we should leave. Okay. Take us back to Earth 2.0." He smiled. "I'm your passenger. I will not change your path, so get it right, and please don't drop us into a volcano. Stretch your senses and return to where we just were."

"Seriously?" I scoffed. "You know, mentioning a volcano right now was a terrible idea. If it happens, it's your fault for putting it in my mind."

"Same principal, greater distance." He rubbed my shoulders. "You got this. Don't think of the distance. It doesn't matter. In your mind, millions of miles are crossed in a matter of steps. All you need is a clear view of where you're trying to go."

"Okay." I brought to mind our campsite, the firepit and Piko. Even the weird little yellow bush that wasn't a bush. The bridge slowly formed. I held my hand out to him, and when I felt his palm press against mine, I started my slow skate across the path. When I opened my eyes, I was there.

Metice stood beside me, and Piko jumped into my arms. At least that time, the little guy acted like he missed me. Of course, there was no meat to distract him. He moved to lick my face, then stopped and chose my hand instead.

"First try!" I cheered and jumped around, then started twerking. "Take that. Uh. Uh."

"Great job." He backed up and watched me. "You should do that every time. Shake your ass like that. I like it."

"Oh yeah?" I pointed my ass at him and shook it playfully. "You enjoying the show, big guy?"

He bit his lips like he wanted to do anything but continue our training. "Now, go back to where we just were."

"Back to the desolate place?" My celebration ended.

"Yes." he nodded. "Take us back."

"I...how? I didn't focus on it." My mind raced trying to recreate the image of the world, but it felt impossible. "I didn't get the signature."

"Try anyway," he said sternly.

"Okay, I guess." I closed my eyes and imagined the vast expanse of nothing. When the bridge appeared, it had holes in it, but that was as good as it was going to get. I held my hand out to him, and as soon as I started my skate across, the bridge fell apart.

The connection failed but, lucky for me, we weren't hanging in a freefall. We landed right back at the campsite, just a few feet to the right.

"See? No signature to follow." I threw my hands up. "I didn't know I was supposed to be collecting it while we were there."

"Here's another lesson for you: everywhere you go, you must take in the energy, catalog it. You never know when you'll need to go back." He smacked my ass. "Don't worry. It will get easier, like second nature."

"Okay." If he wanted me to focus, he was going to have to stop doing that, because I wanted to teleport his ass right to bed again.

Metice took the reins. He transported me to the desolate world, and I popped us back to our campsite. Then, I took us *back* to the desolate world. From there, he would take me to new worlds, some boring, others outrageous. Once we landed in a new place, he would call out a previous location, and I had minutes to collect what I needed and leave.

He was right. It got easier each time.

"Last test." Metice grinned after I emptied another bottle of water. "You ready?"

"What do I have to do?"

"Take us to a world you've never been."

I laughed, expecting him to join in, but he stared at me like I'd lost my mind.

"Wait, you're serious? What happened to collecting new signatures? How am I supposed to do that?"

"Do you think I've had the signature of every place I've ever been?" he said with a straight face. "One thing you will learn with this power is that there are places and people whose energy will call out to you. You'll feel them like soft whispers in your mind. Cling to them, and they get stronger. That is how I've been able to see and experience so many places."

I thought about what he said, and it reminded me of my art. There were things I painted I had no explanations for, faces of people who felt foreign and yet so familiar at the same time. I thought of my art and the image of my recent work came to mind.

There it was the whisper of energy, and I focused on it, held it as tightly as I could until it felt like I'd already been there.

"Okay." I held my hand out to him. "Let's hope this works."

Metice grabbed my hand, and I did it. I felt that thread grow stronger. It stretched into a path, and then I ran across it.

"How did you do this?" Metice asked before I could open my eyes to the scene from my painting. It was exactly how I imagined: rolling hills of ice and hazy skies, specks of grass peeking through the frozen land.

"It's real?" I sighed, and my breath turned into a chilly cloud in front of my face. "I never imagined this could be real."

"This is Floushal's world." Metice said. "This is where I learned about you. How did you tap into this place?"

"It is?" It looked nothing like the world he told me about. "I thought you said that place was dried up without water."

"It was when I was there, but it has seasons just like any other world."

"This is the world I've been painting. I didn't know if it was real or not, but it's been so vivid in my mind. I figured I could try it out, and if it didn't work, the worst that would happen is I would end up in my home in front of my easel."

"This is amazing." Metice pulled me into him and kissed me. "You are truly amazing, Rayna."

"It's really beautiful." My voice trembled from the cold. "This is unbelievable. I dreamed of this place for weeks before I started painting. No matter what I did, I just couldn't get it out of my head. And now, I'm here. How many of my other works are real?"

"I wouldn't be surprised if a lot of them are." Metice wrapped his arms around me and warmed my body.

"To think, I could visit those places and experience those dreams." The excitement was enough to make me forget about the icy wind that slammed against my body. "This is wild."

"Let's get back. We can visit this place again when you're dressed for it. This dress isn't enough to protect you from this weather." He kissed my cheek and moved to my lips.

In a flash, we were back in our tent, and our clothes fell to the floor as we moved to the bed.

Metice paused. His lips lingered on my neck as his weight fell on top of me.

"What's wrong?" I ran my fingers along his bare back. "Something is taking your mind away from me. Come back."

"I hate that this has to end," he admitted. "I don't want it to."

"What has to end?"

"Us, here, alone. We can't stay like this forever." He kissed me, and I could feel the sorrow on his lips. "Rayna, I've waited so long for you. I tried to deny it when I first felt you. I did everything I could to protect you from my world, and it feels selfish now to want to keep you in it with me. The thought of you leaving, of not having these moments with you...it kills me."

"I feel the same way, and hey, I thought we agreed to continue. Yeah, we have some heavy shit to sort out, but I don't plan to go anywhere. I'm kind of tied to you now, so it's not like I can just pack my bags and go." I grabbed his face and lifted his lips from my neck to look into his eyes. "Can we just have one more good night before we return to hell and face the demons? Then, after that, we'll figure out how this works."

"One night, maybe two," he growled, and this time, he wasn't so gentle.

It was during our third round, when I rode him like a bull and held on to his horns for stability, that I lost control. Don't ask me why, but just at that moment, I thought of Keri. I wondered if my friend was okay and then boom! I was gone. No longer riding a demon, but straddled across a coffee table, butt ass naked in front of my friend.

"Rayna?" Keri dropped the bowl of cereal in her lap. "Bitch, what the fuck?"

"Oh shit, Keri?" I slapped my hands over my breast and stuttered. "I - I - I was just...."

"I can imagine what you were just doing." She tossed me the small blanket from the couch. "Cover yourself. Glad to see you're alive."

"Yeah, I, um." I caught my breath and tried to regulate my emotions. Being moments from the peak of orgasm and then scared out of your fucking mind was mind-boggling.

"I guess your demon boy found you." She cleaned the spilled cereal from her lap and stuck her tongue out at me. "You two make up?"

"He did, and well..." I wrapped the fleece around me. "Something like that."

"Okay, don't leave me sitting here thirsty. Spill the tea. What the hell happened?"

"Well, I was held captive. Nearly died. Metice killed a bunch of demons to protect me and then had to take me to a witch. She healed me but changed me."

"Changed you?" She perked up. "Changed you how? Did you have to sell her your soul? Are you indebted to her now? Dammit, Earth law isn't going to help us with this, Rayna."

"Keri, calm down. I'm okay. It's a long story, but you know that power I told you about? Well, what she did unlocked it completely, and Metice been training me to use it." I shrugged.

"Right." She looked at me. "Do you have to be naked to use it? Or is that just like a nice little bonus?"

"No, I, ugh, I'm actually great at it, but I guess it's still a little unsteady." I laughed nervously. "I have to think of a person or place. And this is weird, but we were, well, you know. And-"

"Oh, I know what you were doing." She lowered her voice. "Was it rotating?"

"Keri!" My face flushed with embarrassment.

"Wait, you thought of *me* in the middle of that?" She clutched her imaginary pearls. "I don't know if I should be flattered or concerned. Do you secretly love me? Is this how you confess after all these years?"

"Girl, get over yourself! I just had an errant thought and wondered if you were okay." That's when I saw the cast on her leg. "Oh my God, your leg! Shit. Keri, I'm so sorry. I should have raced back here to see how you were."

"Nah." She waved off my concern. "I figured with the difference in how time moves there and the fact that you were probably running for your life, it's been a few days for you. You had enough to worry about. I'm okay. I'm just glad you're alright."

"How did I get lucky enough to have such a levelheaded friend?"

"You're blessed, what can I say?" she laughed. "Now, run your ass in there and grab something to wear, please. I don't need my man looking at your naked ass when he gets back here."

An hour later, I was dressed in a jumpsuit that was too loose on my ass and too tight on my tits. Oh, how I envied the girls who had friends who wore the same sizes as them. At least the sneakers she let me borrow fit.

"So, you're learning your powers, fucking your demon, and enjoying your new life?" Keri gave an approving nod. "Damn, girl. It's strange to say this, considering the parameters, but I'm happy for you."

"Thanks. It's all been pretty crazy. I'm still getting used to everything that's happened."

"Are you okay?" she asked.

"I'm trying to be. Keri, in order to stay alive, I pretty much had to marry him," I admitted.

"Marry?" She coughed. "Hold the fucking phone. You married the demon?"

"Yes." I laughed at her expression. "I mean, it's not like a marriage here on Earth. It's deeper and far more complex. My soul is now forever tied to Metice."

"This from my friend who said she would rather gouge her eyes out than do legal paperwork to get a man out of her life?" Keri clapped her hands and laughed. "I can just imagine your face when you found out!"

"Exactly." I sighed. "And he wants us to stay together. I mean, so do I, but I can't get the image of me as a stoic housewife out of my head."

"Well, at least there's no paperwork, right?" She scratched her chin with freshly manicured nails as she thought through the logistics of my relationship. "To end it, one of you just has to die. Okay, maybe that's a bit morbid."

"But no paperwork." I laughed and then sobered up. "This isn't over yet."

"It isn't? What do you mean?"

"No. I have a feeling things aren't settled in hell. Eventually, we'll have to face that," I explained. "If we ever want to live without worrying about his enemies coming to hunt us down, we need to deal with it. There's something else: I think this is all because of Olian."

"We?" Keri pointed at me. "You said 'we'!"

"Metice and I." I inhaled slowly as I waited for my friend's freak out.

"Oh my God, Rayna, you're a 'we' girl, now!" She laughed. "I know, demons hunting you down, crazy ex-girlfriend, but you said 'we'! I never thought I'd see the day!"

"Shut up." I slapped her shoulder.

"No, nope. I got to tell the girls about this." Keri pulled out her phone and opened the group chat.

"Tell them what, exactly? You're going to tell them I'm spiritually married to a demon?" I pointed to the phone. "Go ahead, tell them. We'll see who gets sent to therapy this time."

"No. I'll say you flew off to Morocco and met a yummy man and that you're never coming back!" She laughed. "Those bitches will be so jealous. Hey, you think you can get a pic with him?"

"You need help," I laughed at her.

"No, what I need are pics!" She cackled. "Those jealous bitches will drown in their envy!"

"Sometimes, I really wonder if you like the rest of our friend group."

"Of course I do!" She waggled her brows. "I just know how they are, and I love to rub shit in their faces. It brings me joy."

"Right. Well, I don't think he's the picture type." My laughter stopped as the quick shot of pain stretched from the back of my head. My vision blurred, and I doubled over. "Shit!"

"What's wrong?" Keri put her hand on my back. "Are you okay? Rayna, what's going on?"

"I think it's Metice. He's in trouble." I straightened, but my head throbbed.

"You can feel him?" She asked. "Seriously?"

"I told you, this marriage is something else." I groaned. "Yes, I can feel him, and I think he's in trouble."

"Okay, what do you need to do?" She reached for the box that held her little friend.

"Put the gun away, girl." I slapped her hand. "Besides, you can't help me. I'm going back to hell."

21

I know Kungfu

"Take it." Keri held the pink gun out to me. "There is no way you're going to poof your ass up out of here without this."

"I don't think that's going to help where I'm going." I pushed the weapon away.

"Look, girl." She grabbed my wrist and forced the gun into my hand. "I dropped two demons with it. Take it. I know you're full of new power, but maybe something human will help. Just bring her back to me, please. It was hard getting that shade of pink, and I don't want to have to fill out all those dumbass forms for a lost weapon."

"Thank you." I took the gun and hugged her. "Thank you for being my friend. I love you."

"Yeah, I love you too." She hugged me back. "Try not to get too much blood on that jumpsuit. I've only worn it twice. Oh, and don't die!" Keri called out as the world shifted.

The shift took me first back to Earth 2.0. I needed to see if there were any clues to what happened, and I could still feel Piko's energy there. I found the little guy hiding behind the bed, frightened.

"Oh, Piko." I pulled him into my arms. "What did they do?"

Piko whimpered.

"It's okay. I can still feel him. He's hurt, but he's alive. We're going to get him back."

While clutching the little blue guy, I shifted from our hidden campsite back to hell. The first place I could think of starting was the cavern, that hideout where Metice took me to heal. Everything was exactly as we left it, even the shadowy corner.

Piko jumped out of my arms and ran to the opposite corner.

"I guess you're not going in there with me?" I laughed. "Don't worry, little guy. I got this. Maybe you can meet us at the next stop?"

Piko actually nodded, as if he knew exactly what I was thinking. Then, he took off running down the narrow path that led out of the cavern. While Piko ran, I walked slowly toward the shadow. Metice told me the lesson he'd gotten from his friend. Walking through shadows was dangerous, and it took practice—practice that usually required a guide.

The shadow rippled like it was beckoning me forward. This was what I had to do to get to the man who could help me, I knew it. I took a deep breath and then headed into the shadows.

And it was a lot harder than Metice said.

The next thing I knew, I was entangled in the darkness. My eyes were blinded, but I had one foot on something hard and the other flailing around, searching for support. Groans of lost souls, foolish people who had no business in the shadows, rang out around me. The icy grip of death tickled my neck, and I stumbled as my foot slipped off the platform and my heart jumped into my throat.

A hand wrapped around my arm, pulling me forward and out of the darkness. I fell to the ground as my heart raced, and I struggled to breathe.

"That was really risky. You're just as nutty as Meti." Metice's friend stood in front of me, rolling a coin across his fingers. "What are you doing here?"

"Metice is in trouble." I stood and dusted my pants off. "I need your help to save him."

"I can't help you." He shook his head. "I already put my ass on the line once. You can't ask me to do it again."

"Look, Cufio, right?"

He nodded eyes locked on the gun I balanced in my hand with Piko. "That's me."

"You helped us once. I know it's a lot for me to come here and ask you to do it again, but the fact that you risked your life for Metice once means something. If it weren't for you, I'd be dead now, which means you care about Metice just like I do," I reasoned. "You know where he is, don't you? I'm not even from here, and I can tell you that wherever he is, Olian's not far away. You're the only person I know who can get me in there. You can use your shadows to help me."

"I told him this would not end well, but I thought it would be on him, not me." Cufio brushed the short bangs from his face as he looked at me with strange cat-like eyes and took a deep breath. "I hope you have a good plan. And I can tell you right now, you're going to need a lot more than shadows."

"Right, and that's why we need to go see one more person."

"Are you going to use that thing on me?" He pointed to the gun.

"Not if you don't give me a reason to." I winked.

"I see you're just as funny as your demon lover." Cufio rolled his eyes. "Let's go."

Moments later, we stood at the entrance of a cave. Cufio was still reluctant to help, but he'd come, and that was enough for me. I only hoped he wouldn't change his mind in the middle of the battle.

We entered, showing the same respect as Metice did the first time. And just the same, she was sitting in her throne next to the pool of water.

"Likosa," I greeted her.

"Ah, Rayna." She stood and swayed over to meet us. "You've returned to me. Don't tell me Meti couldn't keep you happy like I did."

"I'm sorry, what?" Cufio glanced between us.

"Nothing." I waved him off and changed the subject before Likosa gave him a recap of our first visit. "Metice is in trouble, and I'm here to ask for your help."

"So she actually did it, huh?" Likosa clapped her hands and laughed. The sweet trill echoed around the cavern. "I never thought she'd have the guts to pull that one off."

"What do you know?" I asked. "Olian is behind this, isn't she?"

"Of course she is, girl. Olian's been planning to snatch Metice for a long time. But she knew she couldn't do it unless he was vulnerable." Likosa nodded. "He's far too strong for her to take on when he's at his full potential."

"What do you mean, vulnerable?" I asked. "How did that happen?"

"It's you." Cufio pointed at me. "You're connected now, right? You're alive, which means you did the marriage of souls. Your bond makes him weaker."

"Why would he agree to do that if it makes him weaker?" I asked. "That doesn't make sense."

"Was he supposed to let you die?" Likosa laughed. "That man has loved you long before he ever saw you. There was no way he was going to let that happen.

Besides, it only weakens him temporarily. The longer your bond is in place, the stronger you both will become. Bright side is that your human life will last longer because of your connection to him."

"Seriously?" I had more important things to worry about, but I'd be lying if I said it didn't make me happy to know I could have more time with him.

"Yes. I'm not sure how much longer you get, but I've seen this before. I'm talking hundreds of years at minimum." Likosa beamed. "Plenty of time for us to get to know each other."

"Right." The last thing I was thinking about was getting to know her more. "So, it's like falling for a vampire without the bite."

"A what?" Cufio frowned. "What's that?"

"Nothing." I laughed. It never dawned on me that vampires wouldn't be well known in hell. "Anyway, Likosa, I'm here to ask for your help. Cufio can get me in through the shadows, and my powers can get him out of there, but I know it won't be that simple. Olian won't let him go without a fight."

"I know what you need." Likosa ran her fingers across my cheek seductively.

"What's that?" I pulled away. Her touch invoked the memories of our first encounter.

"Have you watched that Matrix movie in your world? Such a good one. The way they download data into their mind? I can do that for you. For your power."

"You can? Why didn't Metice bring me to you to help me learn to shift between worlds?"

"He's old-fashioned." Likosa shrugged. "Also, I'm not sure he knows I can do this."

"What power are you talking about?" Cufio asked.

"Oh, Meti's mate is a powerful psychic. She can manipulate energy—not just to travel, but to protect herself." Likosa pointed at me. "She did it once before. Knocked Olian on her ass."

"How do you know about that?" I frowned. Did Metice tell her?

"Oh, girl. I have eyes in every world, and I keep watch over those who are dear to me." She winked. "You're one of those people."

"You can teach me to control it?"

"Teach? No." She pointed to the water. "But in there, I can tap into your ancestors and pull their knowledge into your brain."

"Wait…" I shook my head. If this was another attempt to get in my pants again, I wasn't having it.

"Don't worry. It won't be like the last time." She smiled. "The water is a conduit. I'll use it to strengthen the magic."

"The last time?" Cufio perked up. "You took her into the pool, Likosa?"

"It was nothing." I blushed. Obviously, Cufio knew what Likosa did in that water. So much for keeping the secret.

We stepped into the water with Cufio's back to us to allow privacy for our naked bodies. As before, the water moved around us, pushing and massaging our flesh. This time was different. It felt calmer, less consuming, more comforting.

Likosa held my hand. "Remember to breathe," she instructed as the water continued to move.

"Okay." I nodded.

She placed her finger to her lips, whispered a spell, and then touched the center of my forehead. My mind went blank like a fresh canvas. For a second, I forgot everything about myself. My life, my memories—it was all gone. And then, strokes of life filled the canvas, but not just my own. It was people who shared my features, living their lives and doing incredible things.

They learned how to use their powers, and I learned with them. They visited new worlds and experienced the greatest loves, and so did I. My heart broke a thousand times for their losses and soared a thousand times for their wins. I fell back into the water, and my own life rushed back to me.

"Did it work?" Cufio stood over me as my eyes opened. "Can you do it?"

"Maybe give her a second to wake up before you badger her?" Likosa laughed and helped me up from the floor. The soft robe covered my body. "How do you feel?"

"I know kungfu." I grinned as I mimicked the famous line from the movie, and Likosa laughed at the joke.

"What?" Cufio looked at us like we were insane.

"I think that means it worked," Likosa explained. "Rayna, try it out."

"Okay." I lifted my hand and felt the inherited knowledge working. Instructions rattled off in my brain like a checklist. *Feel the surrounding energy. Pull it into you. It's only borrowed and cannot be kept forever. Focus on a target and send the energy to it. Four. Three. Two. One. Boom!*

The blast slammed into the wall. The room shook, and rocks broke off from the ceiling and fell to the ground.

"I'd say it did." The triumphant smile spread across my face.

"Works better than that archaic gun of yours." Likosa pointed to the weapon that lay on the ground next to me. "I'll dispose of that for you."

"No." I stopped her. "This belongs to a friend. She'll kill me if I don't bring it back."

"Well..." Likosa sucked her teeth and then produced a bubble with her hand. "Put it in here."

"What?" I frowned.

"Do you think you'll be able to carry that thing around while you're fighting for your man?" She held her hand out. "Hand it over."

I gave her the gun, which she then popped inside the bubble. Likosa focused on the basketball-sized orb until it shrunk to the size of a quarter. "Turn around."

I turned, and she pressed the small orb on my back just above my ass. It felt cold, like ice, but quickly warmed to my body temperature. "If you need it, you can get it. Just press the spot for a few seconds, and the gun will appear."

"Wow, thanks." I touched the spot before I looked at Cufio. "Okay, now we can go get Metice."

"When do we go?" Cufio looked at Likosa.

"I'm afraid I will not be joining you." She shook her head. "I can't get into messy business here—but I can lend my services to anyone for a price."

"A price?" I looked at her. I had no way to pay her.

"Yes." Likosa walked over to me and kissed me on the cheek. "Paid in full."

"She won't be able to take on Olian and all her men alone," Cufio said. "They'll both die in there."

"You're right. Okay, let's get you some help." Likosa paused, then put her finger to her lips. A sharp sound slipped through her lips, bounced off the walls, and then hit the water. We watched as the once calm pool raged. White bubbles covered the surface, and then, from the water, two creatures appeared.

Cufio and I backed up as the two beasts climbed from the water. Their massive bodies dripped on the floor as translucent skin solidified. Their hard flesh was colorful, like the corals from the sea. Through fresh eyes, I could see the aura of white that rippled around their bodies.

"This is Di and Do," Likosa said proudly and pointed to them as they stepped forward. "They will help you."

The one she called Di stepped forward. Its massive hand stuck out to me as if to shake my hand, but before it could reach me, that familiar yipping of Piko rang out. I turned to see his little body leap into the air. I reached for him but quickly pulled back when, mid jump, the cute little blue creature turned into a giant, tank-sized beast.

His body exploded into a wall of muscle and fur that stood at least twice my size. His cute little face became sinister with the graphic change. Sharp razor like teeth exploded in his mouth, with two fangs that protruded over his lip, vampire style. Piko landed in between me and Di. He bared his teeth and growled at the creature to protect me.

"Piko?" I called out. "Calm down, boy."

Piko turned to me, wagged his tail, then looked back at Di and Do. He whimpered like he wanted to attack them, but he could tell I didn't want him to. Piko grunted, and his body contracted. The little blue guy jumped into my arms but kept his eyes trained on Di and Do.

"Wow, you actually bonded with a denati?" Cufio looked like he wanted to cheer. "That's amazing!"

"What?" I held Piko tightly, afraid he would attack Di.

"A male denati can only do that when it's bonded with someone." Cufio pointed to Piko. "That also explains how he found you in the cavern. He's chosen you as his own."

"I-" I looked down at those wide blue eyes. "Piko? You chose me?"

Piko licked my hand as if to say yes.

"This is good." Likosa smiled. "Now you have three beasts on your side. I suggest keeping that little guy to yourself until it benefits you. No one will expect it."

"Smart, okay. Thank you so much for helping us." I looked at Cufio. "Time to go."

22

Two Tentacles and an Arm

Walking through shadows, though still unsettling, was a lot easier with Cufio there. It was also the best way to get into Olian's spot without immediately signaling her and her men of my arrival. As I suspected, Cufio confirmed she could sense my arrival if I used my ability. As far as he knew, Olian had no way of detecting his presence.

"The problem for most of the sensors is that the shadows, especially here in the Bane, are always active. It's nearly impossible to single out one signature, and even if you could, it would take a lot of power to do so for an extended period. In other worlds, where the dark passages are quieter, that's a lot easier to accomplish," Cufio explained while he navigated the darkness with me in his arms.

"Thank you for doing this," I said, more to keep the noise from being limited to the eerie groans coming from the surrounding darkness.

"Of course. Just never tell Metice I had to carry you like this." Cufio laughed. "Last thing I need is him coming for me."

"You think he would?"

"You didn't see what he did to that room you were in. Let's just say the guy is crazy about you. Crazy enough to level a building. I don't need there to be any misunderstandings."

Cufio laughed again, but I could tell by the way his fingers nervously shifted that he was truly worried about what Metice would do. I smiled at the thought of having someone who would go to war for me. For too long, I'd been sitting across poorly lit tables from men who probably wouldn't defend me against a fly. Now, there was one in my life who literally faced demons from hell to save me. Call me a stereotype, but that shit was sexy.

I dropped my hand to my hip to make sure the bag was still there. Our three passengers were still safely secured. There was no way I could walk into Olian's space with Di, Do, and Piko in their beastly forms. I wanted to get in and out and do as little damage as possible. Those babies were my backup plan.

Likosa provided me with a carrying case that felt like something Mary Poppins would use. I watched in complete awe as Di and Do easily stepped into the ten-inch pouch before Likosa held it out to a reluctant Piko. After promising him several times that it would be safe, that I wouldn't leave him locked inside with Di and Do, the little blue guy hopped in.

"All you have to do is open it and they will do the rest." Likosa instructed as she strapped the pouch to my waist. Before we left, she gave me a long hug, and I could damn near hear the suggestive thoughts in Cufio's head.

"We're here." What felt like ten minutes later, Cufio stopped moving. "Are you sure you're ready to go in there?"

"Are you sure you won't go with me?" I asked once more as Cufio lowered me from his arms to stand in front of him.

Through the veil of shadows, I could see the large room. It looked a lot like the one she held me in, only four times the size. I scanned the space. It was empty—and then I saw him, chained to a wall with large bronze cuffs around his ankles, wrists, and neck. The cuffs had an odd glow to them, which had to mean they weren't normal. To keep Metice down, Olian must have used magic on them.

"I think I'll sit this one out." Cufio nudged me forward. "Look, I've never been a fighter. I stick to the shadows, get intel, and leave. What you're in for is a lot more than I'm capable of."

"Thanks anyway." I couldn't blame him. This wasn't his fight, and he'd already done enough to risk his own life.

"Good luck." Cufio waved as he backed away from me, leaving me alone in the shadows.

"Here goes nothing." I took one deep breath for confidence, then left the unexpected safety of the shadows.

My first step from the shadows was a careful one. The ones to follow weren't. My footsteps were like echoes of my heart as I ran across the room to him. It didn't matter the eyes I felt watching me. I knew going in that it wouldn't be easy to save the man.

"Metice." I dropped to my knees beside him and took his face in my hands. "You're alive."

"Rayna, no. This was a trap for you." Blood spilled from his lips as he spoke. "She wanted you to come."

"Yeah, I'm old enough to know how all this works." I winked. It was obvious what Olian wanted. She had to get me out of the picture, as if that would make Metice fall for her.

"Why?" he asked. "Why would you risk coming here?"

"As if I could leave you here." I kissed him. "We already know what you would do if I were locked away like this."

The slow succession of claps echoed off the stone ceiling. Olian, hidden in shadows, stepped from the darkness. It was her grand entrance, the big bad reveal, as if we didn't already know it was her behind the chaos.

"I wondered how you would make your way in here. I'll have to thank Cufio for his help." Olian pointed to the shadow where I'd entered the room. "That is who helped you, right? One of the few allies Metice has in this world. Well, maybe not after today."

"Let him go." I would not play into her banter. Olian was an attention seeking whore, and as far as I was concerned, giving her any more of my energy would only make things worse.

"No." she said. "Why would I do that after all I did to get him here? I had to wait for the right moment. To think, we had to watch the two of you and that puke inducing planet all that time."

"Why would you go through all that for a guy you know doesn't want you?" My hands moved from his face to his neck. Metice was fuming, and I hoped my touch would keep him calm. This fight wasn't his. It was mine.

"You have something I want." Olian lifted a slow, dramatic finger and aimed it at Metice. "If I can't have him…"

"Please, don't do it." I held my hand up, the laughter already threatening to erupt. "Don't say if you can't have him, no one can. Are you really that lame? I really thought, with all your green badassery, you'd have a better line than that!"

"Fine, I'll cut to the part where I take off your head." Olian rolled her shoulders as her tentacles sprouted from her back.

"Give it your best shot," I challenged her, because I knew something she didn't.

She shot one tentacle out at me, and instinctually, I pushed Metice away and jumped out of the target zone. Once clear, I tapped into my own power. I popped away from Metice's side and reappeared just behind Olian as my size ten foot landed in the middle of her back between the nasty appendages.

"Ah, yes, your little trick." She straightened. "How could I forget about that? But exactly how long do you think that's going to help you?"

I popped again and got right up in the bitch's face. Before she could respond, I connected fist to jaw twice, then popped away.

"Let's find out." I wiggled my fingers at her. "I'm actually pretty good at this, thanks to my excellent trainer."

"Too bad that trainer didn't teach you to do anything else!" Olian shouted.

"He taught me enough." Again, I popped from my place behind her, wrapped my hands in her braids, and pulled her to the ground. Her head slammed into the floor.

I tried to move away, but one of her tentacles was wrapped around my leg.

"You're so predictable, it's laughable." Olian stood and held me, dangling upside down. "It's time to end this so Metice can be with who he's really meant for."

I could hear my friend's voice in my head. *Shoot the bitch!* So, that's what I did. I reached behind me and found the spot where Likosa put the bubble. It took a second to reach it, but once I did, it popped open, and Keri's special friend fell into my hand. I quickly aimed for Olian's knee and pulled the trigger. *Pop*!

Olian screamed out and fell to the ground, dropping me on my head in the process. After having my skull crack against the hard ground, the room spun.

"Damn, that hurt." I scooted away from her, waiting for my head to clear before standing again.

Summoned by Olian's scream, the doors opened, and demons entered, led by her orange boy toy. The orange one ran right for me, scooped me from the ground, and slapped a cuff on my wrist that matched the ones Metice wore.

"No more hopping for you," he grunted in my ear.

"It's time to watch her die!" Olian teased Metice while hopping on one leg. "Then you can get over this nonsense and join me like you promised!"

"I will never be with you, Olian," Metice told her. "You kill her, and you might as well take my head off right now."

"How could you say that? How could you throw away everything for a human?" She pointed to the orange demon. "Bring her to me."

The demon grabbed me by the throat and dragged me, kicking and screaming, to Olian. Her demonic minions stood around and cheered for my approaching death.

I locked eyes with Metice, who fought against his restraints. I tried to pop over to him, but I could feel the cuff on my wrist locking me in place. That was how she kept him there: the cuffs.

"Say goodbye to your girlfriend." The sharp clink of metal rang out as Olian pulled out a large blade and held it against my throat. This was her plan, to torture Metice with the thought of my death instead of actually doing what she threatened. I used this to my advantage.

If there was any time to reveal a secret weapon, that was it. I could have said something funny, but my head was still spinning, and I wanted to keep it attached to my neck. The latch on the bag gave me some fight, but after a few seconds of fumbling, it opened.

First came Di, then came Do, and then Piko, in his normal size, hopped out. The room went *wild*. Piko ran to Metice, but Di and Do were on a mission. They immediately identified the threats, and those gentle, rainbow-colored giants turned into terrifying monsters. Their bodies turned a mystic grey as sharp horns sprouted from their heads.

Di's hands turned into double barreled cannons, which he used to blast the enemies with so much water, they struggled to escape and ultimately drowned. Do had another tactic: beneath his head, his torso became a pool of water. When he wasn't chopping off heads, he pulled the smaller adversaries into his body, where they remained suspended until they drowned and fell to the ground beneath him, demon poop.

In the commotion, the orange one picked me up and returned me to Olian, dropping me when Di popped out the bag. The moment he released me, Do snatched him up and threw him across the room. His head smashed into the wall, and he fell limp to the floor. Before Do could finish the job, another demon attacked him. Do turned on the goblin like demon who cut into his back and quickly removed its head before moving on to a new target.

"You think this is enough to stop me from killing you?" Olian growled at me as her tentacles reappeared.

I heard him before I saw him. Piko yipped, leaping into the air and landing on Olian's back. His body exploded as his jaw clamped onto two of the tentacles and pulled. Blood splattered on my face as Olian writhed in pain and Piko tossed the appendages aside. When Olian dropped to her knees, crying, Piko ran to help Di and Do, and I turned to get to Metice. We wouldn't last long without his help. Soon, more of Olian's demons would be on top of us.

"Stop this. You need to get out of here," Metice said as I pulled against the chains that held him. "More will come, Rayna. It's not worth it."

"Shut up," I snapped. "I'm not leaving you here. Now help me!"

"Watch out!" Metice yelled, and I turned just in time to see Olian.

Her broken body soared through the air, the blade above her head.

Alright, last surprise.

I lifted my hand, pulled the energy from the room and... Boom!

Olian's eyes widened as she realized what I'd done. It was too late for her to change course. The blast of energy slammed into her chest and knocked her back across the room.

"How did you do that?" Metice asked.

"Likosa's training is a lot more effective." I winked.

"My arm!" Olian screamed out. The green demoness lay with her back against the wall as blood oozed from the opening at her left shoulder.

"Oh, shit!" I slapped my hand over my mouth. "I didn't mean to do that."

"Maybe Likosa's training isn't so great after all." Metice joked.

The door opposite us flew open, and a line of armored demons filed in, but they didn't join the fight. They lined the walls and held their place. A moment later, a man so large, he barely fit through the door entered. He snapped his fingers twice, and all the demons who fought at Olian's side stopped.

He was massive, his skin the same green as Olian. I thought he looked mostly human. Despite his giant size. That was until I saw the tail on the ground behind him, and the hooves where I'd expect to see shoes.

"Who is that?" I asked Metice.

"My former boss and Olian's dad," he whispered back, and I felt his energy shift from fear to worry.

"What is this?" Boss-Dad roared, his voice so loud, it shook the walls.

"Get me out of this now," Metice said. "Use your power. Break the cuffs."

"Okay." I aimed my hand at the one on his right wrist.

"Carefully," he warned.

The concentrated energy popped from my hand and successfully removed the first cuff. The chain rattled to the ground before I moved to his other hand and did the same. After I snapped the first two, he pulled the others off himself.

The moment he was free of the restraints, Metice's body expanded. I stepped back to give him space and gawked at how quickly he transformed. Not only did he expand in size, but he looked terrifying. Razor-like armor covered his body, and his horns were so big, I could comfortably stand on them. He'd told me about this talent, but I'd yet to see the full transformation in person. Soon, I felt like a child standing next to two giants. He didn't hesitate; Metice walked over to the large man, putting himself between me and the others.

"Klougus," Metice addressed the demon. "It's good to see you."

"Metice." He looked around the room. "You've brought this disaster into my home. Why?"

"I did not. Your daughter did." Metice pointed to Olian.

"The story of unrequited love." He glanced over his shoulder at his daughter. "Still, how can I turn a blind eye to all this? At least twenty of my men are dead, my daughter disfigured, and you've bought three beasts into my home."

"It was my soulmate," Metice spoke about me. "She brought them here."

"Your what?" Klougus frowned. "Since when do you have a soulmate?"

"I've had the marriage of souls." Metice explained. "Your daughter, after learning about this, captured me. And my mate, well within her right, did what she had to do to get to me."

"The marriage of souls." He glanced at me. "This is the woman?"

"Yes," Metice said proudly. "Rayna, my soulmate."

"She's beautiful." Klougus gave the compliment before he addressed his daughter. "Olian, did you know?"

Olian clamped her wound and shouted. "He promised to be with me!"

I felt her heartache, and for a quick second, I felt bad for her. If she at any point felt what I did for Metice, I understood why she wanted to preserve that. Still, the bitch was out of her mind.

"Did you know, child?" her father snapped. "Did you know he'd completed the marriage of souls?"

"Yes," she pouted.

"And yet you still wasted our resources on this foolishness? You know the bond is final. There is no return from it." He turned to her. "Have you learned nothing from your last century of solitude? Would you like to go back?"

"It's not fair. Metice was to be mine," she cried. "You promised him to me."

"Olian, get over it." Klougus waved her off. "All the demons in the world want you. Well, they did before you went and disfigured yourself."

"I didn't do this. She did!" Olian pointed at me. "She took my arm!"

"Get a new one." He rolled his eyes before leaving a new question in my head. *Could she just get a new arm?*

"Metice, I'm sorry about this. It can be so hard to raise a daughter, especially without her mother around."

"It's okay, I get it." Metice stepped back to stand by my side as his form returned to normal size. "I didn't mean to break her heart, but-"

"You found your true soulmate. I know how it is." Klougus nodded. "Only a few are so lucky. Who am I to deny it?"

"Dad!" Olian screamed. "Stop this! Make him leave her."

"Such a disappointment." He pointed to the orange demon who escaped death at Do's hands. "Take her to cool off and repair her injuries."

The orange one picked Olian up and carried her out of the room. The other demon guards followed them out, but Klougus remained as Di and Do climbed back into the pouch and Piko returned to his smaller, cuddlier size.

"Oh, a Denati companion? You got yourself a good one here. Well done, Metice." Klougus clapped as his laughter boomed. He looked at me like he saw a new prize waiting to be claimed. "Remember, my offer still stands. Come back, and you'll have your rank. I could use a guy like you, and your new partner as well."

"I'm not coming back, Klougus. Nothing's changed. I'm done with that life."

"Can't blame me for trying." He turned to leave and called over his shoulder. "Metice, get out of my house."

Moments later, we were back in Metice's home, which had been destroyed by Olian's men. He flipped the couch over and sat down.

"Look at that: I saved you." I flexed my muscles and gave my best superhero pose.

"Yeah, you did." A slow smile lifted on his face as he watched me. "Thank you."

"This calls for a celebration." I turned and started twerking in his face, beat boxing to make my own music.

"Yeah, shake that ass," Metice laughed. "Now strip for me."

"Seriously? You're covered in blood. You need to rest." I planted my hands on my hips. "Is this really the time?"

His eyes darkened, and his horns sprouted from his forehead as he leaned forward.

"Woman, I said strip."

23

A cute little cottage

One month later, I sat in my kitchen across from Keri. She'd finally come out of the relationship cubby long enough to have a meal with me. It wasn't hard to convince her to show up for the meal. My life was changing, and that change meant spending extended periods away from Earth. We would have very few moments to spend with each other.

"So what you're saying is you're going to look like this forever while I get older?" Keri frowned over her drink. "How is that fair?"

"That's what Likosa said. It's one of the benefits of being soulmates with a demon, I guess. The good thing is, I'm not actually insane." I held my drink up to toast her, but she rolled her eyes. "Come on! All that stuff I saw, the mental break I had before, it was all real Keri. I've been to those places. I've met those people. Do you know how much of a relief that is for me?"

"I'm sorry you went through years of everyone not believing you." Keri shook her head. "All that time with everyone judging you."

"I didn't even believe it. How could I expect anyone else to?" I put my drink down. "There was so much I experienced, lives I lived, and to find out it was real? My mind is still whirling, but it's reassuring. Just imagine the possibilities."

"And the plan is to travel the universes, visiting new worlds?" Keri asked, her voice tinged with sadness.

"Yes. I mean, there's nothing keeping me here. Thanks to being away so often, I lost all my clients, and after learning a lot of my art is depictions of places that actually exist, I want to see as many as I can. I'll be back, though." I reached out to touch her hand. "But I'm selling the house."

Her face dropped. "What do you mean, you're selling the house? You love this house."

"True, but with no income to pay the mortgage…" I trailed off. "I figure the money can sit in an account somewhere and collect interest. Maybe when I'm old, I'll return to Earth to retire."

"Yeah, you're right. Damn. I want this for you, but you're basically telling me I'm going to lose my best friend. You'll leave, and yes, you'll visit, but what will feel like a couple of months to you will be years for me. Then, you get to come back here, tits and ass still firm, while I wither away lathering myself with wrinkle cream."

"That sounds so morbid." The thought of losing so much time with her made my stomach hurt, but it also sparked another idea. "I can take you with me sometimes."

"What?" Her eyes widened as she leaned forward and whispered across the table. "Take me with you? Really?"

"There are worlds that are human compatible. If you want to see them, I can take you."

"Human compatible." She slapped the table. "Dammit, I didn't think about that. This means my best friend is an alien, right? Or at least your ancestors were. There has to be a movie about that, right?" She laughed, and I joined her because I was sure there was at least one story written about it somewhere.

"What's funny?" Metice appeared in the kitchen.

"And there he is." Keri pointed at him. "The demon who's taking my best friend away from me."

"Hello, Keri." He nodded to her. "Should I come back later?"

"No, no. I should go anyway." Keri stood and turned her stern expression to me. "Don't poof away without saying goodbye."

"You don't have to go." I stood. "Metice won't bother you."

"I'm not worried about him. I need to plan. We're telling my parents about the engagement tomorrow, and it's gonna be hell." She wagged her finger sporting the diamond. "I don't care what happens—your ass better be on earth for my wedding."

"There is nothing in the universe more important than my best friend's wedding!" I placed my hand over my heart, a silent promise that I wouldn't disappoint her.

Keri pointed at Metice again. "You better make sure she doesn't."

"I know, or you'll shoot me." Metice laughed like he thought she was being silly, but I felt his concern. He knew better than to doubt my bestie. "She'll be here."

"Smart guy." Keri patted Metice on the shoulder as she walked away.

"I have a surprise for you," Metice said as soon as the door shut behind Keri.

"What's that?" I asked as I cleared the dishes from the table.

"Come." He held his hand out to me.

I placed my hand in his, and the kitchen disappeared. When my vision cleared, we were standing on a hill in a land covered in ice: the place from my painting, where Floushal first told Metice of his soulmate.

Just to the left of us was a small cottage with the cutest little porch, an easel set up looking out over the property. Next to it was a stand stocked with a fresh canvas and paintbrushes. Piko slept in a rocking chair covered in a pink blanket.

"You did this?" I looked at Metice.

"This is where I first learned about you. Where it all started." He pulled me into his arms. "I figured we could start our lives together right here."

"That's so sweet of you." I lifted up on my toes and kissed him.

"That's it? No celebratory twerking?" He peered over my shoulder at my ass. "Not even a little bounce for my good deed?"

"I see. That's why you did this?" I slapped him on the shoulder. "And what do you think twerking will lead to?"

"Oh, the places my imagination takes me."

"Bring it on." I looked at him with a devious grin. "Demon boy."

THE END

ABOUT THE AUTHOR

Jessica Cage is an International Award Winning, and USA Today Best Selling Author. Born and raised in Chicago, IL, writing has always been a passion for her. She dabbles in artistic creations of all sorts but at the end of the day, it's the pen that her hand itches to hold. Jessica had never considered following her dream to be a writer because she was told far too often "There is no money in writing." So, she chose the path most often traveled. During pregnancy, she asked herself an important question. How would she be able to inspire her unborn son to follow his dreams and reach for the stars, if she never had the guts to do it herself? Jessica decided to take a risk and unleash the plethora of characters and their crazy adventurous worlds that had previously existed only in her mind, into the realm of readers. She did this with hopes of inspiring not only her son but herself. Inviting the world to tag along on her journey to become the writer she has always wanted to be. She hopes to continue writing and bringing her signature Caged Fantasies to readers everywhere.

Thank you to our Kickstarter Supporters!

I want to give a special thank you to everyone who helped fund our Kickstarter for the Audiobook Production of I Accidentally Summoned a Demon Boyfriend! Thank you all so much for your help with making this happen.

Alecia Watkins

Alejandra Herrera

Aleta Braziel

Alexandra Corrsin

Alexis Hornsby

Alicia

Alicia Hintzen

Allison Grier

Amanda Law

Amber Cherne

Amy Peterson

Angelique

Ann

Anna

Anna Greenman

Anna Muhovich

Antoine Bandele

Arielle Graves

Arlene Gates James

Ash Raven

Ashleigh Baham

Ashley Writes Romance

Asia Prieto

Author Z. Knight

bloop42

book.cmw1987@gmail.com

Bri

Brian

Brian A.

Briana

Britiney

Brittany Iceman

Brittany Miller

Brittany Williams

Brittney Weaver

Bryan Cohen

Candace

Candice Gary

Cecilia

Cerissa Howard

Champrea

Chandra Lewis

Chanel Holm

Cherelle Hopper

Chris

Chris & Carol Ellison

Christina Logan

Christine Meekins

Cira

Colby Poe

Connor

Corrina

Cynthia

Cynthia Johnson

Daniel Askew-Hargreaves

David Hankerson

Dejah

Demetrica

Denis

Diane Hansebout

Dorian Tobias

Drizzy$256

Elisha Bryant

Elizabeth Falcon

Elizabeth Tanner

Ellena

Emily

Erica Dechene

Erin Free

Evangeline Lacey

Folkloress

Gabby Angelica Beasley

Glenda Brown

Gloria

Golden Harshaw

Greene County Creative

Greg Burnham

Grey

Guðrún Emelía Sigurbjörnsdóttir

Hattie Jacks

Helena

Hollie White

Holly Todd

Iona Woofter

J.C. Walker

Jacklyn Salazar

Janevah

Jasmine

Jasmine Nicholson

Jasmyne

Jay Lofstead

Jazzi Smith

Jeanette Charrette

Jeffrey Mason

Jen (Fantasy girl)

Jessica

Jessica Arden Cline

Jessica Cage

Jessica Karcher

Joela

Joey Evergreen

Jordan Kearns

Kaitlyn VanderPloeg

Kalia W

KARINE ELSEK GAUDREAULT

Kat Price

Kathy Lickel Storms

Katrina W

Keema

Kelly Buiter

Kianna

Kimberley Mayfield

Kristie Redmond

Kristin

Kween Of Swords Comics

Ladybug

LaKevion Trotter-Clark

Lakishia Broughton

LaSasha Flame

Laura Unsworth

I ACCIDENTALLY SUMMONED A DEMON BOYFRIEND

Lenoir

Lisbeth Toth

Liz Hernandez

Lourdes White

Luna

Lwandile Mthethwa

Mahealani Young

Marissa Krause

Mary Marzette

McKenna Hubbard

Mila

Molly Celaschi

Morgan Eccleston

MVmedia, LLC

Nadia Hasan

Natasha Tucker

Natasha Wimmer

Nekia T

Nese Gordon

Nicole

Nicole Banks

Noah Lekas

Noriboo

Octavia C. Jones

Olivia Sanchez

Patrica Jená Bridges

Rachel Walker

rachmarie

Rane2k

Raven McCandies

Rellim

Rielle McGee

Rochelle Lowe

Ruthenia (Ruth) Dillon

Samantha Clark

Samantha Newberry

Sanjhiyan

Sarah James

Seren

Serena Sharber

Shalaunda Lewis

Shannon Bond-Cover

Shenita Wiggins

Sierra Wanzer

Simo Muinonen

Sonya Bundschuh

Sophie Rich

Stacey-Marie

Stefanie B

Summer Pace Robnett

Susan Tenzer

Tanita Rosscady

Tanya Young

Tara Williams

Tati M

Tatiana Perry

Taylor

Tea Nielsen

The Creative Fund by BackerKit

Theresa Derwin

Tia

Tyrisha H.

Victoria Mallard

Victoria Sullivan Wu

Waldo

Wendy Highland

Wright Elise

Yaritza Howard

Yemayla

yunique

Made in the USA
Columbia, SC
11 July 2025

67b8e708-6793-4d4f-bd94-54e04820a4c3R01